Seeking Philbert Woodbead

THE FAIRWEATHER SISTERS SERIES: BOOK 2

ANYA WYLDE

Copyright © 2012 Author Name

All rights reserved.

ISBN:1514758407
ISBN-13:9781514758403

DEDICATION

For John , Portia, and Arya

CONTENTS

Acknowledgments	vi
Prologue	7
Chapter One	9
Chapter Two	19
Chapter Three	23
Chapter Four	31
Chapter Five	41
Chapter Six	51
Chapter Seven	58
Chapter Eight	64
Chapter Nine	74
Chapter Ten	79
Chapter Eleven	89
Chapter Twelve	93
Chapter Thirteen	101
Chapter Fourteen	107
Chapter Fifteen	113

Chapter Sixteen	121
Chapter Seventeen	126
Chapter Eighteen	131
Chapter Nineteen	137
Chapter Twenty	143
Chapter Twenty One	148
Chapter Twenty Two	158
Chapter Twenty Three	166
Chapter Twenty Four	173
Chapter Twenty Five	178
Chapter Twenty Six	185
Chapter Twenty Seven	192
Chapter Twenty Eight	198
Chapter Twenty Nine	204
Chapter Thirty	211
Chapter Thirty One	219
Chapter Thirty Two	226
Epilogue	264
About the Author	

ACKNOWLEDGMENTS

John, thank you for your unconditional love.
Portia, you are my little stress buster.
And finally, a big thank you to all my readers for your encouragement and support.

PROLOGUE

In the latter part of March of the year seventeen hundred and something, a large schooner rested on calm blue waters off the coast of England.

It was mid-afternoon, the water was unruffled and crystal clear, while the sky above had sent its grey clouds to London.

The sun beamed down on the deck where gentlemen with missing toes, feet, teeth or hands lay draped around the schooner attempting to snooze away the day.

Now, this schooner was no ordinary schooner (as you might have guessed from the hint above referring to missing limbs and such) but a piratical schooner, and the gentlemen were not really gentlemen but looters, marauders and plunderers.

Yes, sir, they were murderous, unscrupulous adventurers and stinking water rats.

They were all pirates. Each one of them were pirates. The whole blasted lot of them were pirates. In fact, they couldn't be more piratical if they tried. And they tried. Oh, how they tried to be more devilish than the devil himself.

And one of them came close to being the devilishest ... if that is a word. If it is not, then it should be because it perfectly described the tall, muscular, grey eyed man with his long silver streaked black hair and cruel mouth. This man was so wicked that the mere reference to him caused the afternoon light to dim, the wind to blow more urgently, the men to wake mid snooze, the tea to jump out of the cup ... Where were we?

Ah, yes, the captain of the ship, the head pirate, the Black bloody Rover, whose name was enough to frighten the children of the world into behaving, was the owner of this piratical schooner called *The Desperate Lark* and the leader of these dim muscled men.

He stormed now onto the middle of the deck sending the seagulls screaming into the air. His appearance caused the men to scatter while his frown had them cowering in the bilge. While they cowered, the Black Rover grabbed the cuff of a one legged man, his most trusted aide, and in low, clipped cultured tones asked, "Who stole it, Tim?"

"George Rodrick Irvin, the future Earl of Devon currently holding the courtesy title of Viscount Elmer," squeaked Tim. "The one we call Lord Wicked."

"Kill him." The Black Rover was a man of few words.

Tim bowed in response.

"And kidnap the cooks," the Black Rover continued.

Tim dared to frown, "Cooks?"

The Black Rover glowered. "And the chefs. I want every single person who can cook to be kidnapped and tortured until we get it back."

"Torture?" Tim asked uncomfortably. "Can't we simply kill them and be done with it? I don't like torturing. It is a messy job, and I don't like it when they cry and they all cry."

The Black Rover smiled harshly. He leaned closer to Tim and whispered in his half bitten ear two words, "Pigeon feathers."

"Arr." Tim's sparsely lashed eyes widened in admiration. He shook his head at his captain's intelligence. The most learned man, Tim thought proudly, was right here.

Pigeon feathers ... The Black Rover was a blooming genius.

CHAPTER ONE

It was the first of April and an unearthly hour of seven in the morning. Finnshire was bathed in a dull grey light and the wind was blowing cold, misty and fetid. The bees and the grasshoppers were gloomily sitting under sodden leaves while the birds were chirping and tweeting miserably.

The farmers of Finnshire lingered over their breakfast hoping for the sun to break through the clouds, while the children of these farmers snuggled under covers turning a deaf ear to their mothers shrieking at them to wake up and milk the cows. As for the cows themselves, they too sniffed unhappily at the chill in the air, their tails swishing half-heartedly at the few enthusiastic flies fluttering about.

It was supposed to be spring.

It was also one of those days that tried one's spirit, and the world felt sucked dry of vitality. It was the sort of day when no one in their right mind would venture outdoors for the sake of enjoyment. It was certainly not a day to take a walk, but Miss Celine Fairweather was out doing just that.

To be fair, Celine was not enjoying her walk. It was more a duty, a habit and a matter of discipline. *Mrs Beatle's book for accomplished English ladies* clearly stated that a lady must rise early and go for a ride or take a walk. A spot of exercise was supposed to be good for the constitution.

Which was why Celine was trudging now through the familiar country path, her brown half-boots sinking into the muck and her normally attractive face flushed an unsightly red.

And as she walked, her cheeks inflating and deflating like two tiny scarlet balloons, she failed to notice the beautiful bird with a shiny green neck perched up ahead on the branch or the silver half-moon still glittering in the pink sky. Nor did she stop to admire the handsome farmer hacking away at some wood, his muscles rippling and sweat gleaming on his skin.

Instead, her eyes were trained on the muddy ground, her small, delicate feet carefully circumventing the worms, beetles and blobs of manure in her path. And while her body marched ahead battling the chilly wind and fetid scents, her mind was busy planning the day, for Celine Fairweather was not a fanciful sort.

She was also not ninety years old with loose skin and white hair. She was a young woman of marriageable age whose days were spent in being good and dutiful and cultivating the refined and gentle manners of an accomplished English lady.

In short, Celine was dry, dull and dusty, and something needed to be done urgently before she progressed from being mildly pedestrian to excruciatingly proper.

That something happened to occur right at that very moment when Celine turned the corner that led to her house and found a handsome carriage emblazoned with the crest of Blackthorne hurtling towards her from the other end of the road.

Both she and the carriage halted at the sight of the other. She was stunned, while the carriage felt nothing, for it was an inanimate thing.

The driver recognized her and leaped down from his seat.

"Is all well?" Celine asked worriedly.

The driver shrugged. "The duchess sent this letter for you, Miss. Tis' urgent."

"Go to the kitchens, the cook will have something for you," Celine replied. She took the letter and nervously traced the duchess' seal.

The Duchess of Blackthorne was her beloved friend and stepsister Penelope Radclyff. Celine quickened her steps. Penelope was eight months pregnant ... Surely nothing had gone wrong?

She pushed open the gate and strode down the path towards the house. Her mind was filled with questions. Why had Penelope sent the letter in this manner? Why send the carriage?

She should have waited until she reached indoors to read the letter. It was what Mrs Beatle would have advised, since patience was a virtue all ladies must cultivate.

Celine decided to cultivate it later and slit open the envelope.

She quickly scanned the contents and came to the end of the page. She turned it over and then back again. She was reading it for the third time when a cold drop of rain fell on her nose.

She lifted her head, her eyes dazed.

Another icy drop snapped her back to the present.

She opened her mouth and disregarding for once Mrs Beatle's advice on how a young lady must never raise her voice yelled like a crazed tribal warrior, "Pack your bags, Dorothy. We are leaving for London in an hour."

The clouds parted and the bright sun blazed in its full golden glory upon the inhabitants of Finnshire. The warmed up birds, bees and grasshoppers sang more cheerily, and the breeze turned sweet and pleasant. Spring had finally decided to flutter down and grace England.

Celine and Dorothy smiled widely. It was a beautiful day for travelling.

"It will rain the moment your journey begins," Lily remarked.

Both Celine and Dorothy ignored their sister. Instead, they focussed on the footman, maid and carriage driver, who were busy shoving travelling cases into the back of the carriage.

"Mark my words," Lily continued ominously. "A deadly tempest is on the way. I suggest you delay your journey by a few months."

"Penelope needs us now," Celine said shortly. She directed the driver to place the smaller bags under the seat. The longer ones were strapped onto the roof.

"How many years are you planning to spend in London?" Lily asked as yet another bag was squeezed under the seat.

"A little less than two months," Celine answered.

"I fear the carriage won't hold," Dorothy spoke up. "The long bags are going to break through the roof and land on our heads, and the ones under us will explode, for we had to have three people sit on each one of them before they could be fastened."

"I hope they do explode," Lily said.

Celine scowled at her. Lily had made a pest of herself from the moment she had found out that she and Dorothy were heading to London without her.

"Twenty one bags," Dorothy remarked, "is a little excessive, Celine."

"Every one of them is essential," Celine replied firmly.

"We should be going with you," Lily whined suddenly. "We are eighteen years old, while that imp Dorothy is only thirteen."

"We?" Celine asked in confusion. No one else present was eighteen except Lily ... unless ... She grabbed Lily's hand and gently stroked it. "Lily," she asked carefully, "how many people live in your head?"

"The royal we," Lily sniffed. She snatched her hand back. "Truly, Celine, you can be dreadfully dim at times."

"You are not royal," Dorothy sniffed back.

"I could be royal," Lily said. "After all, if Penelope managed to snare the Duke of Blackthorne, then I can surely find a prince."

Celine pressed her lips together and refrained from comment. She had told everyone that Penelope had requested that she bring Dorothy along when quite honestly Penelope had done no such thing.

The truth was that Lily was a facsimile of her mother. Celine could have overlooked Lily's greed, biliousness and temperamental liver, but what she could not ignore was the fact that Lily was not only all these things but she was also nosy, and that was simply unacceptable.

"Dorothy, ask Gunhilda to hurry," Celine said turning her back on Lily.

"Can't we leave her behind?" Dorothy asked hopefully.

"Afraid not, my love, your governess has to come," Celine replied, patting her sister's head.

"Taking care of the duchess is not going to be fun," Lily said watching Dorothy race towards the house.

"It will be hard work," Celine agreed.

"Is she going to yield up the ghost?"

"Penelope is perfectly healthy, Lily. She is going to give birth within two months and she simply needs someone to help her run the mansion for a while."

"She has the dowager to help her."

"The dowager has broken her leg in Bath. She and the duke's sister Anne had gone there to visit an ailing relative."

Lily smirked, "You won't have a minute to yourself."

"True."

"You know nothing of how to run a duchess' household."

"The steward, housekeeper and Penny can guide me."

Lily smiled more widely. "It sounds tedious. I doubt you will get a chance to visit the sights or attend parties."

"Penelope cannot leave Blackthorne, and I cannot possibly go exploring London on my own."

Lily leaned on her parasol looking far more smug and pleased with the situation. "I wonder how you convinced mother to let you go. It is no secret that she dislikes Penelope."

"She may dislike her stepdaughter, but she does care about her own children."

"Meaning?"

"I reminded her that the duke has plenty of friends."

"Male friends?"

Celine nodded.

"Unmarried friends?"

"Looking for wives."

The dark glower returned to Lily's face.

Thereafter, the two sisters waited in silence until Dorothy came skipping back towards them. The governess and Celine's lady's maid followed close behind.

The next ten minutes were spent rearranging the bags inside the carriage to make it more comfortable, and another twenty minutes were spent detaching Lily from the carriage wheel.

Finally, goodbyes were said and the carriage with the Blackthorne symbol emblazoned on its doors rolled out of the Fairweather household and onto the road that lead to London.

CHAPTER TW0

Blackthorn, the shrub, is as its name suggests a thorny species with a bark that is almost black in colour. The leaves of this plant masquerade as good old tea leaves while the fruits are mostly useless.

This shrub is generally used to create a sharp, warning hedge to contain animals within a particular area or to prevent pests from sneaking in from the outside.

The Blackthorne Mansion shared many of the characteristics of this plant. Its formidable grey walls protected its inhabitants by keeping out unscrupulous men while keeping in the balmier members of the household.

Nestled squarely in the middle of London and surrounded by lush manicured lawns, the mansion was like a beautiful cactus sprouting boldly from the ground.

The mansion itself had been built in the fourteenth century, and as the years went by and the residing families lived and died so did the original structure grow, flourish and expand. And since fashions change with the ages and tastes differ from one family to another so did the mansion grow and evolve until it had Roman, Greek, Gothic and Oriental elements in its structure.

When so many beautiful styles of architecture are squished together the result is bound to be petrifying, and Blackthorne was no exception.

The Blackthorne Mansion was undoubtedly an unsightly structure. A forthright person was often tempted to say that it wasn't just unsightly, it was, in fact, a monstrosity and a blight upon the good English soil. But the Radclyff family which currently resided in this building defended their beloved home by saying that 'It may be frightful to look at, but no one can deny that the Blackthorne

Mansion has character.'

Celine wished it had less character. In fact, she would rather it had no character whatsoever, for the mansion was not only large with cubby holes that were difficult to clean, but walking through its corridors at night was a daunting prospect. She had been here for a week and she still needed the occasional help of a maid to find her way around its long meandering passageways.

She hung now over the ledge of a window in the breakfast room contemplating life. The London lifestyle, she mused, was so different from her own country world. Her days in Finnshire had been like a wooden boat bobbing down a tranquil stream, while here a whole week had sped by as fast as a frog hurling its sticky tongue out to catch a tasty fly.

The fresh cold morning air bathed her face as she watched clear skinned milk maids fluttering their lashes at the mansion's male servants. A few lads dared to wink at the blushing maids and still others hung around to leer for a bit.

Celine was told that this flirtation between the milkmaids and the servants had become a custom of sorts and not a morning went by when this mating dance was not performed.

She started to roll her eyes at the men and their foolishness when she spotted something odd from the corner of her eye and froze mid roll.

She gasped and squinted leaning further over the ledge.

"Are you trying to kill yourself? Do you want me to push you over the ledge?" Dorothy asked helpfully.

"You should be asleep," Celine said whirling around.

"It is time to feed my pet. I was going to the kitchens to ask the cook for some milk," Dorothy replied trying to slip under Celine's arm to look outside the window. "What were you looking at?"

"Pet?" Celine asked, deftly pushing Dorothy away from the window and moving towards the Grand Staircase. "When did you procure a pet, and did you ask your governess Gunhilda or the duke for permission? This is not our home, Dorothy, and—"

"Why are you running, Celine?" Dorothy interrupted.

"I am not running. I am walking quickly," Celine panted as she leaped over a housemaid scrubbing the marble floors. She continued bounding up the stairs making the parlour maid and the housekeeper, Mrs Cornley, spring apart to let her through.

Dorothy had no trouble keeping up with her sister. "Gwerful is about to go into hysterics. She has never seen you run before. Celine, Stop. Don't run into poor Perkins, you will kill him."

"I repeat. I am not running. I am walking very, very fast. A lady.Never.Runs," Celine gasped. She barely glanced at the ancient butler frozen in terror as her feet danced out of the way and up the stairs and onto the Tapestry Corridor.

Dorothy halted momentarily to check if the butler was still breathing.

He was.

She sprinted after Celine once more. "Who are you looking for? What did you see?"

"Duke," Celine panted in reply, "I am looking for the duke."

Down the corridor she hurried avoiding the bustling servants readying the house for the day. She checked the morning room, dining room and the visitors' area.

She finally found him in the study.

The duke stood in front of the fireplace locked in a passionate kiss with Penelope.

"You should have knocked," Dorothy whispered in her ear.

Celine did not reply. Her face turned bright red as she surveyed the scene.

The duke had every right to kiss Penelope. After all, they were married. But the duke was kissing Penelope in his study, and that too a very pregnant Penelope. He had to lean forward quite a bit, since the belly was in the way.

Celine narrowed her eyes.

He was most decidedly bending forward at a seventy two degree angle over the protruding belly to attach his lips to her lips. On top of that the kiss was a little too ardent, too long … The whole thing somehow seemed improper.

She sniffed disapprovingly. The sniff turned into a sneeze and that one sneeze was rapidly followed by four short delicate little achoos.

"Charles, have I told you about Celine's infamous sneezes? I think that is the only silly thing about her," Penelope said stepping away from the duke and smoothing her hair.

The duke scowled. "You should have knocked. And you look like you have been running. I am depending on you, Celine, to keep this house sane and together. My mother had to go and break her leg, and

Penelope is in no condition to run the household. And here you are the only rational female running around the house—"

Penelope sidled up to the duke again and rubbed his arm. "Oh, do stop scolding her. She must have had a good reason. Celine is always sensible. Her long dark hair is always tied up sensibly. Her clothes are always sensible, and her way of dealing with every situation is sensible. Truly, the only thing not sensible about her are her sneezes and her name."

Celine bristled, "Your Grace, I need to speak to you urgently. We can discuss my sneezes at a more appropriate time, but—"

"I told you she had to have good reason for running," Penelope interrupted triumphantly.

"Can I have a pet?" Dorothy piped up.

"No," the duke said to Dorothy.

"Your grace, a moment," Celine said urgently.

"Your grace," Dorothy pleaded.

"Your grace," Penelope crooned fluttering her lashes seductively.

"I need a drink," the duke muttered.

"It is half past six in the morning," Celine said shocked.

"I will feed and clothe my pet, and I won't let it escape the nursery or my bedroom. Even Penelope has a goat. Why can't I have a pet?" Dorothy cried, her eyes brimming over and threatening a tantrum.

"Keep the pet, Dorothy. Penny, a moment," the duke said gently depositing his wife in a chair. He wrapped a shawl around her shoulders taking care to cover as much as possible of her ample bosom. "Now, Celine, what is it you wanted to tell me?"

"Your Grace," Celine started to say and then stopped. Her eyes darted to Penelope.

"Oh, please, Celine, don't keep me out," Penelope begged catching the look. "If it is urgent, then it means it is something dreadful, and if it is dreadful, then it means that it is exciting. My condition has confined me to the four walls of this mansion. I have had no excitement. Not even walks. I have been told not to move from my bed, since I am close to giving birth. I have had footmen carrying me to and fro on a giant mattress. It has all been very distressing—"

"A handsome gentleman is coming to meet the duke. He will be here any moment," Celine interrupted.

"Ah, and you have fallen in love with this gentleman? Love at first sight, is it?" Penelope asked mistily.

"No, though he is the handsomest man I have ever seen," Celine replied.

"Must be Lord Adair," Penelope said.

"Is that all?" the duke asked, his eyes straying to the clock.

Celine took a deep breath, "I was counting the silver in the breakfast room when I happened to glance out of the window. I saw from the window … I saw …"

The duke nodding encouragingly.

Celine gripped her skirts and blurted it out, "Through the window I saw this handsome gentleman walking towards the entrance of the Blackthorne Mansion. And he was being followed by an equally handsome man dead … No, I mean, a dead man."

CHAPTER THREE

"Are you feeling alright, Celine? You are talking funny," Penelope asked concerned.

"Dead people can't walk," the duke added.

"He wasn't walking. He was being carried by two men," Celine said indignantly.

"It is a pity," Penelope sniffed, "a handsome man dead … Tragic."

The duke frowned, "It would have been tragic even if he had been ugly—"

"They will be here any moment, your grace," Celine interrupted. She opened the door and searched the corridor outside. "Shall I ask a maid to fetch some tea? It is too early for breakfast, but perhaps the cook can rustle up something."

"No tea for the dead man," Penelope giggled and then promptly burst into tears. "I am a horrible human being."

"You are just moody. Women in your condition are always moody and often say the oddest things. Miss Berry back in Finnshire told me all about it," Dorothy consoled her.

"How does Miss Berry know? Is she married?" the duke asked tentatively.

"Miss Rosie Harlington Berry can't marry yet," Dorothy informed him, "on account of her being ten years old. But she does know all about Penny's condition because her mother has produced—"

"Dorothy, go to your room," Celine ordered.

"I will not," Dorothy replied horrified." How could you even suggest such a thing when you know I have never seen a dead fellow before? I am staying."

"Go to your room," the duke tried this time.

Dorothy eyed him for a moment and then said meekly, "As you

wish, your grace."

The duke's eyebrow rose in disbelief.

Everyone knew that since all thirteen year olds are a morbid lot, Dorothy would lurk outside on the landing until the dead guest came through. Only after having a good look and perhaps prodding and poking the poor fellow would Dorothy retire to her room.

The duke stroked his temple, his eyes shooting to Celine.

Celine sighed and nodded. "Dorothy," she warned, "if you see the corpse, then his ghost will haunt you forever."

"I am thirteen not five."

"Well, then you should behave responsibly and feed your pet," Celine retorted.

"My pet," Dorothy squealed, "I completely forgot about Tommy, though he insists on being called Littlebury."

"Your pet talks, does he?" the duke asked amused.

"Not very well, but I am trying to teach him."

Penelope chuckled and called her darling, while Celine eyed her younger sister in apprehension. Something was not right, but before she could question her further, the butler knocked on the door.

Perkins stuck his white head in and announced, "Lord Adair, his servants and a dead gentleman here to see you, your grace."

The study door flung wide open, the wind blew and Lord William Ellsworth Hartell Adair, the Marquis of Lockwood, strode in.

Celine, Dorothy and Penelope let out a collective gasp, the duke straightened his back, the furnishings looked brighter, and even the dying candles blazed with a sudden renewed spurt of energy.

Lord Adair was handsome, and Celine wholeheartedly agreed with Penelope that she had never seen a more attractive specimen. His shoulders were broad, hips slim, features sensual, and his eyes were hooded, heavily lashed and intelligent.

Lord Adair greeted the women in a deep, delectable voice and then proceeded to instruct the servants to lay the dead man on the carpeted floor.

Once the women had fanned away the effects of Lord Adair's good looks from their senses, they turned their attention towards the unfortunate dead body.

The dead man had finely cut features. His chin was stubborn, lips generous, nose aquiline, and his inky, curled hair was rebellious and soft enough to be the envy of all English dandies. He was handsome and perhaps as handsome as Lord Adair, but it was difficult to tell due to his unfortunate pallor which was a sickly mixture of yellow and green.

"Adair, I hope you have a good reason for depositing a dead man on my Turkish carpet," the duke commented irritably.

The dead man emitted a soft snore.

Penelope and Celine emitted an ear splitting screech.

"Your grace, how could you think that I would be so insensitive as to bring a dead man into your home, especially when," Everyone waited for Lord Adair to say the word expecting, confined or indisposed aloud. His eyes skittered away from Penelope's stomach and he finished lamely," when you have ladies present in the house."

The duke's shoulders relaxed. "So have you knocked the fellow out?"

"Nothing of the sort. We were at the Blue Cap last night and had a little too much to drink. George here has a delicate constitution and a great liking for the strong stuff. You can see the two don't mix well. He has been unconscious for the last four hours."

Celine peered down at George lying on the floor. "He does not look delicate," she commented.

"No, in fact, his shoulders are broad, arms muscular, hips—" Penelope began, and the duke growled. Penelope ignored him and continued, "Hips, I imagine, are firm. I cannot tell, since he is lying on his back."

"You are married," the duke reminded her, "to me."

"Pity," Penelope sighed.

"He has lovely dark curls," Dorothy gushed.

"Dorothy, leave or your pet goes to the butcher," Celine whispered.

Dorothy left.

"What do you think, Celine?" Penelope asked indicating the sleeping man.

Celine stared down at the sleeping man, her hands twisting her skirts. She finally gave up the battle and whipped out a pristine, rose embroidered handkerchief which she used to scrub away the dirt mark on the man's left cheek. She went on to straighten his boot, push away the curl from his forehead and smooth out a wrinkle in his sleeve.

"He is not a couch, Celine, whose cushions need to be straightened," Penelope remarked. "Now, stop adjusting his limbs and tell me, do you find him handsome?"

"His countenance is a trifle green," Celine replied, "but other than that he is very handsome. Only a squint eye can take away from his fine features. Is he squinty, Lord Adair?"

"Ah, tea is here," Penelope interrupted. Her eyes followed the plates laden with fruits and toasts.

"Sugar?" Penelope asked pouring Lord Adair a cup.

"Yes, please," Lord Adair replied.

Celine chewed a biscuit. Here they were standing over a man lying prostrate on the duke's excellent Turkish carpet drinking tea out of the duchess' excellent china. This whole situation felt a little bit odd, and yet no one else seemed to find it in the least bit strange.

"I think I dribbled some tea on him," Penelope announced peering down at the sleeping man.

"I think we should sit," the duke said, hastily steering his wife towards the couch. "Then you can tell us, Adair, what brings you here at this hour and who in the world is this fellow."

Lord Adair sipped from the cup. The china looked ridiculously tiny in his large hands. He drained the cup in one gulp and set it aside. "This intoxicated gentleman happens to be Viscount Elmer."

"Adair, you are mistaken. Elmer is twice this man's size with soft bits and two sprigs of oiled hair on his head," the duke said.

Lord Adair sighed. "I see, you have no doubt been busy and are as yet unaware of the slight upset in the Earl of Devon's household—"

Penelope lifted a palm up. "Lord Adair, could you please start from the very beginning. I have been confined to the four walls of this mansion ever since I discovered that I was expecting ... Celine close your mouth, Lord Adair knows far more about women than you can ever fathom. Now, Lord Adair, I want you tell us all about this viscount in detail and slowly. Charles, don't you dare interrupt. I have not seen a single soul for months and months and months. I need to hear another human speak, to tell a tale, a tiny spark of entertainment ...."

"You are surrounded by almost three hundred servants, your two sisters, a husband, and up until last month my mother was constantly by your side ... and of course Sir Henry, "the duke began. A glare from his wife shut him up.

"Yes, well, let me start from the beginning," Lord Adair said once the duke and duchess had settled down. "The ninth Earl of Devon has two sons. The elder of the two, Richard Irvin, recently decided to marry a Spanish girl who knew not a lick of English. The Earl of Devon threw a grand ball to celebrate the occasion. The king himself asked to dance with the bride, and after that disaster struck. The warm blooded, sharp tongued girl was a bit too vocal in her protestations when the king's fingertips started roaming a little too freely during the dance. She failed to comprehend that the fingertips were royal, for her translator and companion, a charming Miss Daisy, failed to enlighten her, since she lay sprawled in the gazebo after drinking a few too many glasses of punch." Lord Adair smiled. "And it was only natural that Richard's new bride should pluck a glass of wine from Dame Melford's hand and dump it on his highnesses' head."

"She didn't," his listeners gasped.

"She did, and what's more she proceeded to pinch the fleshy bit near his waist when he refused to release her. Richard and his bride escaped for Spain that very night."

"Naturally," Penelope commented.

"After that," Lord Adair continued, "the Earl of Devon was afraid of losing his title. He therefore disinherited his eldest son and claimed his younger son, George Irvin, to be his heir. This young man is George Irvin, Viscount Elmer, and the future Earl of Devon."

"Good lord, so this is the infamous George," the duke said, eyeing the fellow with renewed interest.

"Infamous?" Celine asked.

Lord Adair nodded, "He was a terror as a child and he grew no better in his later years. He was thrown out of Oxford which embarrassed his father. As a result the Earl of Devon threw him out of the house. After that began George's truly colourful life. He spied for the French against the English, but really it was for the English against the French. He caused countless scandals by flirting with married women. Half of England's husbands would love to get their hands on him."

"I don't care about his escapades," the duke grumbled, "What I want to know is why have you brought the blasted man here?"

"He is hiding. His father is looking for him, since he is the heir and he wants to bring him back home and train him. But he does not want to be found, and apparently he cannot sail for the time being and he won't tell me why. So he came to stay with me." Lord Adair shut his silver snuffbox with a snap. "I cannot keep him. He steals my tobacco and then dares to puff away in my face. He wears my dressing gown, wakes me up at odd hours, he has people chasing him, I cannot venture out of doors with him. He flirts with my cook, he has charmed my valet—"

"But why have you brought him here? He sounds ghastly," the duke repeated, his facial muscles twitching in warning.

Lord Adair turned his back on the duke and faced Penelope, "He is charming, extremely charming … a big hit with the ladies. I am fond of the fellow. Perhaps I got carried away and exaggerated his unfortunate habits—"

"When you speak well of him, you don't sound convincing. You forget I live in London too and therefore have heard enough about his shady character," the duke growled.

Lord Adair straightened his back and looked the duke in the eye, "I am his third cousin, whereas you, Blackthorne, are his second cousin. Therefore, it is your responsibility to keep the fellow. I have to go abroad on an urgent matter for the king and can no longer have him in my house. It is a sensitive issue. You will have to do your family duty and give this man a roof over his curly head."

CHAPTER FOUR

"I think you are making up this urgent matter just to fob him off on me. You told me you had retired from the spy business," the duke scowled.

"I had decided to retire, but the case is extremely intriguing. I had to take it," Lord Adair replied.

"I don't believe he is my second cousin. You are making it up."

"I spent all of last night looking up my family tree searching for the right person to inflict ... I mean, leave him with. Here, I brought proof," Lord Adair said triumphantly handing the duke the family tree. "Now, my great grandmother Beatrice is George's great grandmother's sister. Therefore, George's great, great aunt Rebecca is my great grandmother."

Three confused faces frowned at the large family tree.

The duke spent a few minutes examining the paper.

"He may be your third cousin, but I don't see any connection," the duke crowed, "to my family. I knew he was no blasted relative of mine."

Lord Adair leaned closer to the duke, "Sophia," he coughed out.

The duke paled.

"Who?" Penelope asked.

"Sophia," the duke mumbled, "my grandmother."

"She is also George's great aunt," Lord Adair said.

Penelope's face cleared, "the one whose name has been crossed out in the family—"

"Yes," the duke cut in sharply.

"Why is her name crossed out?" Penelope asked, failing to interpret the duke's warning look.

"Because—"

"I will tell the tale," the duke snapped at Lord Adair. "She is my grandmother."

Lord Adair's eyes twinkled. He gestured for him to proceed.

"Now, Sophia Radclyff, my grandmother, is someone we do not discuss and we will continue not to discuss in the future," the duke said, his eyes boring into the three faces in front of him.

"After today you mean, that is, after you tell us why she is not to be spoken of in the first place," Penelope agreed.

"What I am about to disclose shall not leave this room," the duke added quietly. It was not a request but an order.

Celine bit her lip wondering if she had any right to learn the duke's family secret. Penelope's hand clamped down on her arm forcing her to remain.

"Continue," Penelope begged her husband.

The duke closed his eyes, "Sophia Radclyff ..."

"Yes," Penelope prompted.

"Had an adulterous affair with a French royal."

"Hmm," Penelope said not impressed.

"She was twenty five at the time," the duke continued. "And then she turned thirty and ..."

"And?" Penelope encouraged.

"She had an illicit affair with a Spanish Royal."

Celine's eyebrows shot up.

"After that," the duke concluded crisply, "she ran away with a sultan. When she came back to England, it was on the arm of a Rajah. She died at the old age of eighty and in the arms of a flea trainer."

"Good Lord," Penelope whispered. This time she was impressed, as was Celine.

A small silence ensued after this revelation.

"But I still refuse to believe that my grandmother is this scoundrel's great aunt," the duke burst out. He grabbed the bell and rang it furiously, "I am going to get my own family tree out and then we will see."

Perkins' old nose appeared inside the door, "Your grace?"

"Get me the Radclyff family tree," the duke barked.

The tree arrived. The duke poured over it. He frowned, traced, counted, held the paper up to the light, and finally glared.

After another minute of going back and forth between the two sheets, he said, "My wife is indisposed and Celine is unmarried. I am not going to have this sort of fellow in the house at this time."

"Gunhilda and I are good enough chaperones for Celine," Penelope broke in.

"No," the duke snapped.

"Someone is trying to kidnap him. I can't leave him alone in England, especially when he is refusing to go to his father for protection. You have to keep him. If he gets too vexing, then just let the fellows kidnap him. Let him stay for a while and then decide," Lord Adair requested one last time.

"Oh, let's wake him up," Penelope cried in frustration." I am sick of the man sleeping away while we talk about him over his head." She picked up a crimson vase from the table, grabbed the lilies in it and savagely flung them aside. She then poured the water from the vase on top of Lord George Rodrick Irvin, the future ninth Earl of Devon, currently holding the courtesy title of Viscount Elmer and having nine thousand pounds of yearly income.

The duke watched her lustily, while the rest eyed her warily.

George Rodrick Irvin finally spluttered awake. He blinked the water from his lashes, and his vivid blue eyes fell on Celine who was directly in his line of vision.

Not squinty, Celine thought, her own brown gaze caught and trapped by his bright blue one. And for someone who had spent the night overindulging and was rudely awakened by the contents of a flower pot he looked remarkably well. She stared at him like a mooncalf, her breath stuck somewhere in her throat, her limbs frozen and her wits cruising.

George's lips curved up in a crooked smile.

She shyly smiled back.

George closed his eyes, opened his mouth and sang in a rich rumbling voice,

Up and down the market town,
Wearing a bonnet and bridal gown,
You hollered, you hollered and you hollered till your face was blue,
That your love was off to Timbuctoo.
Now you are free to join me in my feather bed,
Where we shall play heels over head!

Celine's smile vanished and she inched closer to Penelope. "What is he doing?" she asked from the corner of her mouth.

"He is singing a bawdy song," Penelope whispered back.

"Whatever for?" Celine asked.

"I think he thinks he is in a tavern."

"But he isn't," Celine said. "Should I inform him?"

"No, from the looks of him I suggest we stay silent."

"He does look wild eyed."

"He should stop singing. It is disturbing the men," Penelope frowned.

"I think a wheel in his brain has dislodged," Celine suggested.

"And now that wheel is rattling around in his head," Penelope agreed.

"Not rattling but sloshing around so loudly that he can no longer think, and hence he is spewing nonsense."

Penelope pressed Celine's hand warmly, "I am glad we are related. We can read each other's thoughts so well."

Celine smiled.

"Wench," George stopped singing and addressed Celine, "what sort of an establishment is this? Get me a brandy."

Wench, Celine mouthed in shock, while Mrs Beatle inside her head collapsed in a dead faint.

"Celine is not a wench," Penelope informed him, "she is a lady."

"Pardon me, Miss, you do look like someone starched enough to cut a man in two," George corrected himself cheerfully.

His smile vanished when he spotted Penelope's large belly, "Is that—" he started to ask but never finished, for Penelope swung back her fist and punched him in the face.

A minute of stunned silence later, the duke carefully asked his wife, "My dear, was that necessary?"

"He was ogling my bosom," Penelope replied primly, "and singing a bawdy song. I am surprised you did not take offence, Charles."

The duke wiped his brow, "I would love to agree with you, but I don't think he could see straight or think straight. You might have been a little hast—"

"Lord Adair," Penelope cut in, "I have been told that most aristocrats are related to each other. Is that true?"

"I suppose to an extent, yes," Lord Adair replied, confused at the sudden change in topic.

Penelope chewed her lip thoughtfully. "Do you think Lord Elmer is related to the king?"

"Undoubtedly," Lord Adair said.

Penelope howled in distress. "I have given the king's cousin a bloody nose. I am so, so sorry."

Celine let the duke handle Penelope. Meanwhile, she spent her time ensuring that not a speck of blood tarnished the duke's excellent Turkish carpet. Within a few moments she had every handkerchief in the room laid under George's head and under his nose. She then called for the brandy. The clock was striking eight 'o' clock in the morning, but the way things were going she was sure that everyone would need something far stronger than tea or coffee.

Perkins wobbled into the room with the brandy tray, and Celine picked up a glass and froze.

The silver tray was well polished, and in it she could clearly see her reflection and the fact that not one, not two, but three strands of dark brown hair had escaped her coiled bun.

She frowned.

CHAPTER FIVE

Celine dipped the quill in ink to write a letter on behalf of the duchess politely declining an invitation to yet another party.

The duchess herself sat reading her favourite novel with her feet up on the footstool while a maid fanned her with a bunch of large peacock feathers.

Celine paused to stretch her arms and rub her tired eyes. The morning's excitement combined with precious little sleep the night before was taking a toll on her.

The large grandfather clock struck three times.

Her wits woke as if doused with cold water. She had twenty minutes to finish all the letters before Dorothy was done with her music lessons and half an hour before she would have to insist that Penelope retire to her room to rest. Thereafter, Mrs Cornley would meet her in the …

The duke stormed into the Blue Room. "Lord Elmer cannot stay," he groused.

"He is only here for a day, Charles," Penelope soothed her irate husband.

"Adair should have taken the fellow with him," the duke muttered.

"You know he had to urgently leave town on the King's business. Besides, I invited Lord Elmer to stay for dinner. It would have been rude not to ask him. Mrs Beacon's handbook for housewives that your mother kindly left for me clearly states that—"

"Penny, I don't like him. Adventure seems to trail him or he seeks out danger like an irresponsible child. All my life I have heard of pickles that the fellow has got into. Once I heard he was shipwrecked, another time kidnapped, and then he had kidnapped someone. I remember now, I had met him in a pub once when he had come to return a priceless vase that he had stolen from Lord Belair. He said he had stolen it to see if he could steal it. Then when he realised that he had successfully stolen it and that no one realised that it was him who had done the deed, he decided to return the vase."

"That was noble of him."

The duke's mouth twisted humourlessly, "He said the vase was so ugly that it offended his refined senses. He couldn't sleep with the thing in the same room as him. He was compelled to give it back. He is a thief, a blackguard, a flirt."

"So is Jimmy the highwayman, and he is my friend," Penelope snapped.

The duke gave up and glared at the only other person present in the room … Celine.

Celine smiled. She was used to the duke's moods. He had a heart of gold even if his face wore a constant glowering expression. She picked up the glass which Perkins had just brought into the room and dangled it in front of Penelope. "Here, Penny, drink up."

"No," Penelope said firmly.

"Come, just a sip," Celine coaxed.

"You are trying to poison me," Penelope said, her nose wrinkling in distaste.

"With cow's milk?"

"Where is Lord Elmer?" Penelope asked taking a reluctant sip.

"In bed. Lord Adair suggested that I let him sleep all day and only wake him at dinner time," Celine replied going back to her chair and picking up the quill.

"Do you want to marry him?" Penelope asked, dumping the milk into a priceless vase.

"Marry who?" Celine asked producing another glass of milk.

"Lord Elmer."

"Penny!"

"I could ask the duke to keep him around if you fancied him," Penelope persisted.

"You can safely send him home."

Penelope sighed, "Once this babe is born, I will invite you for a season in London. You will have plenty of men to choose from."

Celine produced a third glass of milk, since Penelope had dumped the second into a potted plant. "Drink … for the babe."

Penelope drank.

★★★

Later that evening Celine caught Lord Elmer on his way to the dining room. She scrutinised his pallor from beneath her lashes. Sleep had done him good. He was only a trifle green and looked far handsomer than he had that morning.

She swallowed and peeked again.

He smiled, his vivid blue eyes crinkling at the corners.

She searched his bright clear gaze for a hint of tragedy, a crumb of madness or a smidgen of sorrow. She waded through the sparkling intelligence and dug through the humour. Alas, all she could find was an odd alert expression, which she realised after a moment of contemplation was happiness.

He cleared his throat.

She did not hear him, her brain whirling speedily as she judged, dissected and guessed what sort of a man-beast stood in front of her. It was a habit of hers to liken men and women to various creatures of the animal kingdom. It helped her understand them better. For instance her father was a scrawny hen and her mother a wild angry goose who often honked and waved her wings at him.

Now, Lord Elmer seemed the sort of man that women, animals and children adored on sight. He was a dog, not one of those small moody creatures but a large dog with a pleasant, easy countenance that would, if one insisted, eat a banana peel just to oblige you. Though, he was by no means an idiotic dog but a smart one. One that looked muscular enough to take down a couple of robbers with well-placed bites using sharp, white teeth ….

George waved his hand in front of her glassy eyes. "A penny for your thoughts," he said and then chuckled at his own joke when he noticed Penelope waddling towards them.

"I was wondering what dog … err … Did you sleep well?"

"I did. The mattress was stuffed with a sufficient amount of goose feathers."

Celine didn't know what to say in reply to that, so she quickly moved on to the reason she had accosted him. Thrusting a silver tray with a selection of moustaches towards him, she said, "Here, Lord Elmer, choose a moustache."

George promptly picked up a full, bushy red moustache. He patted it into place and asked, "How do I look?"

"Moustached."

He smiled and waggled his eyebrows, "Come, admit you have never seen a more handsome specimen."

"I have," Celine said smiling back, "Your third cousin, Lord Adair."

"Dashed cousin! Your words wound me, my dear. Couldn't you cushion your darts?"

"We will be late for dinner." She handed the silver tray to a passing maid and made her way towards the Grand Stairs.

"Ah, you are one of those," he said softly.

She halted, her brow rising in query.

He took hold of her elbow and gently tugged her forward.

"What do you mean?" she asked, refusing to budge until she had an answer.

"You are a rational creature. A sensible creature," he expanded.

Her mouth tightened.

"Or you pretend to be. I will have to find out which it is."

"You have an entire evening, Lord Elmer, to dissect my personality, but it would be better if you spent your time appreciating the food. We have a wonderful chef who has gone to great pains to impress you with his culinary skills."

"Celine?" he said, pausing outside the dining room.

"You may call me Miss Fairweather."

"I shall call you what I like. After all, I am here for just one evening. Now, Celine, be a good hostess and tell me why am I wearing a fake moustache to dinner?"

"Sir Henry is the duke's maternal grandfather and he does not like men who do not wear moustaches. He does not think men without moustaches are ... well, mannish. He is very old, so rather than distress him, the duke presents a moustache to all the bare faced guests and asks them to stick it on in Sir Henry's presence."

George nodded unimpressed.

Celine hurried on, "Also Sir Henry may keel over and die any moment, so please be prepared for that. He may cough, choke and wheeze during the dinner as well. Ignore it unless the duke clearly indicates that this time he has definitely set sail for heaven because you may think he is dead and bewail the occurrence only to find out that he has only fallen asleep while eating his soup. It can be embarrassing. I speak from experience," she finished and breathlessly waited for his response. He was sure to have questions. Everyone did.

"I hope we have peas. I am fond of peas," George said and walked into the dining room.

***

Penelope and the duke were already seated at the dinner table when Celine and George joined them.

Sir Henry arrived a moment later carried on a red velvet chair by four muscular footmen. He barely nodded at George. His hungry eyes were on his pocket watch. At eight sharp his hand slammed the tabletop signalling that the first course be served.

The soup arrived and everyone picked up the right spoon, dipped it into beautiful bowls, and expertly avoiding chins sipped correctly and noiselessly. The servers too were like shadows, flitting in an out, removing, filling and replacing food and drinks at regular intervals. It was a perfect aristocratic meal that was conducted in ear splitting silence.

The second course arrived when all of a sudden George flung down his napkin declaring that he couldn't help it, he had to break the silence and speak.

Spoons halted in mid-air. Disapproving heads turned his way.

George kept his eyes fixed on Sir Henry, bravely ignoring the icy atmosphere. He had to speak, he said, for he could no longer hold back his admiration for Sir Henry's remarkable, envious, a thing of legends moustache. He had to ooze and compliment and positively kiss the hands that kept such a moustache well groomed and shining.

Sir Henry's valet in charge of the grooming was quickly called forth and his flattered hands dutifully kissed.

The moustache, George declared, turning his attention back to Sir Henry's hairy upper lip, was even more beautiful in the flickering candle light.

It sparkled, it glowed. It was, he roared, a masterpiece.

Sir Henry simpered, thawed and finally melted into a warm puddle of pleasure. No one had dared to be so bold, so daring and so rebellious in his presence for a long, long time. George had behaved like a man. In fact, he was almost heroic in the way he had declared his admiration for the moustache. George was paying homage to Sir Henry's most prized asset, and every one of those hairs on Sir Henry's white moustache was charmed beyond words. In fact, they were so thrilled that they almost blushed pink.

The aristocratic silence had been broken, and with Sir Henry's happy mood, the room turned warm and informal. Spoons scraped plates, glasses clinked and voices rose and fell.

Conversation was now part of the meal.

"I had a letter from old Gomfrey," Sir Henry excitedly wheezed across the table.

"He is as old as you, Grandfather," the duke replied.

"He is a month older. His cook has disappeared. You are the duke, find him," Sir Henry rasped.

"Find who?"

"The cook, you blasted boy."

"That's odd, I had a letter from Lady Marianne, and she told me that just last week her cook disappeared. He came back within four days, but he seemed traumatised, and he now squeals every time anyone mentions pigeons or if he even sees one," Penelope added.

"I heard about that, "the duke said wiping his mouth, "Cooks are disappearing and appearing all over England. No one knows why. Apparently some masked men keep the cooks and ask them for recipes for treacle bread. Then they are tickled using pigeon feathers to ensure that they have nothing more to spill. They are then sent back home. It is all very strange."

"Two of our chefs are embroiled in a complicated love rectangle. We have one chef left who ensures that we get our meals on time, and I hope he is not the one kidnapped. He is a sensitive sort of fellow. Suffers from nerves," Penelope said worriedly.

Celine snuck a few green leaves onto Penelope's plate when she wasn't looking. George winked at her from across the table.

"I saw that," Penelope said catching the wink. "Lord Elmer, our Celine won't fall for your flirtations. She is too—"

"Sensible?" George asked smiling.

Penelope smiled back, "yes, but there are two silly things about her. Firstly when she was fifteen years old she read a novel and the heroine of that novel was called Celine. Since then she has insisted that everyone call her Celine. She wouldn't answer to anything else."

"Her name is not Celine?" the duke asked in surprise.

"No, it is—"

"Pass the salt, Penny," Celine interrupted, her foot stamping Penelope's under the table.

"What is her name?" George probed.

"Well, the other silly thing about her is the fact that she only sneezes during spring, and all through spring she sneezes a lot. And when she does sneeze, it is five little achoos in rapid succession and no more or no less."

"What is her name?" George persisted.

"It is—"

Celine sneezed, drowning out Penelope's answer. She sneezed four more times. Thereafter, George didn't get to ask any more questions because after Celine stopped sneezing ... Sir Henry set his beard on fire.

It all happened because of a particular variety of fish called Perch. Now, Perch was in season again, and Perch made into a dish called water-soochy happened to be Sir Henry's favourite dish.

When Perkins brought this dish in, Sir Henry's nose caught the scent and he brightened. Once the plate was placed near Sir Henry, he promptly pulled the candle closer to inspect the contents of the dish.

Sir Henry was a little bit blind. Hence, he needed to put the candle right up to the bowl and bend his head forward a good bit to see properly.

Sir Henry, apart from being blind, was also forgetful, which was why he had forgotten that he happened to have a long white beard made up of lots of ignitable hairs which naturally burst into orange and yellow flames when they came into contact with the fat beeswax candle.

Penelope saw the flaming beard and screamed.

George smelled the smoke and yelled.

Celine squeaked politely, and the duke roared.

In a trice the water from three jugs was flung at Sir Henry's flaming beard. George threw the stewed calf's ears and the pork in Robert sauce, since that was all he had close at hand.

One thing led to another and the smell of burning hair permeated the entire meal ruining it for everyone. It was all very traumatic, but the positive thing, as George cheerfully pointed out after the flames had been doused, was the fact that the beard was gone but the moustache with only a few singed hairs remained almost unscathed.

It was, he announced, an immortal moustache.

A beard had been set on fire and a moustache saved, Celine

sighed, as she got up from the dinner table. Surely nothing more would go wrong this day?

CHAPTER SIX

As per the midwife's instructions, the duchess had to retire right after dinner. She was predictably reluctant and not at all sleepy. Hence, the duke, as had become a ritual of sorts, went along to keep her company in the bedroom.

Sir Henry, who was rumoured to be over a hundred years old, only ventured to the dining room every day for dinner and thereafter spent his time in his room dictating letters to his old friends, most of whom were dead but no one had the heart to tell him so. Which meant that Celine and George were left staring at each other over cups of fragrant coffee.

"We don't have a chaperone," Celine commented.

"We don't want one," George responded.

"Speak for yourself," Celine muttered, her eyes darting to the door.

"Are you expecting company?"

Celine's cup rattled in the saucer, "No, why would you think so?"

"You are impatiently eyeing the clock."

"I think I shall retire for the night."

"Retire? Are you feeling alright?" a young feminine voice asked from the doorway. "I was hoping to find you in library. I wanted to know all about the handsome–"

"Guest," George finished for her. "Why don't you ask him yourself?"

"That is my sister Dorothy who should be in bed at this hour," Celine said, "Dorothy, this is Lord Elmer."

"I can't sleep," Dorothy said, scrutinising George.

"You have a lot of sisters. A lot of beautiful sisters," George commented, standing up and bowing to Dorothy.

"Six sisters in all," Dorothy replied, her lashes fluttering expertly.

She dipped in an elegant curtsey, skirts flared, knees bent almost to the point where she was sitting in mid-air. She thus remained suspended for a few seconds before rising and offering George a practised smile, just the right amount of teeth gleaming through, lips stretched but not too wide, and eyes crinkled at the corners.

"Dorothy," Celine warned.

Dorothy ignored her, her eyes on George. "How long are you staying here?"

"I am not sure, but after meeting you, I hope I can stay for at least a few days."

Dorothy giggled, "Are you flirting with me?"

"Yes, do you mind?"

"I like you,"

"And I," he said soulfully, "like you too."

"Let's get married," Dorothy suggested shrewdly.

George straightened and eyed her with respect," How old did you say you were?"

"I didn't. I just turned thirteen"

A tiny sigh of relief escaped him, "Yes, well that is what I thought, but one can never be too careful."

"Does that mean you don't want to marry me?"

George smiled, a dimple flashing in his right cheek. "I do but—"

"Enough," Celine snapped. "My lord, you should not be putting ideas into her silly head. And you, Dorothy, go back to bed."

Dorothy pouted.

George stuck a pencil up his nose.

Celine spluttered.

Dorothy laughed.

Celine narrowed her eyes, and Dorothy eyed her back though narrowed lids.

War was declared and silent battle ensued between the two sisters conducted by blinking, rolling, glaring and finally squinting of the eyes.

The war was won by Celine who punctuated her squint by pointing firmly at the door.

Dorothy conceded defeat and departed with good grace.

Celine peeked out into the corridor to ensure that Dorothy had truly departed for bed. She waited until Dorothy's blue skirts disappeared around the corner. Satisfied she turned back to find

George standing near the revolving glass cabinet that held various liqueurs, desert wines and cordials.

He offered her a glass of Chartreuse. She shook her head, "I apologise, Lord Elmer, but my head is aching dreadfully. I think I will retire early tonight. If you will excuse me."

A hint of disappointment crossed his face before he covered it with an expression of boredom.

Her feet dragged as she moved towards the door. She wished circumstances had been different and allowed her more time with him.

She looked back at him one last time. This was goodbye. He would be gone the next morning and perhaps they would never meet again.

He was busy fiddling with his snuff box and didn't notice her parting look.

She walked to her room feeling a little guilty. She should have been a better host. After all, he had no one to amuse him all evening ... but what else could she do? Not only was it improper for her to spend all evening with him alone and unchaperoned, it was also the only hour that she got to herself when she could pursue her own investigations. Time was short, and once Penelope gave birth, she would no longer have a reason to stay in London. It would be a year before she returned to the city for a season and by then it could be too late.

❦❦❦

Exactly one hour after leaving George in the saloon, Celine once again materialized on top of the Grand Staircase. She appeared wearing a long black cloak that was meant to conceal the wearer, and Celine believed herself to be well concealed.

She took short cautious steps down the staircase, her trembling hands clutching three short, fat tallow candles, while her eyes darted hither and tither. Like an unseasoned creature who was reluctantly dipping her toes into the pool of misconduct, she tiptoed her way towards the library.

It was clear she was an amateur at the art of deception, for she was certain that if she was found and her aim discovered, she would be ruined.

She was a greenhead, for fearful thoughts raced through her mind as she snuck down the stairs, muscles tensed and ears pealed like a

Yorkshire terrier for the slightest sound.

She was a dabbler in all things wicked because a distant thump and a fluttering moth almost had her screaming and flying back to her room.

She was certainly a novice, for a finely skilled miscreant would never meander down the hallway like an ill tutored, badly dressed assassin at nine in the evening.

Nine 'o' clock is not a frightening hour. Nor is ten or eleven. The sort of fear that Celine was experiencing rightly belonged to any hour after midnight and before five in the morning. And yet she was shaking, her resolve tested over and over again by the flickering lamps that lit her path casting shadows that loomed, trembled and leaped at her every now and then.

She wondered why sneaking around the Blackthorne Mansion had not become easier. With practice one would have expected it to, but it hadn't. She still felt as terrified as she had the first time when she had snuck into the library three days ago.

Her entire journey from the top of the Grand Staircase to the library had been emotionally taxing but uneventful. The million eyes that she had imagined were following her every move melted away only after she had pushed open the large wooden doors and entered the library.

The darkness and the familiar scent of tobacco, leather, books and ink calmed her nerves. Feeling slightly silly she pulled out a tinder box from her pocket and lit a candle. Firmly closing the door behind her she quickly moved towards the back of the library.

The library was a large circular room located on the ground floor of the family wing of the Blackthorne Mansion. The front of the library contained a pleasant reading area with two sofas piled high with plump cushions along with a day bed, a few chairs and a large wooden table.

Not a speck of dust sat on the books placed on the tall ornate wooden shelves, and if one pulled out *Romance of Hoggy* sitting on the fifth row of the third bookshelf, then a secret entrance to the basement would open up behind the main fireplace.

Celine did not know about the secret entrance and nor would she have cared. She nipped smartly to the back of the library, her stride purposeful and confident.

The back of the library was slightly different from the front. For one thing the back was chillier, darker and somehow smelled mustier. The sort of smell that one gets when one enters a dungeon. The back had no windows. A cold fireplace sat in the corner, and in front of it was a long unattractive wooden table with four hard backed simple chairs.

Celine set the candle down on the table and walked up to the fireplace, which by the looks of it hadn't been used in years. She reached up into the chimney and felt around the sides. Almost immediately she found what she was looking for. She pulled out the cloth made out of thick blue wool that was hidden in a crevice in the chimney and took it to the table. Thereafter, she sat down and taking out the papers from the bag spread them on the table and got to work.

Half an hour later she set her quill down and stretched. She was halfway through rolling her neck when a deep voice behind her said, "It appears to be a love letter ... or rather a love poem."

Celine squeaked and sprang out of her chair, "Lord Elmer, give me that," she growled, noticing the paper in his hand. Somehow he had snuck up behind her and stolen one of the sheets from the table.

"Not yet," George grinned, lifting the letter above his head and well out of her reach. He squinted at the paper and started reading aloud. "For Celine, my beloved kitten, here is a love poem." He frowned, peered at the writing and then chuckled. "It is a love poem titled, 'My Darling Dormouse'."

"Lord Elmer, be reasonable. This is not proper," Celine pleaded.

"I am unreasonable, and I happen to enjoy everything that is improper," George replied cheerfully. "Besides, the title has intrigued me." He cleared his throat and started reading,

Your green eyes are bright,
They take me on a flight,

Celine suddenly leaped at him, "Give that back now, my lord, or I will scream."

He ignored her and swiftly moved until the table was between them. She chased him around the table, and he continued to read whilst easily evading her,

Your green eyes are bright,

They take me on a flight,
To lunar land.
Your red lips they pout,
Like a bird's snout,
While pecking the blue insects to death.

He smiled and tucked the poem in his pocket. "My dear Miss Fairweather, that poem should not have ended like that. A tad depressing, wouldn't you say? And your poet seems to have given up on the last line. The beginning shows promise and the bird with the snout ... err ...."

Celine dug her nails into his arm, "I am a very peaceful person, my lord. I don't want to hurt you, but I might just have to. Please be a gentleman and give me back the letter."

"But things have just become interesting, Celine. I thought you were a charming, slightly pretty, level headed young miss. But what's this? A young girl praised for being sensible, taking care of the confined duchess, a respectable young lady who one would think was too old for fanciful notions has gone and fallen in love with a poet. A poet called ... let me see ... ah yes, Philbert."

Celine stepped away from him. Her eyes turned cold. "What do you want?"

"A lot of things, but let me start with a question," he replied. His hand shot out and gripped her chin. He tilted her face this way and that, his brows furrowed in confusion. "Philbert the poet wrote this love poem for you. It clearly says so in the beginning so no point in denying it. He loves you and yet he writes those lines completely forgetting that your eyes are, in fact, brown. Why?"

Celine scowled and wrenched her face away, "Sometimes they look green."

"Dark brown eyes can look green?" he asked sceptically.

"Fine, he was just learning to write, and he said that green is far more romantic a colour than brown."

"I beg to differ," Lord Elmer said softly.

Her eyes shot up to his and she froze. His eyes were blue. Blue like an ocean on a sunny day, and she was a river plunging into its depths ....

He blinked.

She came crashing back to earth.

They both cleared their throats.

"Wha—" she started to say.

"I was—" he said at the same time.

Again throats were cleared. Finally she asked, "The letter?"

"I will give it back to you,"

She smiled.

"But," he said.

The smile faded.

"You have to find a way for me to stay here at the Blackthorne Mansion until Lord Adair returns from his trip abroad or else …."

CHAPTER SEVEN

Celine paled, "I cannot. Lord Elmer, what you ask is impossible. Penelope is currently indisposed, and the duke will never allow a strange man to stay here at such a sensitive time."

"Find a way," he said stubbornly.

"Be reasonable, Lord Elmer. How can I convince the duke? I am Penelope's younger sister and here to help with her household duties and that is all. This is not my house. I am a guest just like you—"

"Not exactly. You are the duchess' beloved sister."

"Stepsister."

"Beloved nonetheless," he argued. "You grew up with her. Surely you know a way of convincing her."

"I don't," she said crossing her arms. "I can however suggest the stables to you as an excellent lair. The hay loft above the stallion named Sultan is particularly airy. I won't tell a soul, I promise."

"Please?" he begged opening his eyes wide, "I would rather have a feather bed."

"No."

"I refuse to share space with horses. Think of my excellent lineage," he reminded her haughtily.

"The horses are the best in England. They are also of excellent lineage ... practically royalty. You will feel at home," she smirked.

"I am not going back to my father's house."

Something in his voice made her look up. She bit her lip and frowned.

Noticing the slight softening in her expression he grabbed her hand. "Will you hear my plight? It is very sad."

Celine eyed his doleful face, and her heart in spite of herself squeezed in sympathy. She nodded.

A brief smile touched his lips. He led her to the chair and gently pushed her back into the seat. "I was thrown out of Oxford—" he began.

"I know," she interrupted, "the duke told us."

"He did?"

"Yes, when you were asleep this afternoon."

"Did he tell you anything else?"

"You were shipwrecked, kidnapped—"

"No, about my family?"

"Your brother was meant to be the heir, but his Spanish bride insulted the king. Your father is not fond of you—"

"What about my mother? Did he say anything about my mother?"

"Mother? No."

"I knew it." he exclaimed.

Was it relief or pain in his voice? She couldn't make out, for he had moved into the shadows away from the candle light.

"My mother," he said unhappily," died when I was but a young lad."

"How young?"

"How old is Dorothy?"

"Thirteen."

"Yes, that sounds about right. I was around her age when she died."

"How did she die?"

"I am telling a story here. Have the courtesy to let me tell it my way. Do not interrupt," he said irritably. "Now, my mother was happiness, love and joy bundled up together in a neat little round package. We loved her. All of us loved her. Each one of us loved her. In fact, even her lady's maid loved her. One day I overheard a footman cooing in the chambermaid's naked ear about a circus that had come to town. I had never been to a circus and being a young, sane boy I naturally wanted to go to this circus. However, my father refused outright."

Celine clucked sympathetically.

"My father had refused but my mother, my brave mother who everyone loved, decided to take us all by herself ... By us, I mean my brother and I," he clarified. "She took our tiny hands and walked into the circus tent. And that was the last time that she walked," he told her sadly, "for the circus had a snake charmer and the snake charmer was a very bad snake charmer. He didn't know how to charm snakes, and that is why one of the poisonous creatures escaped and bit my mother. I still remember its black sinewy body moving towards her, baring its teeth and sinking its fangs deep into her flesh. I screamed and my brother swooned—"

"You said she took your tiny hands and led you into the tent. But before that you said that you were as old as Dorothy when your mother died. You must have had large hands by then. I know my neighbour's son is thirteen and his hands are fairly large—"

"I was a small child," he said through gritted teeth.

Celine blushed, "I am sorry. I didn't mean to question you. Losing your mother at such a young age must have been tragic. Is that why you refuse to return … because her memory haunts you?"

He shook his head, "No, because soon after her death my father married again and brought home a woman as kind as my mother had been. She was a wonderful stepmother. We loved her. Everyone loved her. In fact, even her lady's maid loved her. My wounds were healed."

"And then?"

"She died."

Celine gasped, "How?"

He took a deep breath, "One balmy day, I found my stepmother swinging on a tree branch. You see, her wits had unhinged and raced away never to be found again. It was a tall tree and the branch fairly high. She was swinging, singing and searching. She said she had lost her monkey up the tree and she was trying to coax it down with a song."

"She must have been a wonderful singer," she said in a hushed voice.

"My stepmother was an awful singer, but that never stopped her," he sighed. "She was full of life, singing and swinging on that tree branch, her wits wondering in some whimsical land. I will always remember her like that. It was just before she fell and broke her neck."

"Good lord, no!"

"Yes, well, that was not the end. My father did not give up."

"Bless him."

"He went and procured a third bride."

"Did you all love her as well?"

"No, because the day she got married she disappeared."

"Oh my. Did she also die?"

"No, but her wits did ferment. She went loony on the wedding morning, and my father learned the truth only on the wedding night."

"And then she died?"

"Can I tell the tale?"

"Sorry, continue."

"Are you sure?"

"Yes, please."

"Right, my father told us she was dead."

"That's—"

"And then," he spoke over her, "one day I was sleeping in my bedroom. It was a warm summer night and I was sixteen years old. I had kept my windows and room door open to encourage the reluctant breeze. I was in the half asleep, half awake state where you are exhausted and yet so warm that you can barely sleep. My eyes would open and close …"

"And then?"

"I heard it."

"What?"

"The pitter patter, pitter patter of tiny feet walking on my room's cold stone floor. I squeezed my eyes shut, my breath froze and my whole being stilled to hear the next sound. The pitter patter stopped, but someone was in the room with me. I could feel it in the air around me. My fears were confirmed when I heard something pant. Something was panting in my room, some creature, and then came the pitter patter again. Pitter patter, pant pant, pitter patter, pant pant. I sucked in a breath and steeled myself and opened one eye. One single eye. My lashes lifted up and I dared to look. The moon light streaked in through the windows and what I saw—"

"You saw?" Celine asked breathlessly.

"I saw blood dripping from a dagger held in a thin white hand, the other hand held a burning candle, its hot wax dripping onto her fingers. The owner of these hands wore a torn dress, her long matted hair hanging over her shoulders. And with her was a large hound, a vicious looking creature with a frothing mouth and large wild red eyes. And then… and then the clock went tick tock, tick tock …"

"Tick tock, tick tock," Celine breathed.

"Yes," he whispered, "it went tick tock, tick tock in the house somewhere. The feet of the dog went pitter patter, pitter patter. Tick tock. Pitter patter. Tick tock, pitter patter. And that was when I screamed and my father came rushing in, and I realised that the woman standing with a bloodied knife and a mad dog was no other than my third stepmother who my father keeps locked in the attic. She wanted to murder me."

He whirled around and looked Celine in the eye, "She wants to murder me, Celine, and I cannot blame her, for she does not know her mind. It seems my presence aggravates her, which is why she has tried to kill me twice already. How can you ask me to return knowing that my very own stepmother wants to kill me? I don't want to die. I am too young. It would be tragic if I died. Think, Celine, not about my young life being snuffed out but of all those feminine hearts that would break at the news. You have to help those beautiful young women who want me to live. Help for the sake of your kind. Do something for your country women, my dear. You have to save my life."

A small silence ensued while Celine digested this story. After a while she said, "I am so sorry. Your life sounds incredible. The tragedies ... I am surprised you can even smile. Looking at you no one would think you have had such a hard life."

"I hide the pain well," he said modestly.

"But I can't help you. The duke will never listen to me."

"Celine," he pleaded. "Won't you try?"

"You can stay at an inn. Or a friend's house? You must have friends. What about taking a cottage in the country until Lord Adair returns?"

"Nowhere else is safe. The Duke of Blackthorne is one of the most powerful men in England, and no one would dare trifle with him. Besides, no one even knows he is in England. They think he is in the country with his wife and Blackthorne is lying empty. It is exactly what I need."

"Your stepmother is in in your father's house. In his attic. Locked up. How will she discover you at an inn in London?"

He glared at her. "You ask too many questions. If you want the letter back in your hands and not someone else's, then find a way that lets me stay here or ..."

"Are you blackmailing me?"

"You are not leaving me with any other choice. You won't do it out of kindness knowing I have a mad stepmother and a rabid dog out to get me."

She stared at him in shock.

"You have until ten o clock tomorrow to convince the duke."

"How can you?" she asked, her heart thundering. Her situation suddenly became clear to her and she was terrified. If he spread the word, she would be ruined.

"You left me with no other choice," he repeated.

He avoided her eyes as he walked out of the library.

She stared after him in abject horror.

CHAPTER EIGHT

The sun rose above the horizon and amazingly the clouds over England parted to let the rays through. The birds lifted their beaks up to the sky chirping a greeting, the cows mooed, horses cantered and the dogs barked in pleasure. It was a wonderful morning, but for Celine everything seemed tinted in shades of grey.

She had spent the night wishing all sorts of painful things upon Lord Elmer's handsome head and wondering how to coax the duchess into letting him stay. All those hours of thinking had resulted in only one thing, and that was a headache and no solution.

Now she sat trying to find answers in a tepid cup of tea with occasional glances across the breakfast table at Penelope. She slathered a piece of toast with dark red jam and then proceeded to stab the centre of it with a butter knife. Repeatedly. It was hard to behave like a lady with puffy eyes, no sleep and an overwhelming desire to pummel every inch of the guest in the house.

"Air them out," Penelope commented.

"Eh?" Celine asked.

"Your views, ideas … your thoughts. You should always air them out. Give them an opportunity to run around the room a bit or they get musty."

"I see," Celine frowned.

"I see that you don't see. What I mean to say, my dear, is that something is troubling you and I would like to know what it is. Now out with it."

Celine bit into an egg and chewed.

Penelope watched her chew.

"Nothing is worrying me," Celine finally said.

"Then why are you eating an egg?"

"Because I am hungry."

"You hate eggs and never eat them unless you are upset. And when you are upset all you do is eat eggs. Father is the same, except with him it is rabbits and mushrooms."

Celine pushed her plate away, "Penny, don't you think we should ask Lord Elmer to stay with us until Lord Adair returns?"

Penelope put the spoon down and looked at Celine. "Why?"

"You said you were bored and he is entertaining."

Penelope sighed, "It is very sweet of you to think of my amusement, Celine, but Charles will never agree. Lord Elmer is not exactly a kitten that I can beg to keep so I can tickle him under the chin when I please."

A few moments of silence ensued while Celine spooned the porridge and plopped it back into the bowl.

Penelope buttered the toast and delicately sniffed it. She waited for a minute and then ate it.

"I think you should ask him to stay," Celine repeated. She was feeling particularly dense that morning.

Penelope picked up the tea cup, sniffed it, clapped her hand to her mouth and rushed out of the room.

Celine ordered the serving maid to remove all traces of tea.

Penelope sailed back into the room. "Why are you so keen on having him stay?"

"I haven't spent much time with you because I am busy running the household as well as taking care of Dorothy. And I know how dull you have been feeling lately with nothing to do and nowhere to go. A new face around the house will improve your mood, and Lord Elmer will make excellent company. You seem to like him," Celine finished, pleased with how convincing her argument sounded.

"I do like him. Whatever Charles may say, he seems to be such a nice, likeable young man. But would it be proper?"

"He is the duke's second cousin. He is family," Celine reminded her.

Penelope carefully nudged away the jam pot and searched Celine's face. "Have you taken a fancy to him?"

An automatic denial rose to her lips, but Celine bit it back down.

Penelope took Celine's silence as assent. She immediately brightened and cooed, "My dear sister, you do like him. This is wonderful. This is exactly what I needed to restore my mental equilibrium. It was awfully good of you to go and fall in love with

Lord Elmer," she said rubbing her hands together, "It will give me something to do. A man to help catch, a wedding to plot ... Oh, I can barely contain my excitement."

"I am not in love," Celine feebly protested. She wasn't sure if she should protest, and yet she thought she should, but perhaps not too much ... Confused, she frowned, "Truly, Penny, I don't ... I mean ... well ...."

"Oh, look at you blushing and stuttering like a dim witted virgin. It's sweet," Penelope smiled.

Celine had not turned red but green. She had a feeling things were getting a little out of hand. "You are mistaken—"

"Oh, this is splendid," Penelope said, clapping her hands and completely ignoring Celine's protests.

"What is splendid?" Lord Elmer asked, entering the breakfast room.

Penelope shot Celine a wink. "Why, Lord Elmer, the fact that the duke has agreed to let you stay here at the mansion for as long as you like."

Celine's mouth dropped open. Penelope had just lied. She had lied without remorse and with complete confidence. The duke had done no such thing. She eyed her sister with renewed respect.

"Thank you, I would love to accept your kind invitation," Lord Elmer said ladling four boiled eggs onto his plate.

Penelope beamed at Lord Elmer and Celine in motherly affection.

"Penny," Celine hissed in her ear, "you have not asked the duke. What if he refuses?"

"He won't dare," she retorted with a militant look in her eye.

Celine released Penelope's sleeve. The duke was an intelligent man. Penelope was right. He would never dare. Now the only worry was getting the letter back. What if Lord Elmer decided to hold on to it until the next time he needed something from her?

Her troubled thoughts received a brief respite at the sight of Lady Bathsheba, Penelope's pet goat, prancing into the room. She bounded into the room wearing a flowery bonnet, and a pink ribbon was tied to her tail.

"This is Lady Bathsheba and this, Lady Bathsheba, is Lord Elmer," Penelope introduced.

Lord Elmer politely bowed to the goat and offered it a bit of his apple.

Penelope was charmed. "You chose well," she whispered to Celine.

Celine forced her lips to lift at the corners.

"Your mother loves animals as well doesn't she, Lord Elmer?" Penelope asked, scratching Lady Bathsheba's glossy back. "I remember meeting her at Lady Davenport's ball."

"You must be mistaken," Celine said uncomfortably. Since Penelope had become pregnant, she had also become forgetful. How painful for poor Lord Elmer to hear her sister speak about his dead mother.

Penelope shook her head adamantly, "I am not mistaken. I clearly recall meeting Lady Elmer. I am certain of it, for she had a charming little pug with her, and I could never forget a face that has dared to bring a living animal into Lady Davenport's home. I fondly recall how Lady Davenport had a silent fit, her mouth contorting in the most fascinating ways as she watched Lady Elmer feed the choicest bits to the pug off the refreshment table. What was the little dog's name? Oh yes, Mr Smith. It was a gentle little thing. I fed it a bit of biscuit and he licked my fingers clean. Lord Elmer, am I right? Doesn't your mother have a pug called Mr Smith?"

"Penny, his mother has been dead for years. He has a horrible stepmother who has lost her mind and a snarling, drooling giant dog," Celine whispered urgently.

"Nonsense, Celine. Lord Elmer, is your mother dead? Has your father married again?"

Lord Elmer pushed his plate away. He avoided their eyes as he said, "I wonder where the duke is?"

"He is in his study," Celine said through clenched teeth, "but before you go let me ask you again, Lord Elmer, do you have a stepmother?"

"It is a lovely day," Lord Elmer said standing up. "I would love to spend some time with you, your grace, but I just recalled that I have not informed my valet Nithercott that we are staying. If you will excuse me." And without waiting to be excused, Lord Elmer disappeared from the room.

"Celine, you can't whisper such ridiculous things to me. He must have heard you. Saying his mother is dead and all that nonsense. Truly, Celine, I did not expect this of you." Penelope admonished. "Now you have hurt his feelings. Go and apologise."

"But—"

"No buts. Go."

Celine stabbed the sausage a few times before abandoning it and going in search of Lord Elmer.

How could he tell her all those outlandish stories? Telling her his mother was mad, locked in an attic with a large rabid dog when, in fact, she was a sweet old thing with a little dog … She stopped and a reluctant smile tugged at her.

She giggled.

The story that had seemed only too plausible in candlelight seemed preposterous in broad daylight. It was partly her fault for being so gullible and believing him. Sensing a slight softening in her stance she firmly reminded herself that Lord Elmer still had the letter. She had to find him.

She found him in the library.

"You lied," she accused.

"I was desperate, Celine. I have to stay here. I was trying to gain your sympathy. You see the truth is that—"

"I don't want to hear any more lies. Just give me the letter."

"I am sorry," he whispered, hanging his head in remorse. He peeked at her hopefully, his blue eyes shimmering and begging for forgiveness.

She looked at him and felt a tug at her heart strings. "The letter?"

"Here," he said quickly producing it. "Am I forgiven?"

She nodded and turned to leave.

"Celine?" He caught her sleeve.

"Yes?"

"Where are you going?"

"To talk to the housekeeper."

"After that?"

"After that, I will go over the household accounts with the steward,"

"Why do you have to do them?"

"Because Penny has been told to rest. I am here to help her and temporarily take over her duties."

"After you do the accounts?"

"I will go to Penny's room and she will dictate letters—"

"What are the other members of the house doing this morning?" he interrupted.

"The duke will be working in his study, Penny takes a nap after breakfast and then again in the afternoon and evening. Dorothy is busy with her lessons, and Sir Henry never leaves his room unless for dinner."

"I see. Thank you."

Celine hesitated.

An adorable lock of hair fell onto his forehead. He looked at her mournfully, his eyes dirge-like at the prospect of nothing and no one available to entertain him for the rest of the day.

She wrenched her eyes away. He had tried to blackmail her, the cad. Squelching every bit of sympathy for him she ignored the blasted curly lock, the mournful eyes, and the pouting lips, and walked out.

She refused to be responsible for his amusement.

CHAPTER NINE

You did your part
You tore my heart
Into tiny, tiny, tiny, tiny shreds

"Lord Elmer," Celine gasped. She quickly slammed a book on top of the maps and turned around. "Give me back the poem."

"This one is truly terrible," he grinned. "Hold on, I will give it back to you, just let me finish reading it first."

Celine lunged and grabbed the sheet out of his hands.

"You shouldn't have done that," He snatched another sheet off the table, "And since you did, I will read this one aloud just to see you blush."

She blushed.

He grinned and cleared his throat,

Observe here, my dear friends,
The sentimental night sky.
It expects to twinkle upon kissing lovers in dark lanes,
Instead, it brightens the path for rogues, thugs and prisoners in chains.
Observe here, my dear friends,
The sentimental velvet couch.
It expects to warm the buttocks of lords and ladies, earls and viscounts,
Instead, it heats up the backsides of footmen that bounce the kitchen maids in return for small amounts.
Observe here, my dear friends,
The sentimental window pane.
It expects lovely women to peer out of it and observe the world outside,
Instead, it finds your ugly nose squished to its panes,
And your putrid breath fogging up the glass on the inside.

Stop observing, my dear friends,
For you are blocking my view through the new optical lens.
Didn't you hear me, you fool,
You mangy blockhead, go away, shoo shoo,
For you are covering my shoulders with green hued drool.

A small silence ensued after he had finished reading.

"I shouldn't have read that," he said in a small voice. "I feel wronged somehow. I cannot believe I read the deuced thing and the whole of it. I couldn't stop. I tried, but the words they were so ... I was compelled to read it until the end. I feel tortured, abused—"

"What are you doing here?" Celine cut in.

"I was looking for a book." He continued slyly, "Why were you looking at maps?"

"I wasn't."

"You are a bad liar. You should spend a few minutes every day in front of the mirror practising how to lie. It is a talent worth nurturing. Now, look at me, widen your eyes ... not too much, a little less ... very good. Now tell me without twitching that you were not looking at maps."

"Lord Elmer–"

"You are blinking too much," he interrupted. "It is an art, my dear. Do not disrespect it. Now, let's try something different. I can clearly see a map peeking out from below those tomes in front of you. Therefore, look into my eyes, and this time without blinking and with complete earnestness tell me that you like maps, you adore them, in fact, you simply have to carry one everywhere you go. You cannot live without maps. Maps are your life. You were looking at them because they make you feel adventurous or something of the sort. Whatever you do don't deny their existence or look guilty."

She blinked at him lugubriously, "I am sorry, I am busy. Can you go plague someone else?"

"No."

"Penny will appreciate your company."

"I was with her in the morning room. I had to escape. She was slathering blackberry jam on chunks of venison and eating it."

"It doesn't sound so bad."

"The venison was swimming in gravy."

"I see."

"Before that she was crying."

"Why?"

"Because in her words, I have a head full of ringlets, and the curls are so poetic that she couldn't help it. She had to weep."

"I promise you, Penny is perfectly sane. But I am sorry, I have work to do, I—"

"Let me stay here. I will sit quietly in that corner and read. I promise not one word will escape my lips," he requested.

"Has Penny made you uncomfortable?"

"No, she has terrified me. I am scared in broad daylight."

Celine giggled. "Stop, she is not so bad. You can stay, but please don't try and read any more of my letters."

"I wouldn't dare," he said and then pulling out a book from the shelves sat down to read.

Celine dragged another letter towards herself and got to work.

Half an hour later the silence was broken.

"I cannot stand here and let you continue like this," he exclaimed. "Miss Amy Montrose Fairweather, what in the world are you doing?"

"Penny told you my name?" Celine cried.

"Yes, and Amy suits you far more than Celine does," he said gazing at her, "Amy. Short, sweet, simple."

"Don't call me Amy."

"Amy, tell me what are you doing?"

"No."

"Please. Perhaps I can help."

"I don't trust you," She shook a quill at him, splattering his stark white shirt with droplets of ink, "and why would you want to help me?"

"Because it will give me something to do, and you did help me by asking the duchess to let me stay. It was done reluctantly, but you still did it."

"I am not sure."

"And I think you are pretty. A pretty damsel in distress, and it goes against my nature to leave you suffering like this—"

"I am not suffering," she replied blushing.

"Disturbed then. I want to help."

"No."

"What if I told you something about myself that no one knew?"

She pushed away the letter and looked at him. She hated to admit that she was intrigued.

He smiled and fluttered his lashes, "Ask me anything, Amy" he said huskily.

Celine wanted to slam the book on top of his head. She eyed his practised romantic expression, all pouting lips and dreamy eyes, and frowned.

A sudden thought struck her. Perhaps it was better to learn some of his secrets. After all, he knew hers, and in case he decided to blackmail her again in the future, she would have something to protect herself with.

But to ensure that he did tell her the truth she would have to behave like a simpleton. Inwardly grinning she let her shoulders relax, her chin slightly tilt up and her eyes grow large. A soft smile played on her lips.

His dreamy expression faded and his hooded lids sprang up, his entire body going into alert mode.

"Tell me," she asked, a single finger making concentric circles on the wooden desk. "Why don't you want to go home?"

He gazed at her as if he had never seen her before. "I don't want to be the ninth Earl of Devon. My father threw me out of the house and I had to make my own way in the world. Now that I have found my place he wants me back because it is convenient for him."

She eyed him sympathetically. This time her emotions were genuine. "Your pride and honour are holding you back."

He turned his back to her. His voice was cheerful when he said, "Can you see someone like me becoming the Earl of Devon? Being responsible for an estate and human lives? My brother has been groomed since the moment he was born. He is the heir."

"Are you afraid?"

"Yes, I am afraid of becoming the earl and living a life of utter boredom until my dying day."

"But why do you want to stay here at the Blackthorne Mansion? It can't be amusing. You don't know any of us, and surely you have friends all over England?"

He sighed and came and sat down next to her. "I did tell you to ask me anything."

She nodded.

"It has to do with my last occupation. Before I was summoned to England by my father, I was apprenticed to a Pirate."

CHAPTER TEN

"A pirate?" Celine asked intrigued.

"Yes," George replied. He took out a cigar and lit it.

"And before that what did you do?"

"I was in partnership with a highwayman," he said, smoke curling out of his mouth.

"Was his name Jimmy?"

"No, not the Falcon. How do you know the Falcon?"

"Penny knows him well. I met him during the wedding. Nice fellow."

"I see. I was working with a highwayman who you may know as the White Tiger. I had to leave when I realised that too many highwaymen were sprouting up all over England and the magnanimity of the job had become diluted. I then became an apprentice to the Black Rover."

"Good lord!"

"Have you heard of him?"

"No, but he sounds frightening."

"He is intimidating. Six feet five inches, long black hair streaked with silver which is constantly whipping around in the roaring ocean wind. His jet black eyes are like the darkest part of the night, and his fine velvet clothes always smell like the freshest and finest fish in the ocean."

The two of them became silent out of respect for the Black Rover.

He cleared his throat and continued, "He has a mother. She sails with him. She is an excellent cook or so I heard from the Captain. The crew calls her Sordid Sandy. She owns a large treasure chest filled with recipes that she has collected over the years. I stole one."

"Stole what?"

"A recipe."

"You did not."

"I did."

"You couldn't have."

"Are you trying to annoy me?" he asked testily.

She shook her head, "Why?"

"Why what?"

"Why did you steal a recipe? If you had to steal something, then shouldn't you have pinched something more exciting, like say ... a jewel filled treasure chest or a solid gold statue, that sort of thing?"

George leaned back in his chair and pressed his fingertips together. His head tilted slightly to the right while his eyes took on a faraway expression. "It was a beautiful cloudless night. *The Desperate Lark* sat bobbing in the sea a few miles off the coast of England. The black flag with skull and bones had been replaced by a cerulean flag depicting a fig leaf. We were once again in the guise of rich merchants, the blood washed away from the decks and the treasure buried in a faraway land—"

"Lord Elmer, kindly come to the point," Celine cut in.

George glared at her. "Fine. My faculties were impaired by alcohol. I was intoxicated and my cranium was fogged up. I was befuddled, foxed, pickled. In a word ... drunk."

"I see."

"It was Belcher's fault. We shared a cabin. He encouraged me to drink a fair amount of dark rum. The result was that I found myself crawling into the Black Rover's mother's room, opening her treasure chest and grabbing the first bit of paper I laid my hands on. The next thing I recall was waking up in the kitchens with a treacle bread recipe clutched in one hand, covered in flour, wearing only a shirt and no breeches."

"You could have sneaked back in that night and replaced it."

George nodded. "Except that I received a letter from my father that morning. He wanted me back in England. He said my mother was ill and I like a blooming fool believed that old rusty guts. I left immediately and only recalled the recipe once I was in a carriage oscillating my way to my father's house. I realised Belcher is a bootlicker and at the first opportunity he would have told the captain about the theft. I know the captain, and he is normally a patient man unless it concerns his mother."

"Men are often wary of their mothers," Celine agreed.

"Wary, my dear? Captain Rover is not wary of his mother. He is terrified of her. In her presence he becomes a booby, a looby and a betwattled mopsey. Which is why I quickly changed directions and made my way to Lord Adair's house. Captain Rover knows where my house is and who my friends are, whereas Lord Adair is a distant enough relation, and his residence is well protected on account of his own life being in constant danger. I knew I would be safe with him. Once at Lord Adair's residence, I learned the real reason my father wanted me back. The rest you know."

"I see. Lord Adair had to leave on the king's business and the duke is supposed to be in the country with Penny. No one knows that you and the duke are related, and hence Blackthorne is the safest place for you to hide." She sucked on her bottom lip, "And is that why cooks are disappearing all over England?"

"Yes, the pirates are trying to get the recipe back."

"What will happen if they catch you?"

"Well, I dared to steal from the Captain's mother and that in The Desperate Lark's book means violent death."

"How violent?"

"Starting from my big toe they will burn me inch by inch until they reach the top of my head."

"Egad!"

"Precisely."

"I could almost believe you."

"I am not lying," he said fumbling around in his pocket. He took out a fish hook, twine and a pair of pink drawers. He quickly shoved the last item back into his pocket.

"It is a bang up tale. Just like the story about your two stepmothers," she remarked, "but this time I shall not be bamboozled."

"Here is the recipe," he said pulling out a yellowed parchment.

She glanced at the title 'Treacle bread for ye when a cobra or a scorpion has bitten thee in the fleshy part of—" She stopped reading.

"Do you believe me?"

She pulled the maps towards herself and ignored him.

"It is your turn now. What are you trying to do?" he persisted.

"Nothing."

"You promised to tell me."

"Yes, if you told me something honestly."

"I was honest."

"Pooh," she said, waving him away.

"What the devil," he cursed in anger. "You cannot pooh me. No one dares to pooh George Irvin."

"Pooh," she repeated, hiding her smile behind a large map.

"Would you like this back?" he asked politely.

She looked up and found one of her letters once more in his possession. Her smile vanished, "Give it back, Lord Elmer. This is not amusing."

"I will give it back but first apologise."

"I am sorry," she said.

"Good, now tell me what you are doing?" he asked gesturing towards the desk.

"No."

"Yes."

"Stop being childish and give me back my letter."

"Not childish. I simply get what I want, even if I have to use dishonest means."

"And you wonder why I don't trust you."

He grinned cheekily. "Now tell me everything."

She glared at him.

A dimple appeared in his cheek.

He had an awfully infectious smile. She ordered her own features to behave and remain frozen in an expression of annoyance.

He waggled his eyebrows suggestively.

She gave up and smiled. He already knew enough to ruin her. He might as well learn the whole of it. "I have nothing much to tell. I am trying to find Philbert."

"He is lost?"

She nodded unhappily, "He told me he had to leave for London to find his fortune. He couldn't marry me at the time because he had no money. And then a year ago his letters stopped arriving."

"Perhaps he lost interest in you?"

"No, I don't think so. And it is very horrid of you suggest such a thing. He could have written and been honest and said that he no longer wanted to see me."

"So you are trying to find him. Didn't he tell you where he lives?"

"No, he did. I told him I understand all his poems, so he told me the clue to the place where he is staying in London is woven into the last poem that he had sent me. The trouble is I cannot decipher it. It is unlike his other poems.

"Which poem?"

"This one."

"This is not a poem. This is a splotch."

"A painting," she corrected.

"A splotchy painting," he agreed.

"He was branching out into creative poetry. He wanted to paint his poems."

"What does that mean?"

"How am I to know? I am not a poet."

"So this awful painting is the only clue you have?"

"Yes, and it is not awful."

"I don't think he wants you to find him."

"Don't be ridiculous."

"He has done his best to make things complicated."

"He has a very sensitive deep soul."

"More likely he is a handsome, brooding emaciated poet with a questionable soul. A woman is bound to fall for such a fellow."

"He is not thin. In fact, he is fleshy and not handsome at all. He has spots on his face and thinning hair."

"A fat poet? Whoever heard of such a creature?"

"Oh, go away."

"I won't. What's his name? It may be easier to discover his whereabouts."

"You want to help me?"

"Yes. A poet who paints his location and calls it poetry and a lovelorn girl who sets out to find him in a strange city. It is a sort of thing that intrigues me."

"I suppose there is no harm. His name is Philbert Woodbead."

"A fat ugly poet called Philbert Woodbead?" he enquired.

She nodded.

"You are bamming me."

She shook her head.

And that was when he laughed.

CHAPTER ELEVEN

"Dorothy, stop teasing Gunhilda." Celine pulled her sister out from under the table. "You cannot keep running away every time you have lessons. And the housekeeper informed me that your bed sheets were covered in soot. Were you trying to climb up the chimney?"

"Madame? The dinner—"

"Ah yes, Miss Cornley, Lord Elmer will be joining us for dinner again. In fact, he is going to remain with us indefinitely."

"Is he really?" Dorothy brightened. "Can I have dinner with him?"

"You know Sir Henry will never approve. Don't pout. You can meet him in the evening."

"I would like that," Dorothy said. Her shoulders straightened and she ran a hand through her hair. "How do I look?"

"Like an imp."

"Can I wear my pink velvet?"

"Why, where are you going?"

"I shall ask George to walk with me in the oriental garden."

"Don't be so forward, Dorothy. Address him as Lord Elmer, and you are going for a walk not a ball. You will look silly wearing the pink velvet. Wear your brown paisley."

"I don't like brown."

"Blue spotted?"

"Oh, alright," Dorothy replied sourly. She raced up the stairs yelling for Gwerful to come and do her hair.

Celine turned back to the waiting housekeeper. "I am sorry, Miss Cornley. Where was I? Oh yes, sprinkle some tea leaves and rose powder on the carpets in the Jade Room. And can you request the house steward to meet me in the garden. I need to discuss the menu. Perhaps we can have some Gumballs, boiled fish, sugared plums, cheese wigs and a few peacock pies—"

"Amy," George called out.

"My name is Celine, Lord Elmer," Celine said briskly. She nodded a dismissal to the housekeeper.

"Amy," he repeated more firmly, "what are you doing?"

"Putting on these white gloves. It helps spot the dust."

"And after that?"

"I will walk around the mansion spotting dust."

"Can you spare a few moments from your dust spotting? I need to—What was that?"

She tilted her head to one side, "I don't hear anything."

"Hush," he said placing a finger on her lips. "There, did you hear that?"

"It sounds like someone is screeching." She glanced at him worriedly.

"I am sure it is nothing, but perhaps we should check?"

"It sounds like Penny," she said racing towards the music room.

She skidded to a halt outside the library when she spotted a bosom heaving, vein throbbing, enraged duchess facing a subdued duke.

"Have you listened to a word I have said in the last six months?" Penelope asked in a soft dangerous voice.

"I thought you liked fruit cake," the duke replied confused.

Penelope eyed the duke and then the large fruit cake he held on a silver dish. "You did not want to cheer me up. This is your underhand, evil plot. You want to make me fat."

Celine and Lord Elmer retreated a few steps.

"I did not want to make you fat. You could never be fat ... a little plumpish but that is pretty—" the duke spluttered.

"Plumpish?" Penelope asked taking a small step towards the duke.

"Not that you are plumpish. But even if you do become plumpish, I will still find you just as beautiful."

"Charles, do you recall on our wedding day I told you about the sign, the sign that made me realise that I loved you?"

The duke frowned, "Your toes curled every time we kissed and that is how you knew that you loved me. But what does that have to do—"

"I can no longer see those toes."

The duke cleared his throat nervously, "Penny," he began and then trailed off into an indistinct mumble.

Penelope took the cake and squashed it on top of the duke's head. "You eat it," she growled.

Bits of cake slid down the duke's hair and onto his excellent shoulders.

Penelope snatched a mop from a trembling maid and took a step towards him. "Let me clean you up, your grace."

The duke thought the time had come to run and he did. He flew the coup, deserted the army, and abandoned ship. In other words he turned tail and sprinted down the corridor as fast as his muscled legs could carry him.

Penelope narrowed her eyes to slits and waddled after him. She chased him down the corridor throwing all manner of things at his fast disappearing back including a priceless ornament, an ancestral bust, a branch pulled out of a potted plant, and a rolled up rug.

She glared at her hands. Her aim was terrible. Everything she threw fell just a few paces away from her. She roared in frustration making the walls of the mansion vibrate. She gritted her teeth, lifted her skirts, and once again shuffled after him.

She stormed down the passageway like a lion headed, serpent tailed Chimaera breathing forth flames of red tipped fire. She was an unnatural creature, a creature not quite human and yet mortal.

She slithered and hissed her way towards the carved pillar behind which Celine and Lord Elmer were attempting to hide, her eyes pinned to the duke's disappearing coat tails.

But before the bugaboo in the garb of the duchess could discover them, Lord Elmer grabbed Celine and dragged her through the nearest door.

They found themselves in a coat closet where they decided to bide their time until the threat looming outside receded.

A fur coat tickled Celine's nose. She sneezed.

On the fifth sneeze Lord Elmer launched into speech, "Now, listen to me, I want you to meet me in the library tonight after dinner. Get the painting that has the clue of your fat poet's whereabouts. Don't forget, at nine sharp I will see you there."

"But—"

"No buts."

"But—"

He made an impatient noise, "The doting grandmother that is the dowager will come flying home the moment the new babe is born. And you, my dear, will be politely but firmly sent back to Finnshire. The babe will be here soon, Amy, and we are running out of time. Your chance of finding Puff Guts, I mean your poet, is now."

"I know that."

"Then why are you wasting so much time. We have to work quickly. I will see you tonight."

"I don't think it is seemly."

"You are having an affair with a fat poet called Woodbead. You are doing this behind your beloved sister's back, and you are telling me that my innocent offer of helping you is not seemly?"

"I don't think you should get involved. This is my problem."

"Celine, this job needs a man of wit, sensitivity, poise, creativity and good looks. How can you even doubt that I am not the man for the job? This problem of yours needs me, Celine, me," he said jabbing a finger into his chest. "Besides, I am a man and you can't do half the things that I can without questions being asked."

"If we are caught?"

"You should have thought about that before you went and fell in love."

"Well...."

"Do you even love him?"

"Undoubtedly."

"You seem reluctant to find him. I mean a woman in love is passionate. She is desperate to find her beloved, willing to jump of cliffs and whatnot, and here you won't meet me at nine in the evening to research?"

"I shall meet you at nine."

He smiled like a well fed cat, "Good, now let me leave first and you can follow in five minutes."

"Fine," was all she could manage before he had reached the door in one stride and was out in another.

★★★

The clock struck nine. It was time to meet Lord Elmer, but Celine did not move. She closed her eyes and leaned against the cold window pane in her bedroom. She wondered where her Philly was with a slight twinge in her heart.

She opened her eyes and gazed across the garden at the glistening lily pond. She did not notice the pretty yellow lamps reflected in the dark, opaque water. Instead, she saw her beloved Philly racing towards her on a bright summer morning.

She recalled how he had come skipping towards her, his bulbous cheeks pink with pleasure. His feet had pounded on the grassy meadow frightening the birds and the bees, his dumpy form lit from behind by the sun. He had looked like a cherub without wings, his smile frenzied, rolling towards her at great speed, clutching in delicate soft hands his latest poem.

She clutched that very poem to her chest now. Her mouth moved silently while the words danced in her head,

> *My love for you, my dear red haired lass, is eternal,*
> *I promise, my love, it is not nocturnal but diurnal.*
> *You are my Neapolitan ice on a hot summer's day,*
> *And stuffed game and wine when the world is cold and grey.*
> *My heart beats harder when I see you smile,*
> *Than when I am confronted by hungry tigers and poisonous reptiles.*
> *Let me confess, I spotted your ankle uncovered,*
> *I blush when I think how it left me bewildered.*
> *Believe me, my dear, I love you eternally,*
> *Truly, my darling, it's a love not external but arising internally.*

She heaved a great sentimental sigh. Philly had said it was a love poem for her. He had spent an entire week agonising over every sentence. Her Philly was a perfectionist, she mused fondly, with his big cornflower blue eyes fogged up in excitement and his … She frowned. Did he have a dimple in his chin? A variety of puffy weak chins floated by in her mind. None of them seemed to fit her Philly. A horrible thought struck her. If she loved him, then shouldn't she remember what his chin looked like? Surely a woman in love remembers her lover's chin.

She gripped the curtains, her bosom heaving in turmoil. What sort of a woman in love was she? A cruddy sort, that's what. Not remembering her own lover's chin, the horror.

She shoved the poem into her pocket. Women in love, Lord Elmer had said, were willing to jump off cliffs for their beloved. Would she, she wondered, jump off a cliff for Philbert?

What if she did jump, and instead of hitting solid earth she found a deep dark sea waiting to engulf her?

She gulped.

Perhaps jumping off cliffs was a little dramatic. After all, her mother said that she most decidedly at times loved her father, and her mother wouldn't jump off a hay cart for her father, let alone a cliff.

She did love him she told herself firmly. After all, the feelings were still fresh in her mind. She may not recall his chin, but she well remembered the anticipation and excitement she felt whenever she met him. The tickle in her belly when they had kissed for the first time and how her heart had skipped a beat when he had confessed his love for her one frigid winter morning.

She watched a servant go by holding a flickering lamp in her hand. She wondered why she was dithering. Lord Elmer was offering her his help, and with his help, she was sure Philbert could be found ... and yet her feet refused to move in the direction of the library where no doubt Lord Elmer sat pulling out his hair in boredom.

It had been a year since she had seen Philbert and six months since she had last heard of him. What if he no longer loved her?

The servant disappeared from her view, and with the fading light, she came to the conclusion that she would find him. She would risk taking a stranger's help, telling him her secrets, not for sensible Amy, but for the Celine in her. This would be her adventure, and after that she would devout her life to being good, dutiful and an ideal accomplished lady.

With a firm nod, she picked up her diary and the sheets of poetry and made her way towards the library.

CHAPTER TWELVE

"I don't think this is a good idea," she said the moment she spotted Lord Elmer in the library.

He eyed her quizzically.

"I mean finding Philly and—"

"You call him Philly?"

She ignored him and continued, "I don't want your help."

"But why? I already know your secret, and if you live in fear that I may tell someone, then isn't it better to take my help in finding the fellow and marry him before you are disgraced in society."

She didn't reply.

"Do you even love him?" he persisted.

She caught the sneer in his tone. "I do. I just …"

"You just wanted to play at finding him. You did not really intend on acting out your fantasy. Is that it?"

Her mouth trembled.

He took her elbow and gently pushed her into a seat. "Shall we try and see how this evening goes? Now that you are here we might as well make use of the time. If you decide not to take my help from tomorrow, then I promise not to bother you. I will find something else to amuse me."

She glanced at him and then looked away. The blasted man was looking kind. Not scornful but kind and slightly sympathetic. She nodded reluctantly.

He immediately spurred into action. The sheets of paper were spread out, the ink and the quill readied, more candles lit, and various maps pulled down from shelves. Finally, he turned to her and asked to see the painting.

A little breathless from how quickly he seemed to get things done she unravelled the parchment.

He eyed her actions with pursed lips.

She scowled. If he did not find her manner of unrolling a scroll sufficiently romantic, then she didn't care. She wasn't going to spend ten minutes cooing at the paper and caressing it with loving hands. If he could be quick, then she too was efficient and practical. Romance would come later once she met her darling Philly.

The painting was unrolled efficiently, not romantically, and she smoothed it out and placed it on the table.

They stared at the painting.

He picked it up and turned it over.

They frowned.

He brought the candle closer, letting the light illuminate the back of the painting.

They chewed their lips.

He made her hold the painting and then walked across the other end of the room and looked at it.

They strained their eyes.

He walked back towards her, and this time he peered at it with one eye closed and the other open. He then switched things up by closing the open eye and opening the closed eyed. He finally closed both eyes and fingered the paper testing its weight and texture.

They scratched their heads and stroked their chins.

He finally asked, "Has he painted a camel hump? Hills? Mountains? A pig with a stick and mountains?"

"Don't be silly," she replied irritably.

"Then why don't you explain it to me?"

"Well," she frowned, "I haven't figured it out yet. If I had I wouldn't need your help."

"You must have some ideas?"

"I suppose, but they are not very good."

"Tell me one."

"No."

"You have to. Otherwise how am I supposed to help you? You know him best. Now what could it be?"

She fidgeted for a moment and then said, "This here is a man with a crown on his head. See these points."

"The only thing I see is a pig. Those points are ears. If it was a crown, then it would have more points. Now, what about this here?"

"I suppose it could be a kidney?" she offered hesitatingly.

"A kidney?
"Yes, a kidney."
"Why a kidney?"
"It looks like a kidney."
"A human kidney?"
"A fish's kidney."
"Do fish have kidneys?"
"Well, then a human one."

He tilted his head to the side, examining the painting anew. "Do you know doctors dig corpses out of the grave and then cut them up? And then they pull out all the innards and draw them."

"How do they know that a living person's innards are the same as a dead person's? What if they shrivel up the moment a person dies?" she asked curiously. "Do they also cut up people who are alive?"

He looked at her bright, eager face and said hastily, "Let's stop speaking of shrivelled up innards. It is making me feel queer. Instead, let us discuss why your poet would draw a kidney suspended in empty space over a pig. I for one don't think it is a kidney. It looks more like an inverted hill." He looked at her again but this time from the corner of his eye. "Why did you think of a kidney and not an inverted hill? Tell me, do you have violent fits? Have you ever woken up in the stables or a guest's bedroom with blood on your hands and no idea how it happened?"

"Are you calling me insane?"

"If I am, then do you feel a bloodthirsty urge to pick up the letter opener and pepper my body with bleeding holes for revenge?"

"No, and you asked me what I thought the painting depicted. I was trying to help. No need to criticise."

"Amy—"

"Celine," she automatically corrected.

"Amy," he repeated, springing out of the chair. He started pacing the room, "Are you sure your poet wants to be found. I mean, he knew you could understand his poetry. Hence, shouldn't he have written you a poem with his address in it? Or better still, tell you directly and clearly without the need for rhymes. Why did he paint it?"

"I received the painting with a note attached that said that if I ever wanted to contact him, then he could be found at this place. He said if I truly loved him, then I would be able to decipher the painting."

"I think I need to know more about your love story," he said looking baffled.

She hesitated, a faint blush creeping up her cheeks.

He looked away and cleared his throat, "I only want to know the spirit of tale not the details."

She kept her face carefully averted from him as she spoke, "We have an inn called The Tears of a Tankard in Finnshire. Mrs Reed runs it. She also sells pickles, jams, and other condiments. I went to purchase her raspberry preserve when I ran into Philbert. He was staying at the inn in hopes of finding poetic inspiration and because his father had thrown him out of the house."

Lord Elmer smiled. "He must have read one of his poems to his father."

She glared at him. "That's not true."

"Then why was he thrown out."

After a moments silence, she said quickly, "hisfatherdissaprovedofhispoetry"

"His father," he repeated agonisingly slowly, "disapproved of his poetry. In other words he had read one of his poems."

She gave a short nod.

He curbed his smiled and gestured for her to continue.

She continued, "I bumped into him and spilled the raspberry preserve all over his green, moth eaten patchwork coat. It was my fault. I had not been watching where I was going, and I had failed to tighten the lid of the jar." Her voice became dreamy, "He was very nice about it and his pink cheeks puffed in and out, in and out, and once again in and out—"

"Your eyes trapped each other's, heads swam, the beggar on the street corner started crooning a song, and your lashes fluttered, lips moved, mischief occurred under bellowing skirts, and you fell in love," he interrupted. "I know those bits. It is the same for everyone. What I want to know is what in the dickens ruined it all?"

She fiddled with the quill as she spoke, "He left a letter for me every night on our doorstep. I would wake early every morning and get the letter before anyone else discovered it. One day I did not wake on time and my mother found the letter."

"Dash my wig," he said mildly.

She dug the nib into the sheet making a hole.

"I am listening," he encouraged.

She took the nib out of the hole and continued, "She forbade me to write to him or meet him. He continued to write for some more time unaware that I could no longer read them. My mother was burning the letters. I did manage to get the last letter he ever wrote before my mother could get her hands on it and I found the painting. He thought I no longer loved him, so he painted the place with a note to say that if I loved him, I would know the essence of the painting and understand where he will be every day, all day, in London. He said he will wait for me forever. He left Finnshire that day and I have not heard from him since."

"Your love story came to an abrupt end because you overslept. Tragic."

"Oh, to hell with you, "she stood up. "I told you it was a bad idea. Let me find him on my own. You need not worry your pretty head over it."

"I have been called handsome but never pretty. I am sorry. I will not tease you. Come sit. Let's make a note of all the places in London that have mountains or hills in them. I am certain this is a hill and not a kidney. Then I will get my valet Nithercott to visit these places and make discreet enquiries."

Some of the steam went out of her. It did sound like a good idea. Better than she had in days.

Half an hour later she set her quill down and rubbed her tired eyes. She pushed the sheet towards him, "These are all the names I could find."

He poured the sand on the paper, "I will get Nithercott to investigate. Your Philly should be easy enough to find. A fat poet named Philbert Woodbead. He already sounds unique." He grinned. "Don't be so serious, Amy. A little fun never hurt anyone."

She eyed him in frustration. He was being so kind in helping her, and yet he had an aggravating habit of getting under her skin. She wanted to throttle him and kiss him at the same time. She blinked at the last thought. Kiss him?

He looked at her quizzically as he put the names in his pocket.

"Are you ill?" he asked concerned. "You are looking very odd."

"No, I was just thinking," she said hurriedly.

"About?"

"The poem. This poem here. It is a wonderful piece that Philbert wrote for me," she said grabbing the sheet closest to her.

He took the paper and read the contents. "This is a wonderful piece?"

"Yes," she said defensively. "You need to have a sensitive soul to understand it."

"I need to have a sensitive soul to understand 'An Ode to the Noble Liverwort'? He calls you his Noble Liverwort?"

"He likes botany," she mumbled.

"Why don't you go to bed?" he suggested kindly. "You are looking pale."

She scrambled up and made her way towards the door only to slap her head and come right back.

"The poems, I need to take them back," she muttered embarrassed.

"By all means take them and keep them. I read another one, 'The Cat and the Parti-coloured Iris', and it managed to frighten away my sleep. The cat ate the iris. I think I shall read anything but poetry until daylight. Goodnight," he said offering her the neat bundle.

She grabbed it.

He held on.

She tugged at the bundle and then looked at him questioningly.

He smiled and pulled out a pin from her hair. A thick brown lock fell covering her left eye.

"You cannot be proper when having an adventure, my dear," he informed her.

Her right eye focussed on his lips … Not her adventure, she thought firmly. Her adventure would be properly proper. Proper. Not improper but proper … Certainly, assuredly not naughty at all but very, very proper.

CHAPTER THIRTEEN

"Good morning, your grace," Celine sang walking into the room with a breakfast tray.

Penelope's annoyed head swivelled in her direction. "It's a blasted morning. I cannot believe the silly midwife thinks it's time for me to be completely confined to the bed." She straightened up and sniffed. "And don't call me your grace. I hope you didn't get me any eggs."

Celine turned around and quickly spooned the boiled eggs into the head housemaid's outstretched palm. "Not at all, I have some toast and a bit of bacon. Would you like chocolate or coffee?"

"I would like a party," Penelope grumbled.

Celine deposited the tray onto Penelope's lap. "Goodness, what a capital idea."

"I am going to have a baby, but that does not mean that you treat me like a dim witted child. My wits have not slid into my stomach."

"Then why were you wrestling with the housemaid for the broom?"

"I am bored. Everyone knows that. And as for the wrestling, you can't blame me. It is natural."

"Natural? How is insisting on wanting to sweep and scrub the floors when you cannot even see your toes natural? I am not even going to mention the fact that you are a duchess with hundreds of servants at your beck and call."

"Pigeons do it. They build the nest and then clean it up to prepare it for the newborn chicks."

"You are not a pigeon."

"I feel like a pigeon. A trapped, miserable pigeon sitting in a nest waiting to lay her egg while her husband scours the countryside for maggots to bring home for dinner." She shook her head sadly. "Do you know, as a duchess I am invited to countless balls, shooting parties, sailing parties, country parties, dinners and masquerades. Instead of going to them I have been confined to this mansion and now to this bed. I am a pigeon too fat to fly. I want to fly, Celine, and dance. Better still, dance and fly at the same time. Can we not sneak out for one last night in town before the babe is born? We could go to the night garden. It would be our secret."

At Penelope's mention of a secret Celine's mind automatically sprang to Lord Elmer.

"Celine, why are you blushing?"

"I am not. I am a little warm."

Penelope drained her tea and nodded. "It is warm, and yet," she pointed at the fireplace, "you can see that the housekeeper has lit the fire high enough to roast me alive. Now, it is not that Mrs Cornley would like to see me dead because she madly loves the duke and wants to be the Duchess of Blackthorne herself. No, the truth is not so exciting, for you see the reason I am about to sweat away my last breath is because Anne has a cold."

"Anne, the duke's sister?"

Penelope nodded.

"But she is in Bath," Celine said confused.

"Fancy that," Penelope muttered. "Now, I wish someone would explain that to the duke's blooming mother."

Celine's face cleared, "Another letter arrived from the dowager."

"Yes, and I am quickly realising why mother-in-laws are a despised lot in this world. She has written to the housekeeper informing her that I must be kept as warm as possible because Anne has a cold. Just because her daughter has a cold her daughter-in-law must suffer. How is that fair? And why couldn't Anne curb her sneezes. It was blasted insensitive of her. She knows what the dowager is like."

Celine made comforting sounds.

Penelope gestured for the tray to be removed. "Now, Celine, I feel like having a fruit cake. Will you request the cook … thank you … and throw this jug of water into the fireplace, and perhaps open the window slightly."

"Anything else?"

"Ask Mary to fetch my quill, ink and the letters. Oh, and choose some books from the library. I may read for a while. Send the duke to me if he comes home early from his maggot hunting expedition. Come and talk to me in an hour, I may need company…."

Celine spent a few more minutes with the duchess making sure that she was comfortable. Thereafter, she went to check on Dorothy.

The girl was reading in the nursery with Gunhilda.

"I am too old to be in the nursery," Dorothy told her.

"The duke makes the decisions in this house," Celine replied apologetically.

Dorothy nodded and started reading once again.

Celine frowned, "Are you feeling alright?"

"I was reading an account of a man suffering from a brooding liver. I think I have it," Dorothy said bracingly.

"Have what?"

"A brooding liver. I am certain of it. I read the account twice and our symptoms match."

"What are the symptoms?"

"Deep sadness, a feeling of impending doom and a certainty that something has broken away from the lower part of my stomach and made its way to the upper part of it. Gunhilda says that if that had truly happened, then I should be stone cold dead."

"I don't think you are going to die, and please stop reading such accounts," Celine scolded. "Last week you convinced everyone that you were suffering from malaria and having convulsions when all you were suffering from was a stomach ache because you ate too much rice pudding. Now, how are your lessons going?"

"Fine."

Celine lifted a brow at Gunhilda.

The governess assured her that Dorothy was behaving admirably.

Celine frowned. Perhaps the girl was sickening. Dorothy never behaved admirably unless she was ill or guilty.

She eyed the healthy, pink cheeked girl with her bright alert eyes and she was willing to wager her best bonnet that it was the latter emotion making her sister suffer. Now, if only she could figure out what Dorothy had done.

The rest of the day was the same as usual. Celine spent the day dealing with domestic matters and going over household accounts.

She also sorted out an argument between two chefs and a laundry maid. The two chefs declared their love for the laundry maid, and the maid in turn declared her love for the under footman. The under-footman turned out to be madly and deeply in love with the dairy maid, who was happily married to the coachman. The two chefs quit because of a broken heart. The laundry maid and the under-footman sadly followed.

Things became slightly difficult for Celine now that Blackthorne had only one chef remaining. She discussed this matter with the steward as well as the urgent matter of the stubborn stain on the carpet of the Jade Room.

All in all nothing out of the ordinary happened all day, and surprisingly she did not see Lord Elmer either. Perhaps he was no longer interested in helping her? That last thought made her feel partly relieved and partly disappointed as she made her way to dinner that evening.

★★★

She entered the dining room and found Penelope already sitting at the table." I thought the midwife said you have to stay in your room?"

Penelope grinned, "Yes, Beth the midwife had told me that. Now I have requested Mrs Fisher, who successfully assisted Lady Gardiner in giving birth to an unfortunate looking baby last month, to come and attend to me. I trust Mrs Fisher more than Beth because Beth does not like cats, while Mrs Fisher adores them."

"You said you liked Beth because she smelled like roses and not Nelly, the original midwife that the dowager had chosen for you, because she had a look in her eye that was all wrong. You cannot keep changing midwifes, Penny, until you find one that agrees to let you do as you please," Celine scolded.

"Mrs Fisher did not agree to my four pages of reasonable requests. However, she did say that I could walk from one room to another but not up and down the stairs. So I have decided to move to one of the rooms on this floor."

"I see," Celine thought for a moment. "Will the Yellow Room do? It is right across from the dining room?"

Penelope nodded happily. "Now if only Charles would take me dancing, I shall be satisfied."

"Charles will do no such thing," the duke said walking in and dropping a kiss on Penelope's curly head.

Celine looked away. She still wasn't used to the way the duke and duchess were so affectionate in public. It was sweet, a little bit scandalous, and at the same time it made her feel a touch lonely.

Lord Elmer entered the room.

Celine brightened and then frowned. Last evening Lord Elmer had chosen to wear a bushy red moustache. Today he was wearing a full black one. She was about to remind him when Sir Henry was carried in by four burly footmen.

Celine closed her mouth. With a little bit of luck, Sir Henry would fail to notice the change in their new guest. Thankfully Sir Henry's eyesight was grainy and his memory sluggish at best.

The first course of cold fish soup was served.

After Sir Henry's fifth mouthful and no comment on Lord Elmer's appearance, Celine started to relax. Her tensed shoulders had just eased into a more comfortable position when Lord Elmer decided to switch moustaches.

One moment he had a full black moustache and the next time she looked up it was a black, wiry wilting one.

There was no mistaking it.

Lord Elmer had truly switched moustaches.

She promptly sprayed soup, bits of fish and bread out of her mouth.

Lord Elmer's eyebrow rose in question. Not a smile lurked in his eyes.

She searched his face and frowned in confusion. Was she wrong? Had it really been a full black moustache? No one else seemed to have noticed the change. They had, however, noticed the bread and soup flying out of her mouth.

"I am sorry, I think I bit into something unpleasant," she muttered quickly.

"What was it?" George asked.

"What?"

"The unpleasant thing that you bit into?" the duke prompted.

"Perhaps a pepper."

"Perhaps?" Sir Henry asked.

"No, it was a pepper," Celine replied, her cheeks burning.

Sir Henry refused to eat any more soup. Peppers frightened him.

The second course arrived, this one a more grand affair with assorted meats, cheeses and vegetables.

Celine took a bite of the peacock pie and almost choked. Lord Elmer now wore a grey moustache, the sort that curled up at the ends.

There was no mistaking it. And this time she was certain of the change because the duke and Penelope were also gaping at Lord Elmer in shock.

The duke's expression soon turned furious, while a fascinated Penelope leaned forward in her seat.

Lord Elmer continued to eat as if unaware of the interest shown in his moustache.

No one knew quite what to do in such a situation. The duke could not call him out on it, for if he did, then Sir Henry would notice the change. And if he noticed the change, then he would realise that the guest was a wearing a fake moustache. A fake moustache that the duke kept for all clean shaven guests in order to dupe Sir Henry. Once Sir Henry realised what was going on, he would insist on pulling each and every guest's moustache to ensure that they were real, and if they were not, then that guest would no longer be welcome at the mansion. It would also get the duke into trouble for deceiving Sir Henry all these years.

It was no wonder that the duke had altogether given up on the food and now sat boring imaginary holes into the back of Lord Elmer's head.

Celine stopped analysing the duke and once more turned towards Lord Elmer. He had switched moustaches again. This time it was a salt and pepper variety that was fat at the centre and thin at the edges.

She put her spoon down and decided to carefully watch him. Her diligence was rewarded when he pretended to drop a fork and emerged back up wearing a snowy white moustache and beard.

Penelope started giggling uncontrollably. Her cheeks were flushed for the first time in days, and the dullness in her eyes had been replaced by excitement.

Celine was torn. She was amused but at the same time horrified.

Once again Lord Elmer dived under the table mumbling something about shoelaces, and by this time no one was interested in food except for an oblivious Sir Henry.

The servers arrived to place the desert on the table, and from between the mounds of colourful jellies, flower scented ices, and delicate cakes Celine's scandalised eyes watched a plumed hat appear over the edge of the table.

Penelope pressed her lips together, her face red and eyes bulging.

The duke started turning an unflattering shade of puce while the edge of his napkin sat soaking in a glass of wine.

Penelope, the duke, Celine, the serving maids and even the stoic Perkins gasped when Lord Elmer finally emerged from under the table wearing a pirate's eye patch, plumed hat, and a multihued feather boa along with an auburn moustache.

He waved the feather boa at his audience and grinned showing off his two blackened front teeth.

The room froze.

Lord Elmer looked like a cross between an old spinster and a toothless pirate.

Penelope made a strangled sound and finally lost complete control. She dissolved into hysterical laughter, until she was sobbing and thanking Lord Elmer for being the duke's best second cousin.

After that dinner was considered well and truly over and everyone at the table realised that Sir Henry was blinder than he let on. He had not noticed a thing.

CHAPTER FOURTEEN

"Why did you do that?" Celine asked the moment Lord Elmer met her in the library.

He did not reply immediately. He first took a seat and then pulled out a cigar. After clipping it and lighting it, he took a puff. He spoke softly watching the smoke twist and curl in the air, "It is a tragic story. It happened when—"

"I was asking about your little trick with the moustaches. You know the duke is not too keen on your presence, then why did you take such a risk?" Celine interrupted.

He frowned, "I am trying to explain. The story needs to be told with a certain amount of sensitivity. It is an important story. I am sharing a piece of my life with you."

She rolled her eyes.

"Now," he began, "when I was sixteen years old, I had invited some gentlemen friends to my house."

"To meet your crazed stepmother and the drooling dog?"

He ignored her and continued, "And we had a bit of gin like men of my age are wont to do. When the brandy was over—"

"You said you were drinking gin."

"Yes, we began with gin and ended up with the brandy. A lot came in between. At sixteen it all tastes the same. Once the brandy was over, we were astonishingly still awake. We thought we were sober, and most likely we were not, for we immediately decided to raid my father's basement for something more to drink. Now, I was chosen to visit the basement for two reasons. Firstly, no one knew about my gentlemen friends, since they had arrived for the party by climbing the oak tree that grew right outside my bedroom window. Secondly, it was my house and therefore I was the only one who knew the way. It took us awfully long to figure it all out. Finally I went to rummage in the basement with a candle. My friends thought it would be funny to lock me in. They did. They locked me in the dark dungeon with a flickering candle which soon went out. Then the rats, ghosts and the rats who were now ghosts came out to play. It was frightening. I decided that night to never be trapped again in my life."

"How long were you trapped for?"

"Ten whole minutes. I made such a racket that the cook woke up and let me out."

She scowled, "What has that got to do with what happened at dinner tonight."

He sprang out of the chair and knelt in front of her. His eyes blazed as he gripped her hand and said, "Don't you understand? Those rats could have slowly and painfully chewed me to death. I learned the biggest lesson of my life at that tender young age of sixteen. I learned to live. To live fully and completely. Those starved, murderous rats taught me to take risks, Amy, risks that have led me on some strange and wonderful adventures."

"I don't—"

"The duchess, I like her. Her spirits are low and I took that risk to see her smile. For a moment, at least, she was happy."

"You are a very confusing man."

"Confusing and wonderful. Have you fallen in love with me yet?"

"Don't be absurd. I love—" she stopped, catching the teasing light in his eyes.

"The fat poet," he finished for her with a dramatic sigh. "Then let's get to work and give you a happy ending. Give me his poems. Perhaps we can get a clue as to his nature. What he likes and dislikes. It will help broaden our search."

"Why?"

"Nithercott did not find your Blob."

"Woodbead, not Blob."

"Blob," he repeated firmly, "was not found. And while we are mulling over the meaning of this artistic mess," he waved a hand at the painting, "we should also examine the poems. It may give us a clue as to his whereabouts."

She nodded and undid the string from the bundle.

He picked up the first poem.

"This," she said blushing, "was the first poem I ever received from him."

He cleared his throat, "This sort of thing is personal. I will understand if you would rather …"

She shook her head, "I don't mind. If not now, you would have read them at a later date." She noted his expression and clarified, "He was going to try and get them printed in *The Monthly Magazine*."

"I doubt," he said skimming the sheet, "that I would have ever read them. Poets and their work only become known after they are dead, but this," he poked the sheet, "will never be printed. Not when he is dead, not after I am dead. Not even after my great grandchildren are dead. Mark my words, my dear, *The Monthly Magazine* or any other journal of repute will never print this. Ever."

"Are you going to continue insulting Philly because—"

"Is this the letter which accompanied this poem?" he spoke over her.

She scowled and nodded.

"My dearest Celine," he read, "I have finally managed to pen a love sonnet for you. It came to me all of a sudden last night like a madman's fit. Do not be alarmed, my dear, poets often get these sorts of fits, and the result is always beautiful words spewed onto crisp white sheets. It came to me, the fit I mean, right after I dreamt of your lovely face bathed in the grey English light."

He put the letter down and eyed her in concern, "I am starting to see where you got the idea that the hill he painted was a kidney."

She snatched the letter from his hand, "I thought we were reading the poems not the letters. The letters are personal."

He touched the sheet with the poem with trembling hands, "I am afraid to read another one of his works … but I shall be brave. I shall be your knight my distressed damsel and read this," he squinted at the title, this 'Love Song Sonnet'."

She rolled her eyes.

He proceeded to read the poem aloud,

Is that a man? Is that a moon?
Or is that a man on a balloon?
I know you did not expect a love song to start thus,
But I am just learning how to rhyme, hence here I add the words 'yellow puss'.
I see you scrunch up your face in displeasure,
Let me begin anew, my dear, with a love song for your leisure.

Shall I speak of your funeral complexion?
Or perhaps your pink lips or the small brown hairs on your arms on closer inspection?
I am sorry, my love, the last line I wrote ran away with me,
Pardon me, my dear, for I am just learning poetry.
Shall I liken you to my favourite things?
Pies and pigs and cooked birds with wings?
Or shall I compare your willowy form,
To flowers and trees and insects warm?
I saw you smile, my love, and this time,
I truly think I am getting better at creating a rhyme.

The moment he finished reading it, George Irvin, known in polite society as Lord Elmer and in impolite society as Lord Wicked, turned a deathly grey.

When he had recovered somewhat, he stroked his brow with trembling fingers and said, "I don't know what to say."

Celine fidgeted in her seat, "I know he said it is a love sonnet and a love sonnet contains fourteen lines, while this has sixteen, but—"

"That is not all that is wrong with it, my dear."

"But," she continued loudly, "I am certain that between the lines, the poem means something."

"What does it mean?"

"The meaning is well hidden. Alas, I am not creative enough to untangle it."

He watched her trace the untidy black scrawl with the looped l's and the swirly p's. After a moment he said, "The words are engrained in your soul, the meaning remains elusive."

"You understand." she said brightening.

"I understand that you are an idiot," he said flatly. "Here," he took some poems and handed them to her, "go and sit in that corner and note down your observations. I will do the same here with this lot."

"You cannot order me about like this."

"I have to not only read these poems but also try and understand them. I am willing to undergo this torture to help you. Surely my surly mood can be excused?"

She meekly went and did as he had bid.

After an hour George threw the pencil down. "Right, what have you got?"

Celine cleared her throat. "He is kind and loves animals. You can see the references to various animals in the poems titled 'Hamsters in love', 'Oh oyster open thy shell and do not be shy', 'The sad tale of the chicken who was eaten by the king.'"

"Go on," George said looking pained.

"He appreciates honesty. Hence, the poem titled 'Tell me the truth'."

George covered his face with his hands and moaned. "Celine, we have to look for clues on how to find him and not analyse his unstable nature through his poems."

"Well, what did you write?" she asked crossing her arms.

He silently handed over the sheet.

Celine read aloud, "Fellow might be at the zoo, seems to have taken a fancy to porcupines. Seems to like his drink for no sober man would write a poem titled, 'The redhead who kissed me' and send it to his lover who clearly has a mop of lovely brown hair. Nor would a sober man write 'The depressed cat who forgot how to meow.'"

George remained silent waiting to hear her thoughts.

"He was learning how to write," she finally grumbled.

"And he could not change the redhead to brown haired? The fellow is also insensitive."

"I thought we were not analysing his character?"

He rolled his eyes, "Fine, let us move on. Here is a poem titled 'A penny for your thoughts'. This one 'I wager you ten whole pounds my horse shall win', and this 'I wager thee now'. They all point to the fact that Waterbeetle is a gambler. He can be found at a gaming house."

"Not Waterbeetle, Woodbeetle ... I mean Woodbead," Celine corrected. "Now what?"

"Very simple, I will put the word out and search the main gaming houses in the city and the gentlemen clubs. Someone must have heard of him or his family. And you and I will have to come up with an excuse to meet more often during the day. Perhaps go for walks together and on that pretext explore London inns. Most likely he will be at the poet's corner or some such place."

"I cannot go travelling around London. I have to take care of Penny. Besides, it is not seemly. I will be ruined."

"Shall we agree from now on to not mention the words seemly

and ruined? I understand that you are a lady, but you are also a lady supposedly in love. You will have to think of an excuse if you want to continue this undying love story. We will have to sneak out—"

"I cannot."

"Don't you love the fellow? Won't you do it for love? I know Amy wouldn't, but surely Celine would."

She glared at him. This was happening too fast. She had wanted to find Philly but not like this, whatever this was. It seemed worse than what she had been planning.

She frowned. But wasn't this what she had been planning, albeit at a slower pace. Her hands went to her head and she moaned.

"Is that a yes?" Lord Elmer asked impatiently.

She looked up, her eyes dark and wide, "I don't know …."

"Then it is decided. You will meet me tomorrow afternoon at four. We will go explore an inn or two. Good night." He left her still scrambling to collect her thoughts. By the time denial came to her lips he was no longer in the room.

CHAPTER FIFTEEN

"Are you awake?"

Celine's eyes snapped open.

A man was in her room hovering over her head.

She opened her mouth to scream, but a hand clamped down on her mouth.

"It's me George. Don't scream," he whispered.

"Lord Elmer? What in the world are you doing here?" Celine spluttered, yanking up the quilt to cover her nightdress.

"Your nightdress covers more than your evening dress. Besides, you have nothing to fear from me. You love Gilbert."

"Philbert."

"Yes, him. And I love Rosy, Daisy, Mary, Liz—"

"Why are you here?"

He moved towards the desk and started rummaging around. "I am here for the painting. Unlike you I don't have the splotches engrained in my mind. I need to look at it."

"Don't you ever sleep?"

"I sleep as little as possible. Sleeping is a waste of time. Too many things to do."

"Is that the clock? It is past two in the morning. You cannot come into my room like this. It is not done and—"

"Right, I found it. I am leaving now. Sorry for offending your modesty." He paused near the entrance, "Tomorrow at four, we will go on our first investigation. Be ready with an excuse for the duchess."

And with that he was gone.

Celine sat staring into the sudden darkness, blinking in confusion. Was she dreaming? Had Lord Elmer really come to her room? No, that was impossible. Closing her eyes she fell asleep.

Next morning she woke up to find the painting gone. It had not been a dream. Lord Elmer was an amoral villainous creature, a scoundrel and a blackguard … and she was off on her very first adventure that evening at four.

Secretly she was thrilled.

★★★

Lord Elmer had been gone since the sun rose that morning. It was half past three in the afternoon and he still wasn't back. Celine eyed the door for what felt like the tenth time. He hadn't even had the courtesy to leave a note for her. Even his valet Nithercott was missing.

"Are you falling in love with him?" Penelope asked dreamily.

"Eh?" Celine's head whipped around.

"Your eyes are trained to the door. I can only guess that you are anticipating Lord Elmer's arrival. Tell me, how is your romance progressing?"

"I … It is nothing of the sort. I mean, I thought he was handsome, but now I think he is too fickle. He would never settle for a girl like me."

Penelope's eyes brightened. She balanced a tea cup on her protruding belly. "I think I can help you. Make him fall in love with you."

"Didn't you try your hand at matchmaking with the duke's sister? I heard it was an utter disaster."

"Precisely. I made so many mistakes that it is not possible that I haven't learnt from them and become an expert. I also know more about marriages." She waggled her eyebrows, "Do you want to know how babies are made?"

Celine turned hot. After a moment, she said, "I know the details."

"You found the book in father's library?"

"You too?"

Penelope nodded looking disappointed. "I suppose Dorothy is too young to know the details. Would you like to hear them again? Refresh your memory perhaps?"

"No, thank you, Penny," Celine said hurriedly.

"I have forgotten what I was talking about," Penelope said frowning.

Celine did not help remind her. The last thing she wanted was her nosy sister playing matchmaker.

"Ah, how to make Lord Elmer fall in love with you."

"Penny," Celine said firmly, "It will happen if it is meant to happen. I don't want to worry you in your condition."

"But I want to repay you somehow," Penelope sniffed. "You have come all the way from Finnshire to help me and see to my needs. You forget not so long ago I too had come to Blackthorne as a young untutored country bumpkin. You are better prepared than I was, but surely goober, goober."

"What did you say?" Celine asked, shoving a finger in her ear and wriggling it around.

"Goober, goober," Penelope sobbed. The combination of tears, running nose and a mouth full of cake had turned her words unintelligible.

Celine leaped off her seat and ran to her, "Penny, don't cry. I am alright. The housekeeper is excellent and so many servants means hardly any work for me. All I do is order them about, and I am learning as I go along. It will help me when I marry and have my own home to run."

Penelope snorted and blew her nose. "I know running the Blackthorne estate is not fun. And you don't think it is either, so do not lie to me."

"You love being a duchess," Celine hedged.

"I do, but only because I am married to the duke. I appreciate your help, Celine, I truly do, but I wish you could have some fun as well. You should be visiting the famous London shops, gardens and theatres. If the duke was not so busy, I would have insisted that he take you out."

Celine paused, "Well," she began slowly, "perhaps I will take a long walk today. You will be resting at four and I can use that time to stroll through the orchards. The grounds here are lovely, and I haven't had a chance to discover them yet."

"Not just today. You should go walking every single day. Get some fresh air. It will do you good. Knowing you are getting a few hours just to yourself will make me happy."

Celine nodded surprised at how things had neatly fallen into place. She could go hunting for her poet with Lord Elmer every evening, and her naughty maid could easily be bribed to say she had accompanied her on long walks instead. Now all she needed was for Lord Elmer to appear and keep his promise.

The moment Penelope waddled back to her room for her nap, Celine leaped off the chair and raced outside. "Perkins, have your seen Lord Elmer anywhere?"

"I am here," George said from behind her.

She whirled around, and the sight of him killed the question on her lips, "You are drenched. Perkins, get some hot tea and something to eat for Lord Elmer." She turned to George, "I think you should go change, Lord Elmer. I will wait for you here," she said indicating the Blue Room.

He nodded and with a loud miserable sneeze departed.

He arrived just as the tea was brought in. She waited until he had finished a cup before asking him, "Where were you?"

"I went to a few stationary shops. I wanted to see if I could figure out where the paper was procured from on which Hilbert wrote the poems—"

"Philbert."

"Yes, him. If I could learn where the paper was bought, then perhaps his location would be easier to discover. He seemed to have used the same sort of stationary for all his works. I gathered that he had taken a fancy to them. They are unusual—"

"Yes, with the paisley print blue border. That is because he bought them at our local stationary shop. Lord Elmer, I told you he left those letters on my doorstep."

He scowled, "Pardon me for trying to find Gilbert for you. I spent the entire day in the rain sweet talking shop keepers for what has turned out to be no good reason."

Celine couldn't help it, she laughed at his disgruntled face. "Next time just ask me before rushing off. I may have the answer. You just have to ask the right questions. Here, this cake is delicious. Have a slice."

After stuffing him with food, he looked happier. She smiled indulgently. Her father was the same, irritable when hungry.

He swallowed the last bite and leaned back in his seat. "I wonder what he wrote in those letters that your mother enthusiastically burnt to a crisp."

"More poems," Celine said with certainty.

"What if he wanted to call it all off? What if he wrote to tell you about how he had found a beautiful miss who appreciated his rosy cheeks more than you ever could?"

"Or he could have asked me to marry him."

"The proposal," he said cheerfully, "would have arrived in form of a painting, a painting depicting roses and everlasting love, which you would have interpreted as a portrait of Sir John Barleycorn. I think the two of you will run around in everlasting circles destined never to hold hands."

"Snicker all you want. I think he would have stolen me away in a gilded carriage to Gretna Green. No need for pretty words. He is a man of action."

"You forget his destitute state. He cannot afford a gilded carriage."

"Fine, the carriage is not gilded but covered with wild flowers that he has plucked all by himself."

"I see. He arrives in this carriage covered with flowers looking like a complete sapskull and then proceeds to climb the ivy—"

"The ivy wouldn't hold him. He is too fa—" She bit her tongue.

"Fat," he completed for her with a grin. "My dear, I doubt he is in some seedy inn dreaming of your lovely brown locks and beautiful dark eyes. I think he is selling bawdy songs, drinking tankards of ale and bouncing wenches on his dimpled knees." His eyes glazed and a faraway expression graced his features. "That vision almost made me green with envy. Goodness, his blubber cheeks are darned lucky … He was just kissed by the lusty barmaid."

"He is not being kissed by barmaids, Lord Elmer, because …" Here she paused.

"Because?" he encouraged.

"I already told you. He is not handsome."

He looked sceptical. "It is fashionable to say that so and so is not handsome and yet I love him. Take the duke for instance. He wears a constant brooding expression, and I have yet to see him smile. And my friend, a fellow called Lord Crawley with his bushy eyebrows and scarred left cheek, is supposed to be positively hideous. But you have women falling in love with these two men like besotted flies falling into a honey pot because in all honesty these men are not ugly but, in fact, handsome. Women just like to say they are ugly because women like being obscure."

"Philbert looks like a short pig," she said flatly.

A small silence filled the room.

Finally he cleared his throat and said, "I see now how you would not expect him to find a woman. A piggish fellow who is an impoverished poet, and from his poetry I can guess a highly morbid individual." He paused to eye her sympathetically, "A fat poet is in itself unnatural, but to add to that he is called Gilbert Goodbead. Yes, I can see how you can be so certain he has not found anyone. You are an odd sort of woman to fall for such an odd sort of man."

"I admire the man within. His heart is good."

"His head is definitely not good. His heart better be or I will begin to worry for you. I think what you need is a poodle and not a poet. I suspect your maternal instincts have taken over your otherwise rational brain—"

"Thank you, Lord Elmer for trying to help," Celine said standing up on trembling legs. "I think I can take care of my life and my choices. Perhaps it is best that you do not interfere any longer."

"I have a lead. A source tells me that he knows a man that knows where the poet may be. The man, not the poet, can be found at the poet's corner, and he is willing to meet us to tell us more."

Celine lost her steam and collapsed back into the seat, "Truly?"

"Are you ready to leave? I have the carriage waiting outside. We can go and find out right this moment."

"Now?" she squeaked. "I don't think I can. It is too soon. My dress …"

"You look charming my dear," he said yanking her up by the elbow. "What is your maid's name?"

"Gwerful," she replied tugging her arm trying to escape him. "Why?"

He didn't reply. Instead, he addressed Perkins outside in the corridor. "Miss Fairweather here wants to go for a walk. Please ask Gwerful to fetch a parasol. Anything else?"

"My reticule, but—"

"Reticule, coat … and gloves? Right, gloves as well, Perkins, and ask her to bring anything else she thinks her mistress will need on a long leisurely walk. That is all." His hold on her was gentle yet firm. "It is like drinking a nasty tonic. The more you delay it, the more difficult it becomes to drink it. You cannot spend too long thinking about it or you will lose your courage. We will go, enquire and leave."

"I have to bring an abigail …."

"We shall bribe her and send her off to the stables to flirt."

"Someone may recognize me."

"I have purchased a veil for you which is currently lying in my pocket."

"I am not ready."

"You don't have to meet him until you are ready. You can flatten your delightful nose on the grimy inn window and ascertain that he has been found and then leave. At least we will know where your poet is. I am starting to think that he is a figment of your imagination, and that, my dear, is a blood curdling thought."

Gwerful came racing down the stairs and skidded to a halt.

Lord Elmer plucked the things from her hand and expertly slipped a few coins into her pleased palm. A finger to the lips was all the signal the highly philosophical maid needed.

With a nod she disappeared for the rest of the day.

"Put them on in the carriage" he whispered to Celine. "We don't have much time. The place is a good half an hour away. We have to be back before dinner or someone will come looking for you. We cannot have that."

Celine jammed the bonnet on her head, her hands busy tying the strings. Her mouth was full of gloves so she could not answer.

The carriage was well hidden behind a group of large fat trees huddled together like gossiping old men.

"It is a hired coach," Lord Elmer informed her. "Don't call me Lord Elmer. I told the driver that my name is Mr Grey. Remember that."

Celine was speedily attaching the veil now. It was hard work without a mirror or a maid.

He stopped and impatiently tilted her chin up. Quickly he clipped the veil to the rim of her bonnet. "Beautiful. I cannot see even a bit of your face. Now you are Mrs Grey."

"I shall not be Mrs Grey. I am Miss Brown."

"Miss Brown? A young unmarried lady off in a carriage with an unmarried male—"

"Fine, I am Mrs Grey."

The triumphant slap of his cane on the ground was the only indication that he was pleased with his victory.

Celine rolled her eyes and entered the carriage.

Lord Elmer rapped the carriage walls, and they were off on their very first adventure.

CHAPTER SIXTEEN

"Your flashing eyes will soon fall upon the poet's sweaty face. Are you afraid?" George asked, draping a relaxed arm over the back of the seat.

Celine kept her eyes glued to the scenery outside. She refused to answer him.

"Is your heart throbbing? Are you thrilled? Is the vein in your forehead pulsing in excitement?" George continued.

"Lord Elmer," she finally faced him, "My heart, as you say, is not throbbing, nor is my vein pulsing or my eyes flashing. If you cannot help, then stay silent."

"I want to help."

"My nerves feel as if they are stretching under my skin trying to escape, and I fear at any moment they will break free and run away."

"I cannot help."

"Sing a song," she suggested, rubbing her temples.

"I cannot sing unless I am foxed, but I can hum. I hum very well."

"Please by all means hum away."

And George did just that. He hummed away a delightful tune for the rest of the journey.

Half an hour later the carriage halted outside the poet's corner, which turned out to be a seedy inn called 'In the Soup'. It was a place where impoverished poets met other impoverished poets to discuss the mediocrity of the poems written by all the wealthy poets.

Celine stepped out, her cold hands clasping Lord Elmer's elbow in a painful grip. She entered the inn on trembling legs ….

Ten minutes later Celine walked back towards the carriage, her hands once more clasping Lord Elmer's elbow. This time the grip was even more painful.

"That was an utter disaster," she said through gritted teeth. "How could you forget that his name is Philbert Woodbead and not Gilbert Goodbead? I thought you were pretending to mix up his name every time you spoke to me because you derived some childish pleasure in doing so. And I cannot believe that in this world a man truly exists by the name of Gilbert Goodbead. If I didn't know better, I would be convinced you set that whole thing up."

"I confess, I am not good at remembering names."

"You remember Amy without any difficulty."

"I don't have trouble recalling names of beautiful women. Just men."

Celine tensed, her heart skipping a beat.

She asked with a quiver in her voice, "You think I am beautiful?"

"Stunning when angry," he replied banging the carriage door shut.

The answer had come too quick.

She tossed her head in annoyance and her eyes fell on the window.

She froze.

A small, wrinkled head with a missing tooth was peering into the carriage.

Her mouth dropped open, the skeletal face making her flesh creep.

She remained entranced unable to move as she watched the stranger examine the back of George's curly head.

It was her heart that started up first.

It gave a weak flutter, and when that didn't get any reaction from her brain, it began banging away in her chest with all its might.

A small mewling sound escaped her.

George jerked his head around to see what the matter was. He raised an eyebrow at her green face.

She swallowed and then ever so slowly poked him in the shoulder and then pointed at the face outside the window.

George scrutinised the face.

His worried countenance underwent a rapid change. A series of emotions paraded across his features until he settled on blooming cheeriness.

"How are you old Tim?" he exclaimed in delight.

Tim grinned, showing two more missing teeth. "Arr," he said and raised his arms.

George stopped smiling.

Celine snuffled.

And the very air in the carriage stopped swishing around momentarily, for Tim held a bow with the arrow aimed right at George's aristocratic nose.

George's nose was now the centre of attention.

Everyone focused their attention on this beautifully shaped nose. Even George stared at it in a cross-eyed fashion.

The nose unused to such consideration started to itch.

George did not dare to move and scratch that itch.

Oh, how it itched.

And while George's nose was itching, Celine's nose also started itching. Itches are like that, the mere thought of itches makes everyone itch. Hence, now even Tim was itchy but on his back and not his nose. It is another one of those idiosyncrasies of itches. Itches like to travel through air and around the body.

Tim's hand started to sweat and tremble as he tried to forget about his itchy back, the arrow quivering in his grip.

Celine clutched her skirts and thought of England.

George was doing remarkably well. He almost forgot about his need to claw at his face and scratch that blasted itchy spot but, alas, his nose that everyone had almost forgotten about gave up the valiant battle and it … twitched.

Tim snapped to attention and drew back the arrow.

George ducked.

The arrow hit the unlit lantern hanging on a hook with a clang.

Celine's breath whooshed out in relief and George rapped the walls.

Tim placed another arrow in the bow and took aim.

Celine's breath was once again caught in her throat.

The carriage gave a lurch and Tim released the arrow.

Hearts froze.

The carriage started rolling.

Tim's arrow flew in from one window and out the other taking with it a single ostrich feather.

George's nose lived to smell another day, and hearts and lungs eagerly went back to work once more.

★★★

Sitting at the bottom of the carriage Celine asked, "Who was that?"

"One Legged Tim. He was on the pirate ship. The same ship I stole the recipe from. This is a disaster. He has found out that I am still in London."

"That story was true?"

"You doubted my word?"

"It is hard to tell when you are being honest and when jesting." After a moment, she asked, "Did he want to kill you?"

He shook his head, "No, he wanted to discuss how lovely the weather was and then he invited me to a ball. He went on to ask me save a dance for him. Shall I wear my white silk French gown with touches of amber lace, ribbons and silver buttons?"

"Yes, you will look delightful. I will even lend you my maid. She is a genius with hairdos," Celine grinned.

"I will look pretty with a bow stuck in my curls, won't I?" he asked, turning his profile for her to admire.

She admired, blushed and fell silent.

He caught the blush. His eyes gleamed. "Handsome am I?" he asked raising a brow.

She ignored his mirth and instead asked in a serious tone, "Do you think Tim will follow us? Wouldn't that put Penelope in danger?"

"No, I had already planned for such a situation. Nithercott is up front with the driver. He would have bribed the driver by now, and we should be taking a slight detour. Hopefully will lose him on the way." He took a quick look outside the window, "We are definitely being followed, and it appears there are more of them." He turned back around to find Celine rummaging around in her reticule.

He watched her for a whole minute before asking reverently, "Celine, are you knitting?"

"An accomplished lady is never idle. *Mrs Beatle's book for accomplished English ladies* has three whole chapters on it."

"Yes, but we are hurtling away in a carriage being chased by blood thirsty pirates. I am not sure if knitting is the appropriate occupation at such a time."

She finished counting the stiches and looked up. "A lady must use her superior talents for the greater good. If I die, then at least I would have died making a bootee for some poor orphan child."

"Your entry into heaven is guaranteed. Clever, very clever."

She moved on to a purl stitch, "What else am I supposed to do? This could take an hour. I cannot drive the carriage, and sitting here trembling like a leaf, stomach churning, cold with dread will do no good."

He stared at her in awe, "I am slowly understanding why the duchess says that you are a sensible sort of a creature."

After that, for the next forty minutes Lord Elmer sat plotting escape routes and bargaining with the almighty for his life.

Celine, during the same time, managed to do something more constructive. She finished making a green bootee and tied the final knot. When she looked up next, it was to find that the carriage had slowed down.

"Lucky day," Nithercott shouted back into the carriage. "It was only old Tim and two of his cronies. We lost him easily enough, my lord."

Celine stuffed her knitting back into her reticule, "Good, we shall be home in time for dinner."

Lord Elmer smiled weakly and whispered, "Remarkable".

Twice.

And that for some reason made her feel ridiculously pleased.

CHAPTER SEVENTEEN

"Is everything alright, Penny?" Celine asked.

Penelope swallowed the porridge and said, "No, this morning the duke and I had an argument."

Celine made the usual comforting noises.

Penelope took those noises as encouragement to proceed. "We fought about the fact that he is keeping a mistress."

Celine spat out the coffee. "I am so sorry. I never would have imagined. He seems so in love."

The duke slammed the fork down. "I am here. Please don't talk as if I have left the room. And I am not having an affair."

"I saw you," Penelope growled.

Celine frowned in confusion. Penny had her meals in the dining room and slept in the Yellow Room. The duke was not likely to romance a woman on this very floor. Surely he was smarter than that. He could have taken his mistress to the stables ....

The duke closed his eyes briefly and then opened them again. "Penny, your sister is glaring at me. Can you quickly tell her where you saw me and with whom? I am afraid Celine is very close to poking my eye out with the butter knife."

"I saw him with Lady Lydia. The one he was engaged to before our marriage. The same Lady Lydia that creates frozen droplets on the tips of my hair every time she speaks. They were kissing," Penelope announced.

"Terrible, and here your wife is carrying your child. Insensitive I say," George piped up.

Celine dropped the butter knife and took hold of Penelope's hand in concern. "Penny, are you alright? Lydia has not entered this mansion, at least not while I have been here."

"She did too. In my dreams. I saw him kiss her and then we

argued." Penelope insisted.

Celine gaped, "You mean you are stewing because the duke had an affair and argued with you in your dream. All this happened in your head and you know this, and yet you are angry with him? I don't understand."

The duke dabbed his mouth and stood up. He went around the table and soundly kissed his wife. "You can argue with me some more in your head, my love. I am afraid I have work to do and I cannot participate. But my dream self is all yours. Do what you like with him."

Penny's mouth trembled watching him leave. She picked up the jam pot and flung it at the door. "I hate him."

"No you don't, you love him," Celine said smiling.

Penelope's head turned in her direction.

The teapot was lying very close to Penelope. Her hand inched towards the pot, but before she had reached it both Lord Elmer and Celine disappeared from the room.

★★★

"It is a lovely day," Celine said strolling down the garden path. She carefully circumvented the statue of a smiling Phoebe with a half-moon crown on her head. Sir Henry in his younger days had commissioned the marble statue for guests that particularly annoyed him. It was engineered in such a way that whenever someone walked under it, they triggered a hidden mechanism that allowed jets of water to gush out of the crown of the statue instantly drenching the unsuspecting creature.

"Blast," Lord Elmer exclaimed, "I am drenched. Did you know this bloody thing was a fountain in disguise?"

"No," Celine replied, batting her lashes innocently.

He smiled, "I wish I could understand you. Are you a sensible girl who refuses to be called by a sensible name like Amy, a good girl with sparks of mischief, a delicate young thing who barely blinks at the sign of danger, or a well mannered young lady who has had the audacity to fall in love with a fat poet called Cuthbert. You, my dear Amy, are a contradiction."

She winked and handed him a handkerchief to wipe his face.

"Jasmine," he said holding her handkerchief to his nose and inhaling the scent. This time he winked.

She flushed and turned away.

They walked in a comfortable silence for some time.

She was content to gaze out at the beautiful landscape thinking restful thoughts. The sun was bright enough to make her squint and scrunch up her face, the heat welcome after the long cold winter months. She could feel the rays digging into her very bones, warming her up inside and out.

"The duke," George said breaking the silence, "is an acquired taste. Just like fish eggs."

"I adore him," she said.

"Yes, I noticed your dubious taste in men."

"What sort of a girl do *you* like?"

"All sorts."

They came upon an artificial lake and for a moment stood gazing at the shimmering water.

Celine sat down on the garden bench and Lord Elmer joined her.

"Do you have a good dowry?" he asked, closing his eyes and tilting his face up to the sun.

"No," she replied opening her pale green parasol.

"Hmm, and your poet is penniless. How will you live? I think women in love stop feeling hungry. They fail to remember that after marriage you will need to feed yourself and your husband. You will no longer be in your father's house dinning on pigs and wings."

"I will manage," Celine snapped. She had always imagined her and Philly owning a sweet little cottage draped in honeysuckle and wild roses. They would have a tiny kitchen with a maid of all work. In winter they would sit by the fire, sing songs and eat their supper. Now all she could see was a single pea and a boiled potato on her supper plate that she would have to share with not only Philly but also her six wailing children and the dog.

"The duke will give you a dowry. Your sister will ensure it," he mused, failing to notice her glare.

"I shall not take it."

"Does Dimber Mort know that your sister has married the Duke of Blackthorne?" he asked standing up and walking towards the lake.

She followed more slowly. "His name is Philbert. And I am not sure if he knows about Penny. I don't think I told him about it … but someone in the village could have."

"I see." He walked to the edge of the lake and bent to test the water, "Amy, don't mention where you are staying or that your sister is now a duchess to Bacon Fat until the very end of your meeting with him.

After a moment of receiving no response, he looked back to find Celine had halted a few feet away from him.

"Come here," he called out to her. "I think I spotted a pretty fish."

She shook her head and backed away.

He frowned and gazed back at the water.

"What is it?" he asked coming up to her. He took her chin and tilted her face up, searching her eyes.

Celine's heart stopped, her fears faded, and the world narrowed to a point. The warmth of his fingers on her chin coursed through her veins and she emitted an undignified squeak.

One powerful, masculine eyebrow rose in question and she felt her knees go weak. She had to get away from him, away from his earthy scent, away from his crystal clear blue eyes … away from his touch.

She slipped under his arm and hastened towards the mansion. "What is our next step?" she asked in a falsely cheerful voice.

He looked towards the water one last time before quickly following her. "Tomorrow we shall visit The Winged Horse. It is an inn where a number of gamblers meet. A man there says he has met your poet and knows where he can be found."

"Did you say his name right this time?"

"I wrote it down so I don't make a mistake." he said producing the small piece of paper.

"The lump of lard is called Philbert Woodbead," Celine read. "Do you have to call him names?"

"Yes, it is necessary. I am offering my services for free, and in return for excellent companionship and help, please allow me to call your fat poet names. It gives me great pleasure."

Her mouth twitched as she returned the paper.

CHAPTER EIGHTEEN

The sun dipped in the sky and a pleasant spring evening unfurled like the wings of a leathery bat waking up from a good day's sleep.

Celine and George donned their English springer spaniel hats and prepared to nose around London once again in the hopes of catching the poet's scent.

"Perkins," Lord Elmer said, taking the coat and hat from the butler, "lost any teeth lately?"

Perkins slightly unbent his form, and his old bones quivered and rattled. He bared his yellow teeth and wheezed.

Celine pressed her lips together as she watched Lord Elmer slowly back away from the butler.

"What's the matter with the fellow?" he whispered in her ear.

"He is demonstrating amusement, my lord," she replied promptly.

"Is he?" Lord Elmer asked nervously. After a moment, he said, "I don't like it. Tell him to stop. At once."

"Wonders will never cease," Dorothy commented from behind him. "I have never seen a butler giggle."

"That's not a giggle," Celine began and then stopped. She couldn't find an apt word to describe what it was. Instead, she said, "I am going for a walk, Dorothy. Be good and don't tease Gunhilda. And I hope your pet is alive. You haven't forgotten to feed it have you?"

"Certainly not," Dorothy said offended. "I take very good care of him."

"Good, and wash your face. You have soot all over your cheek," Celine scolded.

George cut in smoothly and addressed Dorothy, "Miss Fairweather, you look charming as always. Will you excuse us?"

Dorothy blushed and dipped in an elegant courtesy. "Shall I see you at dinner?"

"I am sorry, but I shall be dinning with the duke," Lord Elmer responded with just the right amount of regret.

"Perhaps next time you can come by for some light supper in the nursery. I will ask the cook to prepare something special if you will inform me in advance," Dorothy invited.

"I would be honoured," he said bowing to her.

"You should stop flirting with anything in skirts," Celine said once they were outside and on their way towards the hired carriage.

"Why?" he asked patting his pockets.

"Because the maids in the Blackthorne Mansion have fallen in love with you, or have you failed to notice?" Celine huffed. "And you shouldn't encourage Dorothy either. The girl thinks she is in love with you as well."

"She will forget about me the moment she goes back home. There is no harm in making her a little bit happy or the maids for that matter," he said in a distracted voice.

"Is that what you are trying to do for me too? Trying to make me a little bit happy?" When he failed to reply, she asked, "Lord Elmer, what in the world are you looking for?"

"For the veil to attach to your bonnet."

"In your shoe?"

"I was being thorough. I think I left the veil back in my room, and we are supposed to be meeting Mr Bindle at The Winged Horse at five. I don't think I have time to run back and fetch it."

"I cannot go without a veil. I would be ruined if someone recognised me," she objected.

"I have a plan."

"Yes?"

"I was planning to disguise myself because as you may have noticed pirates are looking for my head on a platter."

"Yes, go on."

"Therefore, this morning I pocketed two moustaches. One black and one grey. I couldn't decide between the two. I think you should wear the one which comes attached to a beard."

"Wear what?"

"The grey moustache and beard."

"But I am wearing a Parisian walking dress in peach down with border flounces in the same colour and a green pomona silk hat trimmed with ivory lace and rosebuds."

"Gloves?"

"White kid."

"Fascinating. I am wearing buckskin breeches, coat and riding boots. Now, I wonder what could make our attire even more fashionable. By Jove, would you believe it? I just happened to find these two beautiful moustaches. It's fate. We were destined to wear them. They are just the thing—"

"No," she said firmly.

"Do you have a better idea?"

Half an hour later the carriage halted and two faces, one masculine and one feminine but both sporting splendid moustaches, peeked out of the window.

"The inn is at the other side of the river. We will take the boat. It will be faster," he began.

"No," Celine said firmly.

"No?"

"I am not crossing the river."

"Why not? Don't you want to find your poet?"

"Not if I have to cross the river."

"Your dress won't get muddy," he promised. "I will clean your seat with a handkerchief. I won't let the boatman splash water on you. I will look away if you go green and cast up your accounts. Deuced woman, why won't you cross the river?"

She pressed her lips together.

He sat back in his seat, "Are you scared of water?"

She glanced away.

"Nothing will happen to you. I know how to swim," he coaxed.

"I know how to swim," she snapped. "It doesn't help."

For a moment he looked as if he would bang his head on the carriage wall in frustration.

She said in a trembling voice, "I was sixteen when Dorothy fell into the river that runs near my house. She was very young. I saw it happen. I was close enough to help and yet I stood frozen in fright. Thankfully Penelope heard Dorothy's shouts and came and pulled her out. I just stood there like a fool unable to move."

"I see. Well then let me send Nithercott. He can talk to Mr Bindle for us." And that was all he had to say about it.

Celine nodded gratefully. She watched him from the corner of her eye while he instructed Nithercott. Her heart suddenly felt full threatening to spill over. She had not wanted false platitudes or pity regarding her fear of water. She knew it was irrational, and he knew it as well. And yet he had said nothing and accepted it. He understood her.

She beamed at him and he catching her expression beamed back. And with all the back and forth beaming, the atmosphere in the carriage reverted back to being sunny.

For the next forty minutes Celine sat knitting a scarf while Lord Elmer took a short nap in a sitting position. He closed his eyes, tilted his head back and slept. Just like that. It was a talent worth admiring.

And Celine wholeheartedly admired.

The sound of clicking needles filled the air along with George's soft snores. Celine's hands were busy, but her eyes were not. It was only natural, so she told herself, that she happened to spend a good half an hour staring at George.

Her hands itched to smooth away a black curl that was kissing the inside of his ears. She admired the shape of his head, the sensual curve of his nostril, and his long capable fingers. He shifted in his sleep, and her heart sang at the sight of muscles moving underneath his crisp white shirt.

The knitting was forgotten. The blue yarn unravelled unnoticed.

She felt as if some force beyond her control had taken over her limbs. She wanted to … no, she needed to reach across and brush that single lash poised on his cheek.

Her hand lifted … and a rap on the window broke the domestic bliss.

Nithercott had returned from his mission.

Celine shoved the wool back in the bag, and Lord Elmer opened one eye to hear the news.

Nithercott puffed up importantly and said, "I found Mr Bindle lurking outside The Winged Horse. He wasn't happy about the fact that I had come instead of Lord Elmer. He refused to talk to me and stormed off in anger."

Celine clucked in disappointment.

"I chased after him," Nithercott comforted her. "I wasn't going to let him escape without first doing my duty and garnering the information I had been asked to fetch. I followed him down a darkened alley called Gin Lane. I fawned over his leather boots a bit, complimented his dusty tie and admired the shine on his bald head. It soon restored him to a more amiable mood, and that is when I struck."

Celine gasped.

Nithercott nodded, "Yes, I struck expertly, like a viper striking its prey. The moment I spotted that his lips were curving up in the hint of a smile, I asked him for the information. I asked him where the poet was, and because I had put the question to him at just the right moment, his smile did not drop. In fact, he grinned even broader and asked me for two whole pounds for the information. I humbly offered him a copper."

Here Nithercott hesitated.

"Go on," Celine encouraged him.

He looked at her gratefully and continued, "I offered him a copper, and Mr Bindle smelling strongly of gin snatched it out of my hand and took off running. Alas, Mr Bindle knew the alley well, while I did not. He disappeared like a professional crook while all I could do was chew my hat in distress."

Here Nithercott finished his narration and showed George his chewed hat as proof of the aforementioned events.

It was bad news, but worse news was to follow. Lord Elmer's second eye sprang open when he noticed a thin bony hand holding a blunderbuss brushing Nithercott's sweat soaked back. Nithercott had left one crook only to arrive with another shorter, thinner drier one.

"One Legged Tim," Lord Elmer informed her, nodding towards the man with the gun. "Persistent fellow."

"We ran into each other on the boat," Nithercott said nervously. "He wants you to follow him. And if you want to see me alive again, then he says that you had better follow him. I truly hope, my lord, that my service all these years has been satisfactory, and if it has, then kindly save my bacon."

Celine gasped.

One Legged Tim smiled. The left side of his lip curled upwards to show off his solid gold tooth.

"Now look here," Lord Elmer coaxed, "you and Nithercott are old friends. Why don't you take the coach driver instead? You have never met him. A fine specimen Jim is. Broad shoulders, good teeth and sharp ears. Best coach driver I have ever had ...."

A church bell pealed in the distance and Celine gasped again. They had exactly one hour to reach the Blackthorne Mansion to be in time for dinner. She had to get home. Her hands twisted together, her eyes beseeching everyone to hurry up.

Lord Elmer was busy selling the coach driver, Nithercott was sweating profusely, and One Legged Tim was fast losing patience.

She had to act now if she wanted to get back home in time. Every minute was precious. Mrs Beatle's book advised women to be prepared for everything. Never, she had written, depend on a man. Men, she wrote, were ornaments that one pulled out on special occasions or while spring cleaning. The rest of the time they should be safely stored away in either the library or the study depending on where they looked best.

Celine tried to follow Mrs Beatle's advice as much as possible in her day to day life. Hence she dug into her reticule, pulled out a knitting needle, poked her head out of the carriage window and stabbed One Legged Tim in the eye with the pointy end.

One Legged Tim screeched in agony and stumbled backwards.

While he moaned about being blinded, Celine opened the carriage door, yanked Nithercott inside and rapped the carriage walls.

By the time One Legged Tim recovered they were well on their way home.

Lord Elmer held a knitting needle in one hand and all through the drive he periodically tested the pointed end for sharpness. Nithercott spent the entire ride pledging his life to an embarrassed Celine.

The fat poet Philbert was momentarily forgotten.

CHAPTER NINETEEN

"I saw her with my own eyes," the housekeeper insisted.

"The duke let her in?" Celine asked in amazement.

"Her grace wouldn't have it otherwise."

"In other words she started crying."

"No, she threatened to sit on the duke."

Celine dismissed the housekeeper and made her way towards the dining room. What, she wondered, could Penelope want with a soothsayer?

The dining room had been transformed. The heavy curtains had been closed blocking most of the natural light. The long dining table had been covered with a red velvet cloth, and the flickering candles illuminated the altar, which consisted of an ordinary looking rock stuffed inside an ochre hued silk stocking.

This blessed stone was surrounded by odder looking things; namely a bowl of water, a dish of salt, a bell, colourful threads, virulent incense sticks, a comb, shiny buttons and a freshly decapitated bleeding chicken head.

The room tickled her olfactory senses with upper notes of deep sandalwood, soft jasmine, mysterious myrrh, and with the base note of last evening's dinner of boiled pork. It made her feel exotic, spiritual and hungry.

Celine coughed her way towards the table where through the haze of smoke she spotted an unhappy duke, a pleased Lord Elmer, an eager duchess and a beautiful stranger.

"You have candles burning and incense sticks smouldering," Celine informed Penelope.

"At ten in the morning," the duke added with a yawn.

"The dusty spirits and late gods need all these things to coax them into the right mood to answer questions," Penelope replied spiritually."

"Lusty spirits and great gods," Miss Swan's low timbered voice corrected.

The duke chuckled.

"Miss Swan is trying to concentrate," Penelope hissed at him. She eyed Miss Swan apologetically and requested her to begin.

Miss Swan closed her eyes, threw her hands up in the air and started chanting,

> *Come, come, come, oh great elements,*
> *Arsey varsey and sort of malcontent.*
> *Come, come water, wind and fire,*
> *We are willing to throw up our children and all that you desire.*

"I object," the duke objected, "I am not throwing my children anywhere."

Miss Swan opened her dark, mysterious eyes and sent him a sour look.

"Perhaps another chant?" Penelope hastily requested, her hands clutched her belly protectively.

Miss Swan nodded agreeably and opened her mouth and started again,

> *Pooh, pah, pish and Pshaw,*
> *Let us chant equality before law.*

Celine sat down next to Lord Elmer. Once her skirts were arranged just so, she looked across at the energetically chanting Miss Swan.

Miss Swan had a head full of shiny black curls on which perched a yellow turban. Her almond shaped dark eyes were lined with black pigment, and her sun kissed skin and full red lips appeared to be rouged. She wore a long green dress, wooden beads, and a pink rose in bloom was tucked behind her left ear. She had a bowl of water in front of her, and over it she held a pendulum.

Celine reluctantly conceded that Miss Swan surrounded by twinkling candles was a pleasant sight to behold, and by the looks of George, she further concluded, Miss Swan appeared to unattached males as conducive to lovemaking.

"What is going on?" Celine whispered in George's ear.

"Miss Elizabeth Swan is trying to find out if the duchess will have a boy or a girl," George whispered back.

His breath tickled her ear making it itch.

"How?" Celine asked, delicately scratching her ear.

"Magic," George replied.

"Did you tell Penelope about her?"

"How did you guess?"

"You said her name with a lot of—" She closed her mouth.

"Affection," George finished for her.

"Danger," Miss Swan's throaty voice suddenly rang out halting their whispered conversation. "Danger is near. I can feel it."

Celine froze. A trickle of fear raced down her spine. It escaped just before hitting the top of her buttocks.

"I can see," Miss Swan continued, "water, blood, guns, an old gnarled woman, skulls and bones." The pendulum in her hand started swinging to and fro.

Penelope gulped, "I only asked if I was having a boy or a girl," she said staring at Lord Elmer.

"She is in trance," Lord Elmer replied softly. "Listen to her and heed her advice. The trance comes on suddenly and only the chosen are privy to it."

"I don't want to be chosen," Penelope said in a small voice.

"Quiet," roared Miss Swan, "the vision swims, the vision swims … and I see …"

Everyone in the room became deathly quiet waiting for Miss Swan's next words.

Celine leaned forward in her chair when a sudden soft rumbling sound followed by a snort made her jump.

The duke had fallen asleep and was now peacefully snoring.

Miss Swan opened her eyes and glared at the duke.

Penelope stabbed the duke's hand with a fork.

He woke up with a start.

She eyed him meaningfully and he eyed her back fearfully. A swift silent communication passed between them.

The duke's lashes jerked upwards, and his eyeballs whizzed in their sockets. He suddenly looked as awake as Sir Henry did after drinking half a cup of coffee. And good god did Sir Henry awaken if he drank a bit of the strong, fragrant Turkish brew.

Sir Henry drinking coffee was an event in itself. The entire family gathered together to witness this spectacle, and even the upper servants stuck their ears to the door. First, Sir Henry would wait until the coffee cooled down to the right temperature. Thereafter, he would gingerly take a sip. The warm liquid would slide down his gullet and reach his stomach, and that was when the tremors started.

The family would hold their breath, the servants strain their ears, and the duke would ready his flute. By the time Sir Henry finished the entire cup, the tremors turned into vigorous vibrations. His old bones rattled and clicked and squeaked, which the duke took as a cue to put the flute to his lips and begin a tune.

The sounds of shaking old bones and achingly sweet flute would fill the room creating beautiful music. Sometimes the dowager would be moved to add her voice making it a rare musical treat.

Satisfied that her silent threat had had the appropriate effect on the duke, Penelope turned back to Miss Swan, "What did you mean about the danger and how can it be averted?"

Miss Swan's delicate nostrils flared. "What it means only time shall reveal. Meanwhile, you can take some precautions. One way to accomplish this is by ensuring that your husband sings you to sleep every evening."

The duke smirked.

"He must stay with you at all times until the child is born, and he must eat the same food as you do and drink your tonics as well." This time Miss Swan smirked.

"Even the bitter ones?" Penelope asked.

"Only the bitter ones," came the reply.

"This is nonsense," the duke began.

"He must also do a lively spring dance for you every morning," Miss Swan continued loudly. "It shall please mother earth."

"I shall not," the duke spluttered.

"He will have to wear your petticoats and go hunting for a black wolf on a full moon night. It shall please mother nature," Miss Swan chanted.

"I wouldn't object if I were you," Lord Elmer whispered to the duke, "or it will get worse."

The duke closed his mouth.

Miss Swan watched him for a minute, and when no further objections were raised, she said, "Keep this amulet with you at all times. No harm shall befall you while you wear it, and make sure your husband does all that I have said."

Penelope pocketed the amulet which strongly resembled the corpse of a lavender scented rat. "Thank you. Is there anything else I can do?"

"Yes, cross my palm with coin."

Penelope put a coin in her hand.

"Cross my palm with lots of coins."

Penelope handed her a small jingling bag.

"Thank you." Miss Swan said, gathering up her supplies. She shoved the bleeding chicken head into a cloth bag along with the blessed rock and the rest of the paraphernalia.

"Wait," Penelope said. "Am I having a boy or a girl?"

"The powers that be shall reveal in time."

"What does that mean?" Celine asked.

Miss Swan gazed at her mysteriously. "Lord Elmer will see me out."

George nodded and whispered something in Miss Swan's ear making her giggle.

Celine froze, her breath stuck in her throat. All at once time seemed to slow down and Lord Elmer's fingers moved as if wading through viscous air.

Her eyes widened and her refined senses watched in horror as the scene unfolded before her.

It seemed an age before his adventurous fingers reached Miss Swan's round, firm bottom ... and then he flicked it.

Celine was certain that a bottom had been flicked today. And that she had seen it. Her heart sank. "Laced mutton," she whispered, piqued.

Miss Swan in turn sent George a long, heated look before exiting the room. He scampered after her.

Celine fixed her eyes on the tablecloth, her insides in turmoil. She wondered how Miss Swan had achieved that last mysterious expression. She picked up a spoon and squinted at her reflection.

"What are you doing?" Penelope asked, taking the lavender stuffed rat out to examine it. It had eyes.

"Trying to look mysterious."

Penelope tilted her head to the side. She searched Celine's face. "You look like you are about to cast up your accounts." When Celine threw the spoon down, she continued. "Are you jealous of Miss Swan?"

"Nothing of the sort," she said shortly.

"I saw you stick your tongue out at her back when Lord Elmer touched her elbow."

"I did not."

"You also called her a laced mutton. A refined lady using such words." She shook her head and added slyly, "It shocked my bonnet."

"Miss Swan did not tell you if you were having a boy or a girl, and the duke will have to wear a petticoat, and you will have to carry around a dead rat," Celine replied instead. "You have spent the whole morning being bamboozled." She blew out the candles and tossed the incense sticks into the bowl of water.

Penelope held out the stuffed rat towards her as a sort of peace offering. "Would you like to hold him?"

Celine shook her head.

Penelope continued, "I am thinking of giving him a name. What do you suggest?"

Celine grinned.

CHAPTER TWENTY

"You made the duchess name that dead stuffed rat ... George?" Lord Elmer growled.

"You brought Miss Swan," Celine said slamming the bundle of poems down on the table. "Penny thought it was apt if we named it after you."

"Miss Elizabeth Swan happens to be a very fine young woman," he began.

"She is a fraud."

"Perhaps, but it was fun."

"The duke will have to wear a petticoat."

Lord Elmer grinned, "Never in my wildest dreams did I think that things would go so well."

"You really shouldn't tease him so."

"I can't help it. The man never smiles. And don't open that yet," Lord Elmer said, stopping her from untying the string around the bundle of poems. "I am tired of this library. We need a new place to scheme."

"Where?"

"Under the stars," he said pulling her along. "We are going to the rooftop of the Blackthorne Mansion. It is enchanting. I have gone and sat up there two nights in a row."

"Don't be ridiculous. I am not going up on the roof."

"You are," he said plucking the bundle out of her hand and moving towards the door.

"I will be cold."

"I will give you my coat" he called. His long legs already had him at the entrance.

"You are unbelievable," she muttered racing after him.

A few minutes later they were sitting under the stars and a big fat full moon.

"Now, isn't this nice?" he asked gazing up at the sky.

Celine watched the candle flicker out for the fifth time. "It is too windy for a candle. How will we write?"

He pulled out a bottle of brandy. "Would you like a drink?"

She shook her head and repeated, "How will we write?"

He took a gulp from the bottle. "Do we have to write?"

"I suppose not," she replied frowning. After a moment she said, "I am cold."

"You are wearing my coat."

"It is not helping,"

"Take a sip of the brandy. It will warm you."

After a suspicious look at him, she took a cautious sip.

"You trust me," he said in a pleased voice.

"We are friends are we not?" she replied, enjoying the tiny bit of warmth that raced through her.

"I suppose we are,"

She took another sip and then firmly put the bottle away.

They sat in silence for a while. Soon the strong breeze wriggled under her hair pins and coaxed a few locks to misbehave. She slapped at her hair desperately trying to keep what she could under control. Her hair rebelled and won.

"Lud," she exclaimed. Why was everything becoming unmanageable these days?

Lord Elmer offered her another sip of the brandy.

Lord Elmer, she decided, was the crux of the problem. How he had managed to pull the earth from under feet, flip it around twice and then replace it with a bumpier version, she would never know.

"Tell me something about your poet. About the romance between you." Lord Elmer said pulling out a cigar.

"What would you like to know?" she asked sniffing appreciatively. The scent of crushed stale roses, a hint of brandy and the sweet smell of expensive tobacco had filled the air.

"What sort of a man is he?"

"Well, he has a large body, but inside that he is a very tiny person. It is as if he doesn't realise just how big he is."

He nodded understandingly. "What did you like the most about him?"

"He was shy," she said softly. "Insecure. He did not think he deserved a girl like me. His entire face would turn red every time he saw me." She felt Lord Elmer smile in the darkness as she continued. "His favourite colour was blue. I tried to wear something blue every time I met him. He always noticed. It had become a game between us. I tried to add the lightest touch of blue to my attire and he would have to guess where it was."

"Where did you meet him?"

"In the woods behind my house. He used to enjoy writing surrounded by nature. I would sneak out of the house and meet him. He would press a letter into my hand or leave a poem on the back doorstep early in the morning when the entire house was asleep."

"I hope we can find him for you," he said taking a sip from the bottle.

She said softly, "You have a good heart."

"I am helping you to allay some of my own guilt. My presence here endangers your entire family, for if the pirates discover my whereabouts …" He trailed off.

"I never thought of that. Well then you are a scoundrel."

"Birds in their little nests agree," he replied unhappily.

"You are a scoundrel," she said consolingly, "but a good scoundrel. A likeable one. A layered one."

"Layered?"

"Yes, you have a lot of layers. On the very top you are nice, and at times I think that if anyone can catch sunlight in their fist and keep it, then it is you. Underneath that you are a touch … no, plenty mischievous. Then comes a layer of injured innocence. But deep down at the very core you are either very good or pure evil. I haven't figured out which one yet."

"You are not making any sense."

"I am trying to cheer you up. You sound blue," she mused. "Why don't you tell me one of your outlandish stories? It will make you feel better."

"No, we are here to discuss our next step."

"Next step?"

"Sometimes," he said closing his eyes, "I think that if a stranger observed us together, they would come to the conclusion that I love Nesbit and not you. I seem more passionate about finding him."

"Nesbit?"

"Your poet."

"I don't feel like discussing him tonight. Instead, tell me a story."

"You are acting a little strange, Amy. Are you well?" he said catching her chin and tilting it up to the moonlight.

"More than well," she hiccupped.

"You, my dear, are drunk." His eyes dropped to her lips. "Pity," he whispered under his breath.

Her eyes, too, dropped to his lips. He had a tempting mouth. The bottom lip was full, and she wanted to lean over and give it a small nibble. She suddenly raised her lashes and with her eyes wide announced, "I kissed Philbert. More than once."

Lord Elmer grabbed the bottle from her and shook it. It was empty. "I don't think you want to tell me more."

She grabbed the bottle back and hugged it to her chest. "I kissed him and it was ... nice."

"I see."

"Once he licked my cheek. I did not like it. What should I do if he licks it again?"

"Punch him," he advised as he wrestled the empty bottle out of her hand.

"As you say," she said and staggered to her feet. "I am warm now. You can take the coat."

"I think you should go to bed."

She yawned, "I will. I am sleepy."

"Good," he said relieved.

A minute later she still had not moved.

"Come along now," he coaxed tugging on her arm.

"Fine," she said again, but instead of moving she sat down on the ground.

Cursing under his breath he picked her up and flung her over one shoulder.

She hung passively over his shoulder, her head hanging upside down. She watched the ground move through the fog in her brain.

Her eyes slipped to his back and then lower and lower still. She grinned and her arm reached down and pinched his buttock. The action once completed allowed the tension to seep out of her. Her body went limp and her eyes closed in blissful sleep.

CHAPTER TWENTY ONE

"I am not going to drink that. It has green bits floating in it," Celine said turning her face away from the glass.

"Lord Elmer asked me to give it to you, Miss. He said you would need it," Gwerful insisted, "for your headache."

"My head does not ache," Celine yawned and stretched.

"Are you sure?" Gwerful asked. "Lord Elmer said it was bothering you all evening.

Celine frowned and shook her head from side to side, up and down, and then round and round. No, her head felt fine. When had she complained to Lord Elmer of a headache? Last night when ... Her eyes widened. On the roof top, the brandy ... Some of it came flooding back.

"Miss?" Gwerful gingerly poked Celine's shoulder, "are you sure you don't have a headache. You are turning grey."

"My head is fine." Celine splashed cold water on her face. "Is Penelope awake?"

"She woke up a long time ago, Miss. She asked me not to disturb you."

"What time is it?"

"Eleven."

"Oh my goodness," Celine squeaked. "Why did you let me sleep for so long? Where is Dorothy?"

"Lord Elmer took her horse riding."

"She missed her lessons?"

"Miss Gunhilda was teaching Miss Dorothy how to play the piano in the music room, and while the governess was busy playing a tune, Miss Dorothy escaped from the window and went off for a ride with Lord Elmer."

"Where is Gunhilda?"

"In the music room playing the piano."

"You mean you did not inform her that Dorothy is no longer in the room?"

"I did not think it was my place to do so, Miss."

Celine moaned softly. She quickly pushed her arms into the morning dress. "Give me the brush. Now run down to Mrs Cornley and ask her to meet me in the morning room. And the pillows need to be fluffed. Is it sunny? Wonderful, get some footmen to drag the mattresses out from the guest wing and lay them out in the sun. The duke's previous guest who had stayed in the floral room had fleas—"

"Miss, the cook has vanished," Gwerful interrupted.

"He has what?"

"Vanished. No trace of him. He went to the village for a drink and a cuddle last night. He has not been seen since."

Celine sat down on the bed. "Dorothy missed her lessons and the cook has disappeared. Any other disasters unfold while I slept? And don't feed it to me in doses. Tell me the whole of it."

"Well," Gwerful said, "I think that is all, unless … No, I shouldn't say."

"You really should."

"I shouldn't."

"Gwerful, we don't have time to play this game today. I agree that you are a good maid who does not gossip. You are simply doing your duty by telling me what you happened to by accident overhear or see. It is for the betterment of mankind and all that sort of thing. Now out with it."

Gwerful shuffled her feet.

Celine sighed and tossed her a coin.

Gwerful caught it expertly and pocketed it. "The duchess chased the duke out of the bedroom. She threw the entire contents of her dressing table at him."

"That's not unusual."

"He was wearing a petticoat."

"That is unusual."

"That is all."

"Right," Celine said pulling on her slippers and standing up. "I don't have time to eat breakfast. Take the tray away. And don't forget to send the housekeeper to me. We have to find the cook."

★★★

"My lord, I think we should give up," Celine said staring out of the carriage window. They had left yet another inn, and the result had been the same as usual. They had asked the barman about Philbert. The barman had snickered in reply, 'Fat poet, hehe. Not seen that ever. Try the British Museum.'

"We will find him. Until then the cook's apprentice is doing a fine job. The toast was edible and only a touch burnt," Lord Elmer soothed.

"I don't mean the missing cook. I mean Philbert."

"You don't mean that," he said shocked.

"I do. It is hopeless. The painting can mean a hundred things. It is foolish to even try and decipher it. You were right. He would have never made it so difficult had he really wanted me to find him."

"He wrote to you from London. He wants to be found. You simply had the misfortune of not getting those letters."

"Lord Elmer, don't you see, London is big. Much bigger than Finnshire. We have one tiny inn, and here in London there are shops, inns, gambling houses, eateries. How will we find one man among this crowd? I am wasting my time and yours. I am sorry, Lord Elmer, but …"

"Amy, you love him," George reminded her softly. "You will regret not looking for him."

Celine squeezed her eyes shut. "I am wasting your time," she said.

"I have nothing else to do."

"Well I do," she snapped and then immediately felt terrible. He was, after all, helping her.

"Not much of a love is it?" he muttered under his breath.

Celine heard him and scowled, "You should go back home. And—"

"That is none of your business," he growled.

"Philbert is none of your business either. But that surely is mine."

"That?" he asked, his voice rising a touch.

"That," she said pointing out of the window at the carriage keeping pace with them. "We are in yet another life threatening situation, my lord. That carriage is stuffed full of your friends, and I am certain that they are, in fact, your friends, for they have nasty looking guns pointing right at us. Now, my friends are a good deal more polite. They would never behave in such an unseemly fashion."

"Duck?" he suggested.

She ducked and that is when the firing started.

"This time let me play the hero," Lord Elmer pleaded, his survival instincts all fired up. He growled.

She shrugged and took out her knitting, "As you wish."

Lord Elmer smiled a dangerous smile. His body tensed like a panther about to strike a great crested newt. He remained in a crouching position, for if he raised his head, it would be blown off. In a flash he had a knife in his hand which he threw outside the window in the general direction of the carriage.

A shout proved he had hit someone.

"One Legged Tim has got help this time," she said, rummaging around in her reticule for the blue wool. She was knitting a sock.

He did not reply, for he was too busy crawling like a hungry lion entering a wolf's den. He moved closer to the window and in rapid succession started pulling out knives and throwing them out of the window.

She watched from the corner of her eye as he retrieved the knives from inside his shoes, coats, behind his shirt, inside his breeches and underneath his hat.

"All my knives are gone," he informed her. "Can I have a needle?"

"No," she said clutching it protectively.

"Then this will have to do," Lord Elmer said picking up his pointed shoe and flinging it out of the window.

"You wouldn't have to live like this if you went home," Celine said. "It cannot be that bad."

He suddenly dived sideways pushing her head lower still. They narrowly missed another volley of gunfire. "I don't want to be the heir. My father tossed me out of the house because I was thrown out of Oxford. Now that his golden son has offended him I am forgiven?" he gasped.

"The truth is that you are afraid of responsibilities," she replied pushing him off herself.

"And if I am?" Lord Elmer asked, lying down flat on his back at the bottom of the carriage. He nudged her away with his toe to make more room and then proceeded to wriggle out of his breeches. He continued to speak through the entire process. "Imagine spending days locked in the study with an old man who drones on and on about the greatness of my dead ancestors. Imagine me making decisions that affect the livelihood of humans when I cannot be trusted with a healthy turtle. Furthermore, if I do return home, then I will have to stay put in London. No more exotic lands to discover. I will have to marry a tittering young woman—"

"I think we are slowing down," Celine interrupted in alarm.

"Now is the time," George announced dramatically.

"Time for what? Are you standing up? No, you will be shot!"

He ignored her and stood up. He had the breeches in one hand and the coat in another. He first swung the coat around his head in a circle and aimed. The breeches soon followed.

Celine tackled him to the ground.

"Are you crazy?" she screeched.

"I threw the coat at one of the horse's head and the breeches at another. Let me up, I think it worked."

Nithercott's pleased head peered inside the carriage window, "The breeches fell neatly on the black one, my lord. Made it panic and veer off in another direction. The rest of the horses became confused. We have lost them."

"Thank goodness," Celine said thrilled, and after smiling at Nithercott's upside down head for a while, she asked, "Where is the rest of you?"

"I am hanging onto the roof using my toenails, Miss," Nithercott replied modestly.

"Eek!"

"My toenails are strong, Miss," Nithercott comforted her.

"Both of you are stuffed in the head," she scolded, "Did you have to take such a chance? And Nithercott go back to your seat please. We have had enough excitement for the day."

"It was that or we were dead. We were dreadfully outnumbered, Amy," George defended himself.

"Stop calling me, Amy," she snapped as she pushed herself away from his tempting breechless body.

He caught her hand and tugged.

She glared down at him.

He offered her an apologetic smile.

"Did you have to throw your breeches? Couldn't you throw your shirt instead?" she asked.

"In situations of urgency I have only had to dispense off my breeches and never the shirt. It was only natural that in such a life threatening situation I would do what was an engrained habit."

She wondered what sort of urgent situation required him to take his breeches off. She stilled. He was moving towards her with an odd look in his eye.

His breath tickled the back of her neck. She gripped her skirts and was about to move away when he bent his head and licked her cheek.

"Forgive me or I shall do it again," he threatened mischievously.

"You are impossible," she said but with a big wide smile and her wet cheek slightly pink. She couldn't stay angry with him for long, and they had, after all, survived against all odds yet again.

★★★

They made their way towards the Blackthorne Mansion. The duke caught them right outside the entrance.

"Lord Elmer, where have you been?"

"For a walk," he replied. "Lovely day."

"You went for a walk?"

"That is what I said," George assured him.

"You went for a walk," the duke repeated, "wearing one shoe?"

"Yes," Lord Elmer said testily.

"And without a coat, hat, cane," the duke continued, "or for that matter breeches."

"I fell into the river and lost some of the clothes while splashing around."

"You are not wet."

"It was sunny. I became dry in no time."

"Are you done inventing falsehoods?"

"I am telling the truth."

"Celine, why are you wearing a moustache?"

"Err …."

The duke eyed the two of them in disgust. "Perkins informed me that you had hired a carriage which was then hidden on the Blackthorne Estate. He saw you and Miss Fairweather leave the premises alone and unchaperoned."

"We did no such thing," Lord Elmer said trying his best to look outraged. "Perkins is a lumping squealer and dicked in the nob for inventing such falsehoods. How can you trust him? Instead, ask her, your own wife's beloved sister, who happens to be young, intelligent and perfectly sane. She will tell you the truth. Tell him, Amy." He turned to look at Celine. "Tell him the truth. Did we or did we not leave the premises unchaperoned? Amy?"

Celine didn't answer, for she lay prostrate on the ground in a dead faint.

CHAPTER TWENTY TWO

"Celine?" someone called her name. She kept her eyes closed. Her head was pounding.

"Here, make her sniff this."

"I am not going to make her smell Perkins' shoe," someone else replied.

"Trust me—"

"Lord Elmer, really this is all your fault." That sounded like Penelope.

"It is not. I am not the one who forces her to work all day. She never has a minute to herself."

"Miss did not eat anything today," Gwerful wailed. "Nothing, not even a measly lick of butter."

"They went racing around London unchaperoned," the duke roared loudly.

Somewhere Lady Bathsheba bleated.

"I told you Gunhilda was with us," Lord Elmer insisted. "She told you that."

"I think she lied," the duke glowered.

"Don't be silly, Charles. Gunhilda would never lie to a duke," Penelope protested. She waved a bottle under Celine's nose. "The smelling salts are not working, though I could have sworn her nose wrinkled a bit."

"Nooo," Dorothy came racing into room, "Celine can't be dead. I will not have it—"

"I am not dead," Celine said heaving herself upright.

Dorothy promptly turned to Penelope, "Can I have a biscuit?"

Penelope shoved a few biscuits into Dorothy's hand and turned to Celine. "I am so sorry Celine. This is my fault. I have been expecting too much from you."

"That you have," George muttered.

Penelope ignored him. "I will ask the housekeeper to take over most of your duties from now on. She is highly capable, Celine. After all, she has been taking care of Blackthorne for fifteen years. I will deal with my own letters, Dorothy will behave herself—"

"Only until she gets better," Dorothy spoke up.

"I am sorry," Celine started to say.

"It is not your fault," Penelope interrupted. "It is Charles' fault."

"I object," the duke said.

"I agree with the duchess," George added.

The duke spluttered at the injustice of it all.

"Dr Johnson is here," Dorothy announced through a mouthful of biscuit.

"Doctor?" Celine squeaked.

It took half an hour for the doctor to satisfy Penelope that Celine was all right. It took another twenty minutes for George to stop asking questions.

The doctor's prescription was food. Celine had to be fattened up. Penelope took this advice to heart.

"How did you manage to produce fifteen trays of food without a cook?" Celine asked eyeing the mounds of fruits, meats and breads decorated around her bedside.

"Lord Elmer worked as a chef in France. It was part of his disguise as a spy for England," Penelope replied.

"Penny, are you crying?" Celine asked.

Penelope burst into tears. "Please eat something," she wailed.

Celine quickly took a bite.

"Chew," Penelope howled.

Celine chewed. "I am fine, Penny. I am eating, I am eating, but for goodness' sake stop crying. This is not your fault."

"No, Charles is to blame," Penelope agreed wiping away the tears.

Celine made a noise.

Penelope took that as an agreement and it cheered her up somewhat.

"Now, you go to sleep for a while. I will see you at dinner," Penelope said, gesturing to a maid to close the curtains.

"I am not sleepy."

"Yes, you are," Penelope informed her before closing the door behind herself.

Alone in the darkened room Celine stared at the roof. She turned over and stared at the wall. After a minute, she turned back to once again stare at the roof.

She felt as if something supernatural was holding her eyelids wide open. Her eyelashes felt as if they were glued to her eyebrows.

Was this room haunted?

She had never before wondered about Sir Henry's wife who could easily be a deeply unhappy spirit moaning around the mansion—"

A shout had her spring out of bed. She snatched her robe lying atop a chair, and barefooted she hurtled down the corridor to see what the commotion was about.

She paused at the top of the stairs, her ears cocked and moving. All she could hear was an odd ringing sound.

She looked down the winding staircase which quickly proved to be a dreadful idea. Her head started spinning alarmingly, and she teetered on the topmost step of the Grand Staircase.

She was going to fall.

Fall down the stairs and break her head.

She closed her eyes and rocked on her feet.

To and fro her body weaved while she wondered if there would be blood when she splattered on top of the Persian carpet lying on the bottom step. And if there would be blood, then would it be enough to ruin the carpet? She wondered if Mrs Cornley would be able to get rid of the stain.

She also wondered when the falling would begin.

"You fool," someone roared in her ears. A hand grabbed her waist and lifted her away from the edge of the staircase.

Her head stopped spinning, and the scent of whoever held her worked far better than smelling salts would have. And apart from smelling delectable, the person was also tall, warm and comforting.

She snuggled closer.

The arms tightened around her.

"You could have fallen and broken your neck."

Celine tilted her head back and found George gazing down at her.

"You are not smiling," she said frowning.

"No, I am not,"

"I have never seen your eyes so grim."

He pushed her away, "Why did you leave your room? Didn't the duchess tell you to rest?"

"I didn't want to rest. I was bored. Please stop shouting."

"A lady must always be useful," he said sarcastically. "Were you looking for your knitting needles?"

The fog in her brain was fading and she was better able to judge his tone. She had never seen him like this before. His mouth was twisted and his eyes flashed in fury.

"I am sorry, I heard a shout."

"I don't care what you heard. Hundreds of servants in the house could have gone and investigated. You were meant to stay in your room."

"Lord Elmer," she said softly, "I didn't fall. I am alright."

The anger went out of him, and he closed his eyes and rested his head against her forehead.

"You are alright," he repeated.

Her throat seemed too full suddenly to make a sound, so she nodded. Her nose brushed against his.

His hand once again went around her waist and he pulled her closer, "Celine," he began.

"Amy," she whispered back.

"Amy, go back to bed."

She could tell he was smiling from his voice. "We have been chased by murderous pirates and you have never turned a hair. How come a little fainting spell frightened you?" she teased, lifting her lashes and searching his face.

His eyes dropped to her lips, "That was before I knew—"

"Dorothy," someone yelled.

"That was Penelope," Celine cried, slipping under his arms. "I have to see …."

"Amy, stop," George shouted chasing after her.

She ignored his calls and only halted once she had reached the bottom step.

Penelope stood holding Dorothy's hand in a firm grip. The duke was glowering.

"What is the matter?" Celine asked.

"Celine, didn't you say I could have a pet? I asked you," Dorothy babbled the moment she saw her.

"Yes, and I said that you may as long as the duke agrees," Celine replied.

"And he did, didn't he? You were in the room when I had asked."

Celine nodded.

Dorothy turned to Penelope triumphantly." I told you I had permission to keep a pet."

"Dorothy, please introduce Celine to your pet," Penelope ordered in a tight voice.

Dorothy gulped but did as she was told. "Tommy, this is Celine, the greatest sister in the whole world. She is never angry and has the sweetest of temperaments ..." Penelope made an impatient noise and she hurriedly continued, "and, Celine, this is my pet ... Tommy the chimney sweep."

Celine gaped at the little soot faced boy in horror. "This is your pet?"

Dorothy nodded, "Look at his little face, isn't he angelic? Do you know he has to climb up chimneys to clean them, and when he grows older and bigger, he will get stuck up there and never come down? How could I leave the fellow starving? He is the best pet I have ever had. He loves bread and milk ... He learns so quickly and, oh, don't make me give him away."

Penelope's mouth turned down, "Charles, the fellow is so small. Can't we—"

"No," the duke said, his eyes shifting from Dorothy to his wife in terror. "We are not keeping a chimney sweep as a pet."

George chuckled from behind Celine.

"Can't we adopt him?" Penelope insisted, her hand going to her belly.

"Dorothy, go the nursery. Leave Tommy here," Celine said firmly. It was time to sort things out. "Penny, you cannot adopt the boy. His mother will be looking for him. Won't she?" she asked turning to the boy.

The boy shook his head.

"Then your father will be looking for you?"

The boy shook his head again.

"Do you have a home?"

He shrugged.

"Can you talk?"

He stuck a thumb into his mouth.

"How old are you?"

He held up six fingers.

Celine sighed, her hand going up to rub her temples.

Lord Elmer grabbed her elbow, "I think the duke can handle this one dilemma. You need to rest."

She hated to admit it, but he was right. She turned to go when a manly sob made her turn back around.

Hopkins, the duke's valet, was shedding fat drops of tears. "If you don't mind, your grace, can I keep the fellow?"

"I think I am better equipped to keep him," the housekeeper spoke up from behind the pillar.

"He is my pet," Dorothy screeched from between the bannisters.

"Perhaps I ..." Gunhilda started to say.

Celine did not hear the rest. Lord Elmer pulled her away from the scene and up the stairs and into the room. He pushed her inside and closed the door.

Celine lay down on the bed and stared at the ceiling. A moment later she heard another shout, but this time she ignored it and closed her eyes. She was asleep within moments.

★★★

After dinner George walked Celine to her bedroom. It was not what an unmarried gentleman should do with a gently bred woman, and yet the action barely drew a gasp from her. She had somewhere along their acquaintance resigned herself to the fact that, alas, he was not a gentleman and never would be.

"We should be going to the library," she said. "I am fine. I slept all evening."

"Not tonight," he replied firmly. "You need to rest."

"But we need to discuss the plan for tomorrow. Time is speeding away and we have to scheme in greater detail. We were almost caught today," she argued.

"If you don't want to sleep, then don't, but I certainly do. I spent all day inventing falsehoods, and that duke is a sharp devil and difficult to dupe. It taxed my brain awfully. We won't be able to do anything concrete with my brain feeling like something soft and shapeless."

She sneezed and reluctantly nodded.

"Bless you and may your wits come back to you," he said handing her a snowy handkerchief.

She took it and rubbed her itchy red nostrils. "What happened right after I lost consciousness? What did you tell the duke?"

George smiled. "I have worked with the best of ruffians,

scoundrels and swindlers, my dear. I simply used my finely honed wits and—" He stopped at the look in her eye. "I will get to the meat of the matter. As soon as you swooned, I lifted you up and carried you indoors. And while the duchess took care of you and the duke took care of the duchess, I slipped out and begged Gunhilda to agree to the fact that she had indeed accompanied us on our drive into town."

"Where did you say we went?" she asked, pausing outside her room door.

"I told the duke that Gunhilda's sister happens to live close by and she was going through some sort of a feminine pickle. They needed you to sort things out for them. The duke thought it prudent not to dig too deep."

"I see, and how did you convince Gunhilda? I didn't think she could be bribed."

"I did not bribe her, I blackmailed her."

Celine gurgled.

George took that as an encouragement to continue, "A few nights ago I caught her kissing the cook in the kitchen. That disturbing vision became exceedingly helpful when I was trying to convince her of our predicament this evening. I only had to mention it once."

Celine was shocked, but she was also amused.

"How could you do such a horrid thing?" She giggled and frowned at the same time.

"If I had not, then the duke would have insisted that I marry you or he would have shot me through the heart," he said leaning towards her.

The look in his eye made her bite her lip. "Yes, neither option sounds good."

"Would you have married me to save my life?" He moved closer to her. His hand came up to rest next to her head.

Her back hit the door, and she looked at his wrist resting within kissing distance. Her breath whooshed out and did not return for a long while.

His other hand slid around her waist, and his eyes darkened.

Her heart started banging in her ribs eager to leap out of her chest and offer itself to him on a gilded platter.

He whispered softly, "Tell me, Amy, would you rather have the duke shoot me or would you have agreed to marry me?"

She heard the words as if from a distance. His scent teased her nose, his lips curved up in a taunting smile. He was daring her, daring her to be bold, frivolous and not at all sensible. Her back arched towards him, her limbs fighting with the angry Mrs Beatle yowling in her brain.

"Amy, shoot or marry?" he coaxed, his fingers gripping her waist a touch harder.

"Shoot you," she replied huskily. Her hand snuck up and grasped his lapels.

His lips turned up in a wicked smile. "You are the only woman I would allow to crease my coat," he said, his lips a breath away from hers.

"I feel privileged," she replied unsteadily, her mouth parting in invitation.

"What are you doing?" Penelope called.

They leaped apart.

"What were you doing?" Penelope repeated. She raised a brow and her foot tapped as she waited for them to respond.

"There was a fly in her eye," George burst out. "Yes, a fly in her eye which I was removing."

"He is right, fly in this eye," Celine hurriedly agreed. As an afterthought, she fluttered and blinked her right eye.

"You look like you are having some sort of a spasm, Celine," Penelope said. "I thought you were kissing."

"You should be in bed," Celine muttered. "Go to bed."

"I can't sleep when I am hungry," Penelope replied.

"What do you want? I will bring it to your room. You are not allowed to walk around," Celine said hurriedly.

"I want the smelliest fish in the kitchen, and drizzle some honey over it," Penelope requested.

"I will bring it."

Penelope eyed George up and down and back again. Her expression was dubious as she shuffled off to her room.

"I have to go," Celine mumbled, barely looking George in the eye.

"Wait," he called.

She ignored him and gripping her skirts sprinted towards the kitchens.

CHAPTER TWENTY THREE

The moment Lord Elmer's shiny brown shoes disappeared around the corner, Celine crawled out from behind the potted plant. Still on all fours she made her way towards her bedroom. She had managed to avoid him since last night even if at times she had been forced to resort to improper means.

Lord Elmer, she mused, as she turned around the corner and passed between Perkins' shocked legs, was the type of fellow that made the very air around her contort and become conducive to mischief making. Whenever he was in the vicinity, somehow her brain forgot every line of the learned *Mrs Beatle's book for accomplished English ladies* and instead made her feel like an Athanasian wench.

Which was why, she mused, as she circumvented Hopkins knees, she had decided to stop spending time with Lord Elmer.

Truth be told, it wasn't Lord Elmer's fault. It was the kiss that threatened her at every opportunity. Every time Lord Elmer came near her, the kiss became an almost tangible presence fluttering in the background, lurking, tempting and mocking her, and with every passing day it moved closer and closer. Last night it had been a hair's breath away from smacking her in the face.

She sighed as she rose and entered her bedroom. She had to remain loyal to her Philly. As for Lord Elmer, she had to admit he had behaved admirably. He had not encouraged the kiss and lord knew how much she had at sensitive moments wanted him to encourage it.

No, it was best to avoid him for now or at least until the butterflies in her belly that started summersaulting at the sight of him calmed down. And if she had no choice but to meet him, say tonight at dinner for instance, then she would make sure that she had a chaperone with her at all times.

The presence of others would prevent her from leaping across the dinner table, grabbing his face in her hands and … She stopped that thought from going any further and pulled open the windows. She stuck her head out in the evening air and panted for a few minutes. The cold stench of London air soon extinguished all thoughts of Lord Elmer and kisses.

She began dressing for dinner. She wore the heliotrope with pink roses, a colour that particularly suited her. She made Gwerful do her hair twice, and for once a small curl was allowed to escape the bun and kiss her forehead.

"Are you wanting to look nice for the special meal, Miss?" Gwerful asked as she placed the final pin in Celine's hair.

"Special meal?"

"Yes, Lord Elmer wants to dine outdoors."

"Truly?" Celine asked in amusement, "in this weather and that too in the evening?"

"I thought you knew, Miss."

Celine pushed her feet into soft gold slippers, "Lord Elmer will have to dine alone. Neither Sir Henry nor the duchess can venture outdoors."

"But the kitchen has been instructed to prepare a basket for everyone, even Sir Henry. Mary told me that she had it from the housekeeper herself."

"We will have to disappoint him then," Celine said taking a last look at the mirror.

"Amy," George greeted her. He had been lurking outside her room, it seemed, waiting to catch her alone, "you look lovely."

He spoke as if nothing whatsoever had happened last evening. It hadn't, but it could have. Celine scowled, "Lord Elmer, I cannot possibly go outside. It is too dark, we don't have a chaperone. Penelope expects me to dine with her—"

"But this is for the duchess," he interrupted.

"The duke will never allow it."

"But he has," George retorted smiling.

Celine frowned, "I don't understand."

He didn't answer and instead steered her towards the dining room.

"Perhaps this will explain it," he said throwing open the doors.

Celine gaped at the scene within.

The dining room was a sober, elegant room created for the purpose of making every Blackthorne guest feel awed in the presence of its grandeur. It was a large room with a high ceiling from which dangled a low chandelier. And now only the chandelier remained.

The long dining table with its silver candlesticks, the antique chairs with the gold brocade covers, and the dark red carpet with its swirly designs had been removed. The room had been transformed.

George it seemed had decided that since the family could not eat outdoors, then the outdoors should come inside and dine with them. The floor had been covered with a dark green carpet and the room filled with potted plants and perfumed flowers.

The windows were flung open, and the breeze with a hint of rain raced around the room in pleasure. The greenery was thick and lush enough to almost make you believe that you were outdoors. The dining room was further enchanted by pretty little glass lamps that twinkled by the dozen.

In the middle of the room was a bright square cloth on which sat piles of fruits, breads, cold meats, pies and cheeses. Penelope and Sir Henry had been given comfortable ottomans piled high with cushions while the rest were meant to sit on the ground. Amazingly even Dorothy had been allowed to join them for dinner.

"What a wonderful idea," Celine said clapping her hands.

Penelope beamed. "Lord Elmer had the whole household running around the mansion to arrange this meal. It was meant to be a surprise for me to cheer me up. Even Charles reluctantly agreed. Isn't this wonderful?"

Celine turned to him, her eyes shining, "Thank you," she said. He had done it for the duchess and yet somehow deep down she felt that he had also done this for her.

He smiled back.

From the corner of her eye Celine noticed Penelope nudging the duke and pointing in her direction. When Penelope began puckering her lips and smacking her lips together, she asked loudly, "What are we having for dinner?"

"Lemonade, fruit cake, butter cake, biscuits," Dorothy announced.

"Salad, pies, beef, chicken, pork, fish, boiled eggs, peacocks, wild hares, breads," Penelope added in an equally excited tone.

"Mashed peas for me," Sir Henry grumbled.

"And some excellent wine," the duke muttered. "I don't know

how I agreed to this."

"Because you love me and you knew it would make me happy," Penelope said smiling at her grumpy husband.

"It has made everyone happy," George said biting into a piece of cheese. His eyes were on Celine.

Celine blushed and plucked a grape.

"Salt," Sir Henry barked from the top of the silk cushions.

Dorothy grabbed the ivory salter and threw it towards Sir Henry. "Catch."

Celine watched horrified as Sir Henry panicked and dangerously seesawed, the silk cushions not giving enough of a grip for his breeches to adhere to. He somehow found his balance and at the same time swatted the salter. The salter flew into the air, the top came off and the fine grains of salt fell like rain drops on top of all the food.

"I am sorry," Dorothy's lip trembled in remorse, "I didn't think."

"It doesn't matter," Penelope soothed. "We can brush off the salt."

Celine patted Dorothy's head, "Most of the food is fine, Dory."

"I like my food salty," George added.

Even Sir Henry and the duke muttered something comforting.

Dorothy smiled and the merry atmosphere soon trickled back into the dining room.

Celine went back to nibbling on her bread while George tried to catch her eye. She pretended not to notice him.

He flicked a morsel at her.

She brushed it off and turned her back on him.

George on the pretext of reaching for the butter shifted closer to her, his knee touching hers.

She blushed and looked at him from the corner of her eye.

George grinned. He placed a cushion over her hand and now sat holding it.

"Lord Elmer," Celine whispered horrified, "What are you doing?"

"I want to talk to you and this is my way of ensuring that you do not run before I complete what I have to say," he whispered back.

Celine tugged at her hand. Her heart thundered, "Please, I won't run. The duke is going to see ...."

"He won't," George replied confidently. "You have been avoiding me all day." His hand tightened over hers.

Celine twisted her hand in his grip but not too much or the cushion would dislodge. "Please, the duke has noticed something is wrong. He is looking right at us."

"Let me quickly speak—" George started to say when a scream stopped him.

Penelope had screamed because Sir Henry had fallen off his cushion.

"Bloody, blistering fool of a thing," Sir Henry roared.

"Amy," George tugged her hand, "listen."

"Deuced cushions, go to the basted devil." Sir Henry yelled as he was held aloft by footmen while the cushions were being adjusted.

"I am not going to stay at Blackthorne any longer," George told Celine.

"What? Speak louder," she said, finding it hard to hear above the racket Sir Henry was making.

"I will boil the lot of you. Cook you alive. Who bought those villainous cushions? I am going to kill them. Kill them all," Sir Henry shouted as he was gently laid back on top of the cushions.

"There, there," Penelope soothed.

"Can I have some more muscadine ice?" Dorothy demanded.

"This was a farewell dinner," George finally lost patience and bellowed over the din. "I leave tonight, Amy. This is goodbye."

Celine turned to George in shock. The meal, the corset digging into her ribs, and Sir Henry, who was now loudly singing a battle song, faded into the background. He was leaving. Her hand turned cold in his grip, and all of a sudden the most unbearable sadness filled her.

"No you are not," Penelope said, for she had overheard George. "You have to stay. Please say you will stay."

Celine nodded fervently.

"I am sorry. I received an urgent message from a friend yesterday morning. I was going to tell you, but what with Celine swooning and then Gunhilda adopting the chimney sweep ... I didn't get a chance," George said apologetically.

"It's a shame," the duke said perking up. "When do you leave?"

"Tonight."

"If you need a carriage or anything, let me know," the duke said looking positively kindly.

"Thank you," George replied.

Celine refused to look at him. How could he do this to her? He had promised to help her and now he was leaving?

"Is your friend in London?" Penelope asked, her eyes darting from Celine to George.

"Yes," he said, his eyes glued to Celine.

"Then you can come to our dinner party tomorrow," Penelope said pleased.

"What dinner party," both the duke and George echoed.

Penelope pinched the duke hard and smiled at Lord Elmer. "Anne's friend Sophia is coming to dine with us tomorrow. Anne is my sister in law and Sophia, her bosom friend, is as good as family. Will you please join us, Lord Elmer, and make it a small dinner party?"

Celine bit into the cold chicken and chewed. She knew fully well that Sophia was not planning to come to dinner. Penelope had decided to invite her but a moment ago.

"I am not sure," George hedged.

"Bring your friend along," Penelope coaxed.

"I don't—" the duke began. Penelope pushed a slice of cake into his mouth.

"I don't think my friend can come, but I will, "George finally agreed. Penelope had left him no way out, and he couldn't possibly be rude to a duchess.

Celine spent the rest of dinner mechanically eating. She had lost her appetite.

***

"I need to explain," Lord Elmer began.

"No, you don't," Celine interrupted. She had decided not to go to the library after dinner. She didn't think there was any point anymore. They had nothing to discuss. She would find Philbert on her own. And while she was deciding to never ever see Lord Elmer again and stay away from the library, her feet had taken her exactly where she had not wanted to go.

She was in the library sitting opposite George.

"The cook has been kidnapped," George reminded her.

"The cook?" she asked in confusion.

"Yes, the Blackthorne cook. Remember the cooks in England are disappearing and appearing because the pirates are kidnapping them? The same pirate who is looking for his grandmother's recipe. The recipe that I stole."

"Oh."

"I have to leave don't you see? The cook knows who I am. The pirates will interrogate him, and if he happens to mention the guest staying at the Blackthorne Mansion, then all of you will be in danger. The duchess is vulnerable …."

"I understand," Celine replied, her anger melting away.

They sat in silence staring at the cold fireplace.

Finally Celine said, "Thank you for all your help. I appreciate it."

He didn't say anything, so she continued, "I suppose this is goodbye. You are coming to dinner tomorrow … Not really goodbye yet, except …"

"It won't be the same," he finished for her.

She glanced up to find him staring at her. She shifted nervously on the chair.

"Goodnight, Celine," he said quietly.

She stood up and smoothed her skirts. She made her way towards the door. Halfway through she stopped and turned.

He was still watching her.

She smiled hesitatingly, "You can call me Amy."

He nodded, his expression unreadable. "I will."

"Goodnight."

"Goodnight."

She made her way to her room, her steps slow. She was waiting for something but what exactly she wasn't sure.

She stopped twice and turned to look behind her. Both times, she found the corridor empty.

Later that night when she had laid her head on the pillow she was surprised to find her cheeks were wet with tears. She would miss her new friend was her last thought before she drifted off to sleep.

CHAPTER TWENTY FOUR

Perkins, Hopkins, Gwerful and Mary confirmed that George had indeed left the mansion. The news made Celine feel as if one of Blackthorne's beloved limbs had been hacked away and transported to an unreachable location. Her only consolation was the fact that she would see him at dinner that evening.

She moped around all day willing the clock to move quicker, but time was being contrary as usual, for it crawled when she wanted it to race.

Even Penelope seemed out of sorts after George's departure, for all she ate that morning for breakfast was three eggs, buttered bread, a few spice biscuits, some slices of cold meat and a pear. As for Dorothy, the poor girl howled and cried and kicked up her feet until even Lady Bathsheba was moved to tears. The duke spent the day whistling a merry tune.

"Are you going to a ball, Miss?" Gwerful asked as she pinned a sparkling brooch to Celine's Egyptian robe of blue satin shot through with fine silver threads and silver acorn trimming.

"No," Celine said attaching blue sapphires to her earlobe.

"Then are you going somewhere else special?" Gwerful persisted.

"No, why?" Celine placed the white cashmere shawl on one shoulder and the soft grey lace wrap over the other.

Gwerful pointed to the lace wrap in approval. "Because you are taking an awful lot of interest in your dress today."

"I am simply dressing for the dinner party, Gwerful. Surely, I am allowed to take pains with my toilette on such an occasion."

"Yes, but dinner is at six in the evening, Miss, and right now it is only two in the afternoon."

Celine opened her mouth to scold her and then closed it again. Her maid was right. What the devil was wrong with her? She never spent so long preening in front of the mirror like an imbecile. She pulled off the dress, placed the wrap back in the cupboard and replaced the earrings in the jewellery box.

"Pull the taupe silk out," she said quietly.

"I am sorry, Miss. I thought you looked lovely in the blue … Surely the taupe is too dull?"

"The taupe will do."

Gwerful nodded and did as she was told.

Celine entered the Blue Room at six sharp. She wore the taupe silk, her hair was scraped back into a low bun, and a thin gold necklace was her only ornament. She looked sensible and she felt miserable.

Miss Sophia Leech followed close behind her.

"Sophia," Penelope held out her fingers, "you are as pale as a corpse. It is positively enchanting. How did you manage it?"

"It is a new tonic from France. I will send you a bottle," Sophia replied kissing the air in front of Penelope's fingers.

"Miss Leech," George exclaimed the moment he entered the room.

"Geo—I mean, Lord Elmer," squealed Sophia.

Celine watched the enthusiastic greeting with a jaundiced eye. Sophia looked ecstatic and George pleased, while she felt like a colour changing lizard that had blended into the room's furnishings. No one had greeted her yet.

"I gather you know each other?" Penelope asked.

"Yes, Lord Elmer and I knew each other a long time ago. In fact, I knew him when he was still at Oxford. He often came to meet my elder sister Jane. They were extremely close," Sophia grinned. "And I am sure if my sister had not already been married to the old toad Major Wright at the time, she would have married Lord Elmer. Major Wright is now dead, Lord Elmer. A bird dropped a turtle on his head and cracked it wide open. I mean both the turtle shell and the Major's head cracked open. Neither Major Wright nor the poor turtle survived. Jane is still celebrating her husband's funeral."

George cleared his throat, and his eyes finally fell on Celine. "Miss Fairweather," he said warmly.

Celine's mouth dropped open. He had called her Miss Fairweather. Since when did he adhere to propriety? She nodded back coldly.

"Tell me, Lord Elmer, how long are you in London for?" Sophia said snapping open her fan and fluttering with all her might.

"Would you like some tea?" Penelope interrupted.

"No, thank you," Sophia said and then turned back to George. The tip of her fan rested on his sleeve, "You should have called over to our house, Lord Elmer," she pouted. "Mamma would have been thrilled to see you."

"Not your Father," George replied smiling. "He chased me with a very large hunting rifle the last time I dared to set foot in your house."

"You shouldn't have climbed into mamma's room then ... or at least you shouldn't have allowed yourself to be caught climbing in," Sophia scolded.

"Would you like some coffee," Penelope interrupted again.

"No, and, Lord Elmer—"

"Some wine then?" Penelope insisted.

"Truly, no need—"

"You must try some lemonade."

"Honestly—"

"Sophia," Penelope came to the point, "did you know Celine and Lord Elmer are engaged? Why don't you congratulate them?"

Three jaws dropped open in shock.

Sophia changed colours like a peach speedily ripening. She first turned green, then pink, and finally a mixture of red and yellow. "I did not know ... I wish you ... When is the wedding?"

Celine sprang up, "Penny, I mean, the duchess needs to retire to her room for a moment. She needs to take a tonic. A very bitter tonic."

Penelope meekly followed.

Celine planted her hands on her hip, "What were you thinking? How could you tell her that I was engaged to Lord Elmer?"

"I was simply trying to hurry things along," Penelope replied sheepishly. "Besides Sophia was flirting with him and I didn't like seeing you suffer."

"I was not suffering."

"You looked like you were suffering."

"Penny, this is a pickle. How could you do this? And what about Lord Elmer. What will he do?"

Penelope clutched her stomach with one hand and touched her

forehead with the other, "I am going to have a baby. Women in my condition should be cossetted and never scolded … In fact, I think I am having a headache … and oh, I felt a decided twinge in my belly. I think I am going to have the baby now …."

Celine shook her head in disgust and walked back into the Blue Room. She believed not a word of Penelope's mythical pains.

Back in the Blue Room Sophia had gone back to flirting with George. It seemed Sophia was one of those women who believed that if a man was not married, he was fair game for all. And clearly Sophia liked to play. A lot.

Thereafter, Celine spent the entire dinner silently stabbing her meal while listening to George and Sophia flirt and reminiscence about the good old days. She learned about the party in Lord Clifton's country house where George and Sophia had spent a week. George had spent four days chasing everything in skirts. The skirts in turn had chased him back until finally Lady Clifton had declared her love for him in public. Lord Clifton lost his patience, and he too began chasing George but with a rifle and off the premises.

The duke loudly crunched a chicken bone while Penelope slurped the wine. Sophia, being as sensitive as a block of wood, failed to take the hint and continued to babble.

And George … George encouraged Sophia.

Celine felt as if she no longer knew him. The duke had warned them that he was an incorrigible flirt, but somehow she had forgotten. She thought she could trust him, and yet after listening to all the scandalous stories, she felt muddled. He had lied to her and told her outlandish stories. Pirates were chasing him, and he had been a pirate, a spy and a thief … a rogue.

She watched him wink at Sophia and her heart constricted. He did flirt with anything in skirts.

After dinner was over, they moved to the family room. Sophia stroked the piano and hinted slyly, "Lord Elmer, I know you dance exceedingly well."

Celine played a tune to which Lord Elmer and Sophia danced. She banged away at the keys irked by the fact that Sophia knew Lord Elmer could dance, while she hadn't. What else did she not know about him?

Celine finished mauling the piano and retired to a corner with a cup of tea.

Meanwhile, Sophia had progressed from touching Lord Elmer's sleeve with the tip of her fan to touching his sleeve without the fan. She now sat coaxing him to give her a sip of brandy.

Penelope stood up and walked over to Sophia. She pretended to bump into her, thereby spilling a glass of sickly smelling tonic on her lap.

"I am so sorry," Penelope said, looking not the least bit sorry. "I will call the carriage. We cannot have you sitting here wet and dripping. You may catch a deathly cold."

And with that Sophia departed.

As soon as she left, Penelope and Celine turned to George.

He smiled, "Bang up evening, eh? Pity Miss Leech had to leave so early."

"The evening was frightful and Miss Leech ghastly," Penelope growled.

"Penny," Celine scolded half-heartedly, "you shouldn't speak so about a guest."

"It's the truth, Celine, and as for your behaviour, Lord Elmer, I am disappointed," Penelope shook her head sadly.

"Oh, don't say that," George begged. "Be anything but disappointed."

"I am nothing but disappointed," Penelope stressed again.

"But why the devil?" George exploded.

"You are engaged to Celine," Penelope informed him, "and you were flirting with that creature instead."

"We are engaged," Celine said shortly, "in your head, Penny."

"Miss Leech is quite pleasant," George added. "You simply have to dig deeper."

Penelope and Celine glared at George.

George blinked in confusion.

"I spent all evening excavating with the best spade in the country, and even after hours and hours of digging into Miss Leech's head and heart, I found nothing. Nothing, Lord Elmer. The woman is made up of empty paper bags and cotton balls," Penelope seethed.

George turned to Celine.

"Good evening, Lord Elmer. If you will excuse me, I have a headache," Celine responded to his silent query.

"Eh?" George said beseechingly eyeing the duke who intelligently spent the later part of the evening lurking in silent corners.

The duke shrugged. "I hope to see you at Boodles sometime."

With that the dinner party was over.

★★★

Celine did not go to bed immediately. She first spent a lonely hour in the library staring at London maps. The task of finding her Philbert was suddenly no longer fun. Her mind kept flitting back to George's beautiful dimple appearing and disappearing for Sophia's amusement. A soft voice at the back of her head asked her if she was jealous.

"No," Celine informed the bookshelves, "I am not jealous."

The bookshelves in turn looked sceptical.

It was, she decided, time for bed.

Celine climbed into bed and blew out the candle. She closed her eyes and started to go over the evening's happenings. She had just finished picking out faults in Miss Sophia Leech's dress when a hand closed over her mouth.

CHAPTER TWENTY FIVE

"Don't scream," George warned.

Celine nodded and bit his finger.

George screeched, "Why did you do that?"

"What are you doing in my room?" Celine countered furiously.

"I have come to discuss our next step."

"What step?"

"To find your cretin. I mean your poet," he replied. "I say, you didn't think I would give up the hunt, leave you in the lurch and abandon ship, did you?"

"I thought it would be impossible now with you gone from the mansion."

"I cannot see you during the day, but nothing stops us from meeting during the night."

"Lord Elmer," Celine said sternly, though her heart was singing, "I thought we had said our goodbyes."

George placed the candle on the table and sat down next to her. "You thought you were bidding me goodbye? Forever?"

She nodded.

"And you didn't even shed a tear?"

She had sobbed her heart out, but she couldn't tell him that. So she remained silent.

"You did shed a tear," he teased.

"I did not."

"You did."

"Did not."

"Liar," he said wagging a finger at her and winking at the same time. "You sobbed your heart out when you thought you would never see my handsome face again."

Celine started giggling. "Lord Elmer, we cannot meet like this."

"But it is the only way. The servants will tell the pirates that I have left the mansion, and I can sneak in like a thief at night and meet you and discuss the next step. Everyone will be safe and we can carry on with our plans. It is the perfect solution."

"I don't think so. If anyone found you in my room, I will be ruined—"

"Why does society treat women like a bunch of mangoes? If they are not treated a certain way then they will rot. The best way to preserve them is to pickle them or dry them in the sun. It is ridiculous. I don't like pickled or dried up women—"

Celine touched his cheek halting his tirade. "You are sweet," she whispered.

He turned his face and kissed the palm of her hand.

Her heart skipped a beat.

"I found him," he told her abruptly.

The way he said the words Celine knew that this time he truly had.

He jumped off the bed and started pacing the room. "I am sorry I did not tell you before, but I stole your poet's painting and showed it to an artist. He said that what we thought was a camel's hump and three sticks was in fact a pitchfork, and the pig was not a pig or a kidney but the devil. Hence Ludsthorpe—"

"Who?"

"Ludsthorpe … Your poet can be found at The Devil's Pitchfork. It is a gamblers inn. I spent all day greasing the innkeeper's palms. He told me that your poet does in fact arrive at the inn every single day."

Celine took a sharp breath, "You did find him."

He stopped pacing, "I told you I would."

Her eyes widened. He had found her Philly.

"Are you happy?" he asked gently.

Her eyes darkened as he came towards her. She nodded.

"You don't look happy," he said kneeling down next to the bed.

"I am happy," she insisted.

He took her hand. "I have never seen a less happy person."

"I am just surprised. I never thought I would see Gilly … err … I mean Philly again. It is unexpected, sudden …" She trailed off. She didn't know how she felt, and with George holding her gloveless hand, it was even more difficult to focus on her beloved poet.

George tugged at her hand pulling her closer. "Is it different?"

"Is what?" she asked huskily.

"Kissing someone you love?"

"What do you mean?"

"I mean, I have never kissed anyone I have loved before. Only girls I liked. Is it different?"

"I have only kissed one person and I loved him."

"I found your poet."

"Yes."

"It is your duty to help me now."

"How?"

"Let us begin with a kiss," he said slyly, "and then you can judge and tell me the difference."

"Begin with a kiss," she mused. It had been a long while since she had been kissed, and kissing was not all that earth shattering as poets made it out to be. She had kissed Philly often, and she recalled vaguely that it had been a pleasant sensation.

She looked at George's moist parted lips, soft curly hair and the muscles moving under his shirt. What, she wondered, would it feel like to be kissed by him? She shivered at the thought, her mind going strangely numb.

"Amy?" he coaxed.

Oh, to hell with propriety, the devil with being sensible and good riddance to maidenly modesty sang her heart and mind. She forcefully ejected Mrs Beatle from her head and said firmly, "We will begin with a kiss."

"Truly?" he asked shocked.

She lost her nerve and wilted, "No, no, I am sleepy you see and didn't know what I was—"

He silenced her with a kiss.

An earth shattering kiss. A kiss that made her world tilt to never right itself again.

Her senses contracted to a point where all she could feel was his lips on hers. Her hands clutched his lapels in a deathly grip.

Poets were not wrong. A single kiss could contain everything. Philbert's kiss had made her stomach tickle pleasantly, but George's kiss was creating a fully fledged ball in her belly.

Her knees melted like jasmine flavoured ice and her emotions whirled, bounced and ricocheted inside her.

She sighed.

She was a young tender leaf uncurling for the sun, a soft petal letting the dew soak into her thirsty veins, a tiny pup who had found a juicy bone to chew ...

He broke the kiss, but her lips continued to move and seek.

He tapped her on the shoulder and she opened her eyes.

"Now tell me the difference," he said moving slightly away from her.

She gazed at him feeling decidedly foolish. The kiss had sent her wits gallivanting it seemed. "Whaa—?" she asked not very seductively.

"Tell me the difference between kissing someone you love and someone you like? You like me and you love Scroggs."

"Philbert," she mechanically corrected.

"Yes, him. Tell me the difference."

"I can't ... I don't ... It is late. I am tired. I don't think I can think at the moment. You will know one day ..." she babbled in utter confusion, her hands mangling the bed sheet.

He smiled. "Go to sleep, Amy."

She nodded, avoiding his gaze.

He caught her chin and forced her to look at him, "You are going to meet your poet tomorrow, you need to rest. I will meet you in the orangery and we can depart for The Devil's Pitchfork at four."

And with another lingering kiss, he departed taking with him Celine's peace of mind as well as an entire night's sleep.

★★★

At ten minutes to four Celine met George in the orangery. Thereafter, the two of them spent a few moments admiring each other's respective shoes in awkward silence. Another moment went by in clearing throats.

Finally George spoke, "I think we should go and sit in the carriage. I brought the veil for you this time. Here," he said pulling out the dark cloth from his coat pocket.

Celine took it and with numb fingers tried to attach it to her bonnet.

"Let me," George said reaching for her.

Celine took two hurried steps backwards almost toppling over a plant, "No, I can do it."

His face darkened but he nodded.

They walked towards the carriage hidden behind trees, and all through the walk Celine kept a good distance between them. A single kiss had changed their relationship overnight. She felt more aware of him now than she ever had. Once she would have thought nothing of touching his sleeve, and now the very thought set her heart racing.

He too seemed to be behaving oddly with her. His eyes met hers and flittered away only to meet again a moment later. His shoulders were tensed and his mouth was set in a grim line. His whole form seemed filled with suppressed energy. Words perched on the tip of his tongue but were never spoken.

Her heart stopped for a fraction of a second when she had to take his help in climbing into the carriage. Her hesitating fingers clutched his, and even through her thick white gloves the heat of him seared her palm.

He helped her in and quickly let go.

She busied herself arranging skirts looking at anything but him.

He pretended to look for his cigar.

All at once the carriage started shaking from side to side as if someone was energetically bouncing up and down on the roof.

It yanked them out of their brooding moods, and they eyed each other in astonishment.

"Lord Elmer?" Celine asked nervously, "I think someone is trying to cut a hole in the roof."

George did not get a chance to reply, for at that moment two masked men burst into the carriage.

One held an evil looking snickersnee and the other an equally vile looking rifle.

Everyone froze.

George and Celine had frozen in shock, while the muscled men had frozen because it appeared as if they wanted to be admired in their deadly masked forms, swathed in black, holding newly acquired, glinting weapons of destruction.

They narrowed their eyes and snarled dangerously.

Celine stared back at them. Her chin lifted in defiance, and her hands slipped into her pockets.

They smirked at her defiance and lifted up their weapons.

George moved but did not get a chance to do anything more than take a step, for Celine whipped out two glass jars from her pocket.

The men eyed the glass jars in confusion.

This time Celine smirked as she undid the lids and flung the contents of the jars at the men.

The men screeched in agony.

George leaped at the man with the rifle and wrenched it out of his hand. "What was that?" he panted.

"Chilli powder," Celine replied as she twirled and with pointed feet kicked between the other man's eyes. It successfully knocked the man to the ground, and she grabbed the knife out of his hand.

"Good girl," he grunted in reply. He dragged the unconscious men towards the door, and she gave him a helping hand.

"On the count of three," he told her lifting one of the men by the shoulders.

She nodded and caught hold of his ankles.

"Now, one, two and … three," he yelled, and they swung the man to and fro between them before flinging him out of the carriage. They did the same with the other man.

"That was easy," George said, brushing off a little lint on his coat. He turned around and his smiled faded.

One Legged Tim stood in the middle of the carriage. He grinned, his gold teeth sparkling.

Celine looked up. Tim had cut a large hole in the roof of the carriage.

She gasped.

When she looked back down, she found One Legged Tim unconscious on the carriage floor. A dart with a turkey tail feather was sticking out from his buttock.

"This time I was prepared," George said pleased.

"I think some more men are coming this way," Celine announced looking out of the window.

"Why is this blasted carriage not moving?" George growled pulling out more poisoned darts from his coat pockets, breeches, shirt, underneath his hat, shoes and socks.

Celine took some darts and moved to one window while George went to the other window.

Sixteen rifles pointed back at them.

The dart dropped out of Celine's hand. "We are dead."

The carriage lurched.

George flew across the carriage and landed on top of Celine. They both ended up on the floor with a thud.

When Celine stopped seeing stars, she noticed the carriage was moving and the walls were being peppered with bullets.

Finally everything became silent and Nithercott's head appeared at the window. Celine no longer cared if he was hanging by his toenails. She was simply too happy to scold.

"We escaped. It was a miracle," Nithercott grinned.

"How did they know where to find us?" George mused.

"The driver was bribed," Nithercott informed them. "I knocked him out."

"Who is driving now?" Celine asked.

"I am," Nithercott replied.

"But you are here …" Celine trailed off. She heard the hysterical note in her voice.

"Return to your seat," George ordered.

As soon as Nithercott disappeared George pulled Celine into a hug.

It was a hug that was meant to comfort her and it did. She lay her head on his shoulder taking deep ragged breaths.

The panic receded, and she slowly became aware of his arms around her, his chin nestling at her nape and her own hands clutching a fistful of his shirt.

She stilled.

He moved away searching her face.

She looked back at him from beneath heavy lashes, a blush tinting her cheeks.

He frowned.

She tilted her face up softly, her lips trembled and parted.

He hesitated, unsure of what she wanted.

Her chest rose and fell in anticipation. Her eyes dazed, her skin heated and flushed. The air seemed charged, the world outside forgotten. She waited ….

He cocked his head to one side, reading the signs but uncertain. His hand rose and fell back to his side.

She licked her bottom lip in blatant invitation.

Still he did not move.

Her eyes narrowed, and with a growl of annoyance, she pounced. She grabbed the back of his head and kissed him on the mouth.

He was stunned but not for long.

The moment he recovered his wits he was more than happy to oblige her with an equally heated response.

When the kiss ended Celine burst into tears.

"Amy, I am sorry. The attack on our lives was too close for comfort and it simply triggered our deepest instincts and we kissed. It was only a kiss. You still love Harper—"

"Philbert," she wailed, "his name is Philbert."

"Yes, him. Now stop crying please. Here, I have a handkerchief … No wait, it is dirty … This one is clean. Now, in life and death situations things often get out of control and we do things we don't want to, and a kiss is not something to worry about. I am sure Dauncey … err … your poet must have kissed plenty of women … no, no, I never meant to say that. I am sure he has been loyal. After all, who would kiss a fat, dim witted poet, only a fool—"

"Lord Elmer," Celine choked out, "for goodness' sake, do not utter another word."

George nodded and pressed his lips together. They sat in silence until the carriage stopped at The Devil's Pitchfork.

"We have arrived," George said. "Let Nithercott investigate first and make sure everything is in order. I don't want to put your life in any more danger. We will wait in the carriage."

Celine nodded, her mind in turmoil. She was busy dissecting the difference between kissing George and kissing Philly. If George's kiss was like a lavender satin bonnet with rose bud trimmings, then Philly's kiss was like a spinster's cap. If Philly had made her heart beat faster, then her heart thundered at the sight of George. And if the thought of Philly made her smile, then George made her laugh.

She dug her nails into her palm … Her heart and mind were in conflict. A gruesome battle was occurring inside her head while her emotions churned and heaved in confusion.

"He is inside," Nithercott arrived to tell them.

Celine moved and George caught her hand. "Is it safe?" he asked his valet.

Nithercott nodded.

George turned to Celine. "Would you like me to accompany you?"

She saw the concern in his eyes. "I want to do this alone."

He nodded and dropped his hand. "It is time to meet your poet. I wish you luck, Celine."

"Amy. For you my name is Amy," Celine replied, her eyes on the inn.

CHAPTER TWENTY SIX

They were parked near The Devil's Pitchfork sitting inside a holey carriage. Philbert Woodbead was inside the inn and all Celine had to do was walk a few dozen steps and meet him.

After ten minutes they were still outside The Devil's Pitchfork and Celine had still not walked those few dozen steps.

George watched her quietly. He seemed to understand that she needed this time to come to terms with what was going to happen.

Celine stared up at the grey sky through the hole in the roof of the carriage. She was afraid. What if he no longer loved her, or worse, what if he still did?

She wondered if she had romanticised the depth of their love in the time they had spent apart. Had she truly loved him to distraction or was her head stubbornly insisting on continuing a love that her heart had never felt?

A drop of cold water fell on top of her nose.

"It is going to start raining," George spoke up, "and our carriage can no longer shelter us. I think you should go inside."

Celine swallowed nervously but did not move.

A bullet scraped George's hat momentarily distracting her.

George looked out of the window, "It is only an unhappy husband. Hurry, Amy, go inside. Don't worry, I can handle this one man alone."

Celine picked up her parasol and adjusted her gloves. She would have liked some more time to prepare herself, but what with an unhappy husband out for George's blood, it wasn't really possible.

Ready or not, this was it. Taking a deep breath she descended from the carriage and walked into The Devil's Pitchfork.

She looked around the inn.

It was a low roofed, wooden establishment, the wood being dark, dusty and grey. The floor was peppered with peanut shells, and a small fire burnt in the fireplace at the back of the room. The fire did nothing to light the room nor did the windows admit any light. The fire did however contribute to the smoke in the room, for the chimney, it seemed, had never since its construction been cleaned. Her lungs complained and she stifled a sneeze.

She counted five men sprawled over wooden chairs with tankards of ale sitting in front of them. None of them looked like her Philly ... except ... She squinted ... A man in a familiar parrot green patchwork coat sat reading a book right at the back of the room.

She rubbed her eyes and inched closer to the parrot green patchwork coat. She observed the man for some time, her tentative steps getting closer and closer to the table at the back of the room.

Finally her mouth dropped open in horror.

She gurgled and wheezed.

Philbert Woodbead was now, she moaned softly in despair, no longer fat. In fact, he was most certainly reed thin.

It took a few moments for the truth to sink in. She eyed his gaunt face, his thin bony hands and the wispy beard. Another thought struck her. Philly had not only become thin, but he had also become handsome.

Her Philly was now a thin and handsome poet.

She clutched the nearest chair for support. For a moment she felt like turning around and running screaming from the room.

Her eyes squeezed shut and she took a few rapid breaths. So what if he was now handsome? He was still her Philbert and she loved him for his beautiful, immature soul and not for his features or figure.

She slipped her hand into the hidden pocket in her skirt and took out a brandy flask. Taking a big gulp of the contents and letting the warmth give her courage she walked up to the man at the back of the room.

"Philly?" she asked, her voice trembling.

Philbert glanced up, "I am sorry, I will have the money tomorrow."

"Eh?" Celine asked in confusion.

"Didn't Hammer send you? No ... How about Strangeways? Stubbs, Norris or ... let me see... Steering?"

Celine shook her head, her eyes wide.

"Then who the devil are you?"

"Celine," she whispered and then recalled the veil she still had attached to the bonnet. She unclipped it and let it fall.

He stared at her face and then peered and squinted. His face cleared, "Celine Fairweather, how are you? It is wonderful to see. I never thought ..." He half stood up and gestured to the chair opposite himself.

She sat down.

"Would you like something to drink?" he asked.

She shook her head.

He nodded and leaned back in his seat, "So what brings you here? A lady like you shouldn't be visiting this part of town."

"You left the painting ...." She trailed off.

He ran a hand under his collar, "Painting? Ah yes, that was a long time ago. Goodness, time flies and all that."

A barmaid with her ample bosom on display arrived at their table, "Anything to drink?"

"Tea," Philly answered the bosom.

She departed with a lusty wink.

"How are you?" Celine asked, watching Philbert watch the barmaid's hips sway away.

"Good," he replied shortly. He started playing with an empty glass on the table.

"Have you been writing much?" Celine asked after a moment of silence.

"Plenty. In fact, a fellow wants to publish my work. I have asked him to hold off until I can be sure he is a reputable sort. Don't want him running away with my hard work and calling it his own."

"I still have your poems," she tried again.

After a small heavy silence, he said, "Yes, well, about that, I hope you won't mind terribly, but can I have them back?"

"Have them back?" she asked in confusion. "Have what back?"

"The poems," he replied apologetically. "You see, I was robbed by a highwayman. You must have heard of the Falcon? Yes, well he is planning to build a library for his apple dumpling, that is his missus, once he retires. He told me all about it while divesting me of all my belongings. He took the poems for his library, and you are the only one who has the copies ...."

"I will give them back to you," she replied.

He nodded, his mood visibly improving. He pulled out a cigar and lit it.

The stench of stale beer mixed with the odour of cheap tobacco and unwashed feet had Celine quickly reattaching the veil.

Philbert eyed her across the table, the smoke curling out of his nostrils, "London is wonderful, is it not?" he asked. "The modes of transport alone are remarkable. Have you ridden on one of the flying coaches yet? You must. It is an experience in itself. They are sprung, can you believe it? I don't think Londoners can conceive what a jolting the carriages in Finnshire give. And the leather straps that hold the body together—"

"Body?"

"Yes, the body of the carriage. Remarkably strong leather straps. Keeps the carriage from flying apart. And some of the carriages are lined on the inside with velvet. Father never had one of those. And the beautiful silver mouldings and the iron with not a speck of rust …"

Celine yawned into her gloved hand. She wondered if it was time to go.

The barmaid with the ample bosom arrived to deposit the tea.

Philbert thanked the bosom, and before he could once again launch into the description of a chaise or a landau Celine spoke up, "You have lost a lot of weight."

Philbert spat some of the tea out. After delicately dabbing his chin, he said, "Yes, well, father has not called me back, and the world seems to share his opinion of poets. My creativity has not been appreciated, and the pay is not sufficient. What with the costs of staying in London, I quickly spent all my savings. A month of starvation followed where I truly became an impoverished poet."

"Your last letter, it said …" Celine struggled with the words. "It said that you were waiting for me."

"Did it say that?" he asked in surprise.

Celine bit her lip. She did not have the luxury to play games, "Phill … I mean, Mr Woodbead, you said that you would love me forever. You wrote that you were waiting for me, and you painted the name of this inn …" She trailed off.

"Miss Fairweather," he soothed, "really, you couldn't have expected me to wait, and after all it has been months since I saw you."

"You said you would love me forever. Forever means eternity and not a few months," she pointed out.

He hurriedly continued, "Besides, at that time you must admit I was not very pleasant to look at. A fellow like me was thrilled that someone like you fancied him. And now that I am an emaciated, handsome, impoverished poet things are different. And a girl like you deserves marriage, and my financial state is such that I don't think I can even offer you a cup of tea, forget a house and garden."

"I see," Celine said her lips pursed in disapproval.

"I am glad you are taking this so well. You were always a sensible sort," he smiled.

Celine realised that she did not like his smile. In fact, she had never liked his smile. His smile was outright ghastly.

He seemed unaware of her rapidly changing mood. When she continued to remain silent and not shriek and break the teapot on his fragile empty head, he further brightened and asked, "Say, would you happen to have a pound or two to spare. I am sure my poems will be published soon and I can pay you back or you can keep a couple of the poems in return. After all, you had the pleasure of reading them for so many months for free … Where are you going?"

Celine did not answer. She opened her reticule, slapped a few coppers down on the table and started walking away.

"My poems." he called.

"You will have them by tomorrow," she threw over her shoulder.

Back on the street Celine lifted her face up to the rain. That, she felt, had been an utter disaster.

A carriage came hurtling around the corner and George's arm shot out, clasped her around the waist and yanked her inside. They continued to hurtle down the street, this time towards the Blackthorne Mansion.

Celine sat with her hands folded on her lap, her eyes pinned to the arrow sticking out of George's hat.

"I am terribly sorry about picking you up in an unseemly way, but I think Lily's husband is lurking around the corner, and I think he has been practising with a bow and arrow—"

"It's fine," Celine cut in.

After a few moments, George asked, "Are you alright?"

"Yes."

"Are you certain, for I can see your lips quivering? If you would like to cry …."

Celine put her hands to her face and her shoulders shook.

"Amy," George said with a hint of panic in his voice, "don't cry."

When she continued to shake uncontrollably, George removed her hands from her face in order to gently wipe away her tears.

"You are laughing?" he asked in shock. "I thought things had not gone well."

"You were right, things did not go well."

"Did it go splendidly then?"

"He wants his poems back."

"Tragic," he said shaking his head.

"Lord Elmer, I know why I am laughing, but what in the world is tickling you? You are grinning like a fool."

"I am a fool. A beauty-fool," he chuckled.

Celine eyed him in disgust, "Beauty-fool?" and then she burst out laughing. "That," she giggled, "was terrible. So terrible, in fact, that now I am depressed."

"Amy, are you laughing or are you crying?"

"Both," she said, smiling broadly with tears running down her eyes. "I am the fool, Lord Elmer. A silly romantic fool who dreamt of love and roses. I am sensible and practical. I solve everyone's problems. I am dependable. How could I have stuck my head in a cloud of love and froth?"

"Amy," he said sobering, "love is the most beautiful feeling in the world. It is the only feeling that matters. Don't close your heart to it."

She wrenched her hand away, "Love does not exist, Lord Elmer. And if it did, I wouldn't know it even if it bit me on my rosy buttocks."

"You have rosy buttocks?" he asked, his eyes widening. He leaned forward in his seat and then altogether stopped breathing as he waited for her answer.

"It is not seemly to talk about buttocks, Lord Elmer. I don't know why I said such a thing," she said primly. "I think I am distressed. Distressed enough to forget about the fact that I am a lady because … because I thought I loved a fat poet with a good heart called Philbert Woodbead. Instead, I found a pompous, skinny heartless rat."

"Perhaps you needed to meet him to learn the truth, to learn the difference between a passing fancy and everlasting love."

"Love is a risk for a woman in this world, Lord Elmer. I took that risk and now it is time to be rational. You on the other hand have the luxury of experimentation and adventure. You can never understand the world from my eyes."

"I have a mind, Amy, not a block of wood up there."

"You are a man and …" She bit her lip.

"And therefore as sharp as a toothless lion, as able as a one winged bird or as clever as a blunt bonnet pin," he completed.

"How did you—"

"I read that book. You had left it in the library."

"You read *Mrs Beatle's book for accomplished English ladies*?"

"Yes."

"Why?"

"Because that is what you base your life on and I wanted to understand. Listen to me, Mrs Beatle is loony, barmy and mad. She should be locked up in Bedlam. Anyone who asks you to collect broken buttons and make teeny tiny rabbits out of them is—"

"Lord Elmer, that is enough. How can you expect me to take advice from someone who refuses to be responsible in his own life? Who runs away from his father's house like a child seeking fun? Who lives the life of a court jester constantly trying to amuse and be amused? In fact, you cannot step out on the streets of London without a pirate shooting at you or an enraged husband trying to strangle you—"

"I understand you are hurt, but please remember it was that poet of yours that broke your heart. I had nothing to do with it and therefore do not deserve this—"

"You are right," Celine cut in, her voice rising. "You do not deserve to hear the truth. The truth that you are an irresponsible creature with the intellect of a five year old child. You are a thief and a scoundrel who has stolen poor Sordid Sandy's family recipe. How do you think she is feeling? Did you ever consider things from that old woman's point of view? You are so undependable that I would rather walk through Hyde Park with Dorothy's pet chimney sweep than with you. You would get me killed, while the chimney sweep would only get me sooty."

"Listen now, that is unfair—"

"Unfair? Since the day I met you things have gone wrong. My life has been in constant danger, my hair does not stay in place, my heart beats so fast that at times I think it is going to bound out of my chest and go running away ....."

"Your lips seek mine," he continued softly.

She snapped open a parasol and kept it pointed towards him in defence. He had that look in his eye—hooded lids, lips parted and flame tipped ears. He wanted to kiss her. Again.

The carriage came to a halt.

"Lord Elmer, thank you for helping me find Philbert."

"Is that all you want to say to me?"

She licked her dry lips, "I ..."

"Yes?"

"Thank you, and I hope we shall meet again sometime in the future."

"Amy, stop a moment longer. I need to speak to you about something. I wanted to ask you if—"

"Lord Elmer, I will be late for dinner."

"Shall I see you in your room tonight?"

"I don't think it would be proper."

He made a frustrated sound, "Do you have to be so bloody starched all the time? Everything has to be proper with you. You live your life like an unhappy colonel, following that idiotic Beatle's advice on how to be a refined English lady. You don't know if you are Amy or Celine. Stop lying to me, stop pretending to be someone you are not. You want to go off on an adventure just as much as I do. I have seen your eyes glint in pleasure every time you took down a pirate and no point in denying it. You need to learn how to live, to be honest with yourself. Stop trying to make life comfortable for others. Make it happy for yourself first."

"I see," she said quietly. "This is goodbye then, Lord Elmer. I don't want to burden you with my starched self any longer."

She leaped out of the carriage and raced towards the mansion. She ignored his call and only paused once she was safely in her own room. She locked the door and leaned against it.

Was she lying to herself, she wondered. Was she not a genteel young lady but a naughty, wild, fickle young woman who fell in and out of love with the changing seasons, who enjoyed flinging pirates out of carriages and kissing men, specifically a handsome, mischievous man with a dimpled cheek called Lord Elmer?

Her eyes fell on her reflection in the dressing table mirror. Who was she, she asked herself again. A good sister, an obedient daughter, an accomplished lady, or a simple girl who only wanted to love and be loved?

She searched her reflection for answers. Her bun had uncoiled allowing her damp tresses to escape and hang limply over her shoulders, while her skirts were drenched and stained with mud … But it was her eyes that disturbed her the most.

The dark eyes looking back spoke of a love and friendship lost.

CHAPTER TWENTY SEVEN

Celine was amazed at how unhappy she was. In fact, she was so unhappy that her mind had decided to soothe her soul by playing music in her head. It started with the gentle sounds of a violin, which was soon accompanied by a flute and piano. Within a few moments it was as if an entire orchestra was playing inside her head. She sobbed and wondered at the injustice of it all. Her own brain was mocking her, for the music was jaunty.

She wiped her eyes and lifted her head off the pillow. The music was loud, she realised, too loud to be simply playing in her head. The sounds of laughter filtered into the room on the heels of the happy music.

Her misery was momentarily forgotten. Her curiosity was peaked. She quickly shoved her feet into slippers and raced out of her room. At the landing she paused and stared down into the Great Hall.

The sight made her gasp.

She could see people in glittering gowns, giant hairdos and unfashionable wigs milling about. A long table in the corner held dishes piled high with fruits, meats and breads, while hundreds of candles and glass lamps made the Great Hall seem enchanted.

Celine could not believe her eyes. She rubbed them twice and the vision remained.

A fully fledged ball was in progress downstairs.

"Hopkins, wait," she called out to the duke's valet, who was strolling past her wearing a coat and tails. In his hand he held what looked like a glass of champagne.

She blinked at his attire.

He smiled and took a sip from the glass.

"Hopkins, what is going on? How did the duke allow all these people to enter the mansion? I thought only family and close friends were allowed to visit us considering Penny's condi—I don't understand … Hopkins, a ball is in progress. It is, isn't it?" A thought belatedly struck her. What if her misery had caused her to lose her mind and that is why she was seeing Gwerful in a puce coloured dress with prancing squirrels embroidered on the hem wearing a fruit bowl for a bonnet.

Hopkins soothed her, "Your eyes are not deceiving you, Miss. A ball is truly in progress. The ball is for the duchess and no one from outside has been invited. The people below are the servants of the Blackthorne Estate. The duke said the duchess wanted a party and dancing—"

"And he gave her a ball with two hundred people and not a single person from outside. He made her happy and adhered to propriety," Celine finished. The duke hadn't told her because he knew she couldn't lie. Penny would have guessed that she was hiding something, and then the surprise would have been ruined.

"The orchestra is playing in the other room," Hopkins added. "The musicians are not allowed to look upon the duchess. And in the morning room the duke has hidden fourteen doctors and three midwives in case dancing disagrees with the duchess."

Celine smiled, "This was a wonderful idea."

Hopkins took another sip of the champagne. His tongue nicely loosened, he said, "It was Lord Elmer who gave him the idea. Lord Elmer had planned the outdoor meal indoors and made the duchess laugh. The duke wanted to do something bigger and grander than that, so he planned this ball."

She opened her mouth to ask yet another question when a sudden hush made her pause.

She turned back towards the Great Hall, and from her excellent spot on the landing she noticed Penelope enter the room.

It was clear Penelope had just woken up from her nap. Her curly brown hair was trying to escape from her head, her pale blue evening dress was crumpled, and the corner of her eyes were crusted. She shuffled into the room holding her swollen belly, her mouth parted in shock.

The duke who had been sitting in the corner wearing his full evening attire stood up.

Penelope noticed him and her eyes widened further.

He smiled and walked towards her, and on cue the orchestra

started playing a beautiful waltz.

"May I have this dance?" he asked bowing to her.

"Gack!" Penelope managed to say.

The duke took that as a yes and taking the duchess in his arms whirled around on the dance floor.

The servants parted to let the couple through. This was their dance and no one dared to join in for the moment. A few maids sniffed into their handkerchiefs, and Celine had to admit as she dabbed her own eyes, Penelope had never looked more beautiful.

Celine and Hopkins too danced for a bit on the landing before Hopkins departed with the scullery maid who was wearing a chicken feather hat.

Celine watched Penelope laugh at something the duke said. The duchess' face was flushed in happiness. She wiped away another tear. Penny was the luckiest person in the world to have someone love her so passionately. And Lord Elmer would have enjoyed this moment. It was a sort of thing he would think of ….

"Why are you sitting here?" Dorothy asked coming up beside her.

"I can see everything better from up here," Celine replied.

Dorothy sat down next to her and stuck her nose between the bannisters, "True."

"Who adopted your chimney sweep?" Celine asked, her voice still husky from crying.

"Gunhilda. She thought that since she was the governess she was best suited for the job. The duke agreed."

Celine nodded.

"Are you very sad?" Dorothy asked, putting her head on Celine's shoulder.

"No, why would you say that?"

"I overheard Penny telling the duke that—"

"What?"

"Nothing."

"Here, keep this coin. Now out with it."

"Are you trying to bribe me?"

"No."

Dorothy scowled, "Why not? I like being bribed."

"Dorothy," Celine threatened.

"Wait, I am telling you. Penny was telling the duke that you have been moping because Lord Elmer has left. She said you are in love with him. Is that true? Do you love Lord Elmer?" After a moment Dorothy asked again, "Celine, did you hear me? I asked you if you love him or not?"

"Not."

"Are you sure? You don't sound sure."

"I am sure," Celine replied in an unsure voice.

"Why ever not? I think he is loveable. If I was you, I would adore him. He is rich."

"Wealth does not equal love, Dorothy."

"It should. I have seen plenty of pretty girls marry old gnarly men for their wealth. Now if wealth did equal love, then this world would be a happier place."

"Your philosophising is giving me a headache. Go to bed."

Dorothy caught Celine's face in her small hands, "You love him, Celine. Admit it."

Celine's heart almost stopped. Her sister's eyes suddenly looked old and learned, "Since when have you become so wise?" she asked softly.

"Since I started practicing for a play that Rosy is writing. I simply changed Mary to Celine and said the dialogue. What did you think of my delivery? Was it convincing?"

"Your neighbour Rosy? The ten year old Rosy? How does she come up with such lines?"

"She gets inspiration from the novels hidden under the mattress in the—"

Celine put her hand on her ears and shook her head, "Dorothy, go to bed now or ..."

Dorothy reluctantly left and thereafter she too decided to go to bed. She ignored the laughing people, the music and the food, for her mind and heart were desperate to mull over Dorothy's words.

Had she gone and fallen in love with the scoundrel, the blackguard ... the adorable Lord Elmer?

★★★

Back in her room Celine firmly closed the door, and with only the faint sounds of the orchestra filtering through, she got to work.

She took a seat in front of the large mahogany writing table and pulled out a sheet of paper. Next she sharpened the quill and unscrewed the ink pot. Finally she pulled out *Mrs Beatle's book for accomplished English ladies.*

She flipped through the pages, her finger tracing a line here and there.

"Ah," she softly exclaimed. This was what she had been looking for.

Love, she read, was the most confusing of all emotions. Everyone fell in love at least once in their lifetime, and if they haven't, then they are either very young or very cold.

She quickly skipped a paragraph lauding the virtues of love. Her finger paused at another line,

As discussed previously, love is vague and cannot be defined. Yet, everyone falls in love once in their lifetime and some people more than once. The trouble starts when a bright young lady goes and foolishly falls in love with two young men at the same time. In such a situation a dilemma occurs which may cause, amongst other symptoms, heart palpitations and cold sweats. In such cases I would suggest that you take some lavender drops (see recipe, chapter 4) and constant warm baths and marry the richer of the two men. You can, if possible, keep the other man as a lover on the side.

Celine pursed her lip. This wasn't exactly what she was looking for. Further research revealed yet another golden nugget of wisdom.

Women who are dim often cannot understand their own mind and heart. They cannot tell if they love one man or another, and in such cases I request them to follow a visualising, spiritual technique that never fails in determining the true love of your life.

Celine impatiently shifted in her seat and read on.

I have a few options on how to determine whom you love. The first option requires some chicken blood, ground lizards tails ...

Celine skipped to the second option.

For women who are not only dim but also weak of heart, I can understand that wrestling with a wild boar may not be possible. Hence, I offer you another option, and that simply requires a short meditation technique which was taught to me by an old, barely clothed man who spent years meditating on the foothills of Himalayas. Now, sit crossed legged on an uncarpeted floor.

Celine raced to the dressing room which contained a pearly rug. Removing it she sat down on the marble floor and crossed her legs. Opening the book once again, she continued reading where she had left off.

Close your eyes and take ten deep breaths and four shallow ones. Repeat for a few minutes until you feel as if you have drunk a couple of glasses of wine. Hold on to the happy feeling.

Celine sat breathing in and out, in and out. When she finally started getting bored, she decided to pretend she was feeling very happy and drunk. She opened one eye and squinted at the rest of the paragraph.

Let your mind's eye conjure up a vision. In that vision you shall see the two men that you think you love standing in the middle of a deserted road. It is a deserted country road surrounded by tall green trees that are swaying in the pleasant, scented breeze. Next place an unnamed man in the middle of your two lovers.

Celine imagined the road and placed Philbert, Lord Elmer and a faceless man in the middle of it. Once more she peeked through one eye at *Mrs Beatle's book for accomplished English ladies,*

Let the clouds part and the sun shine onto the three men. The sun is shining and the men are squinting. The sun shines brighter and the men squint harder until a carriage led by six wild horses comes galloping around the corner, their hoofs hitting the ground making the dust and pebbles fly. The carriage races towards the three men, and the men, due to the sun shining in their eyes, fail to notice it, and therefore the carriage tramples them to the ground.

The three men are dead.

Now, I want you to dwell on this moment and think. Whose death do you regret the most? I am sure you are upset that three human lives have been lost in your imagination but focus. One lost life is hurting you more than the others. If the death of the unnamed man is hurting you the most, then you are still waiting for your true love. If it is the man on the right lying dead and bleeding on the road that is upsetting you unbearably, then that is who you love.

Think, young lady, think. Whose bloodied body disturbs you the most?

Celine closed the book and stood up. Her trembling hand silently saluted Mrs Beatle and her genius. In her imagination she had seen the carriage run the men over, and her heart had cried not for the unnamed man or Philbert. It had wept for Lord Elmer and only Lord Elmer.

She closed the book and reverently placed it back on the desk.

"Mrs Beatle," she whispered to the red and gold hard bound leather cover, "I have gone and fallen in love with the blasted scoundrel. Love has well and truly bitten me on my rosy buttocks. Isn't that wonderful?"

CHAPTER TWENTY EIGHT

Life had started strutting differently for Celine ever since she became aware of her love for Lord Elmer. The world, she felt, was tinted in shades of heliotrope, which just happened to be her favourite colour.

When the world did not look purplish pink, it looked grey. Grey because Lord Elmer was no longer staying at the Blackthorne Mansion, he no longer winked at her across the table and made her laugh, and he no longer sprang into her path to sweep her off on yet another bone rattling adventure.

She peered at her reflection in the back of a spoon. She wondered if Lord Elmer could fall in love with a girl like her. Wouldn't he want an exotic, wild and wanton kitten? While she was a simple, sober cat with a few sharp claws ….

"If you had been on stage, Celine," Penelope broke into her thoughts, "you would not have needed lines. Your expressions have changed so swiftly in the last half an hour that I can almost hear your thoughts."

"Would you like some more tea?"

"Don't changed the topic, and tell me what is bothering you? Lord Elmer has not written or come calling in the last two days, isn't that it?"

Celine shook her head and pressed her lips together.

"Have the two of you fought?"

"Nothing of the sort," Celine replied crisply. "Children fight and we are no longer children. We don't go into corners and sulk for days without writing to the other person simply because the other person raised their voice once. And if we do, then we shouldn't—"

"Here, wipe your nose before your tears mix with drippings from your nose and fall into the tea cup."

Celine blew her nose and dabbed her eyes, "I am not crying. Truly I am not. Why should I?"

Penelope smiled, "If it isn't because of Lord Elmer, my dear, then my condition is rubbing off on you. It is possible, for even the duke has been getting more emotional than usual. The other day he saw a small white kitten from our bedroom window, and don't tell anyone this, but he saw it nuzzle Lady Bathsheba. He thought a goat and a kitten becoming friends was so sweet that he couldn't help it, he sniffled and allowed a tear or two to leak down his chiselled cheeks."

Celine chuckled through her tears, "I think you made that up."

"I did not," Penelope replied smiling. "Now, do you want me to send Lord Elmer to the gallows? Have him tortured by the king or ship him off to the continent?"

"Good god, whatever for?"

"He made you cry," Penelope replied grimly.

The tears quickly dried up, "Really, Penny, I am not crying, see, and when I had tears running down my eyes, it was because … not because of him," she laughed loudly and unconvincingly.

Penelope narrowed her eyes, "Then why were you crying?"

Thankfully Celine was saved from answering, for Perkins' wrinkled head appeared at the door distracting Penelope.

"A gentle—" Perkins cleared his throat and tried again, "A person is asking to see Miss Fairweather."

Celine's heart leaped. Could it be Lord Elmer?

"Who?" Penelope asked, since Celine looked too hopeful to speak.

"He wouldn't tell me his name," Perkins replied, an almost invisible shift in his expression showing disapproval.

"Why wouldn't he tell you his name?" Penelope asked.

"He wouldn't tell me his name because he said that I had offended him greatly by not allowing him to enter the mansion. After such an insult, he did not think I deserved to know it," Perkins replied.

"Where is he now?" Penelope asked. She was in a mood to ask questions.

"I allowed him take a seat in the reception room. I posted a few muscled footmen outside and one inside to keep a watch on him," Perkins said, his voice rising in passion. "If he tries to lift one tiny sprig out of the mansion, we will have him. We will have him, I say.

And then we will tie him up and throw him in the dungeons with no food or water. He will starve, slowly and surely until—"

"Until?" Penelope prompted.

"We get the snakes from the circus and set them—"

"I smell a Lord Elmer in the air," Celine cut in.

Perkins blushed, "Not Lord Elmer. It is Nithercott, Miss. He and I have become good friends. It is like I have caught a story telling disease from him. My tongue runs away with me."

"I like this disease," Penelope approved.

"I will go meet this guest," Celine sprang up. It had to be Lord Elmer in disguise. It was the sort of thing he would do.

"Miss," Perkins halted her, "I would suggest taking a rifle."

"Why?" Penelope spoke up once again.

"The fellow, your grace, looked at best ... seedy."

Penelope nodded and offered Celine the paring knife that she had been using to cut apples.

Celine took it and slipped it into her pocket and then bounded out towards the reception room.

Perkins hobbled after her with muttered warnings of robbers and fleas.

Celine ignored him and flung open the doors of the reception room.

Her lashes quivered in shock, "Good God, Gilbert Goodgeed," she exclaimed when she spotted the familiar parrot green patchwork coat.

"Philbert Woodbead," he corrected sourly.

"Yes, him. I mean, yes, Mr Woodbead. I thought I had already sent you those poems. Did you not receive them?"

"I did. I also learned from the footman who gave me those poems that your stepsister is now married to the Duke of Blackthorne. Why ever did you not tell me that, Celine? This changes everything."

"What do you mean?"

"Well it changes our circumstances which are now conducive to getting married. The duke is a wealthy fellow. Surely he will give you a fairly good dowry and—"

"Dowry?"

"Yes, dowry," he repeated testily. "You will now have a decent dowry, and with the duke and his excellent connections, we can lead a fairly good life."

"I don't understand."

"Celine, I always thought you were an intelligent young lady, but perhaps such an emotional moment is bound to make you feel dim. I am wondering if we should move to Bath. Buy a little cottage next to the sea—"

"Are you saying we should get married?" Celine interrupted coldly.

"Precisely, my dear. I have come all this way to propose. I suppose I should speak to the duke and ask him for your hand—"

"No."

"No?"

"I mean I will not marry you, Mr Woodbead."

"Don't be silly now. You surely don't mean that. You said you will love me forever."

"Yes, my forever means the same as your forever, Mr Woodbead. It only lasts a few months."

"I understand you are angry. When we met, I wasn't in the right mood. I was taken by surprise and perhaps did not woo you—"

"Woo me? Mr Woodbead, you clearly told me that you no longer loved me because, as you put it, you were now a handsome, impoverished poet and hence have plenty of women to choose from."

Philbert twittered, "I was hurt. You had not replied to my letters. I thought I had been snubbed."

"I am snubbing you now, Mr Woodbead. Consider yourself wholeheartedly snubbed."

"Now, now, my dear, see it is like this—"

"I don't want to see—"

"Give me a chance to explain—"

"Good morning, Mr Woodbead. Perkins will show you out," Celine broke in crisply. She did not wait for him to respond but turned on her offended heel and left the room.

Mr Philbert Woodbead, too, turned on his heartbroken heel and left the room, but he did not venture too far from the mansion.

Over the next two days Celine rapidly learned that poets are persistent fellows. Nothing excites them more than unrequited love, and Philbert, after all, considered himself a good poet. He threw himself heart, body and soul into winning back his beloved Celine.

First sheets and sheets of terrible poems arrived for Celine. Next, it seemed Philbert had exhausted his finances and could no longer afford paper. Therefore, poetry arrived written on socks, torn shirt pockets, moth eaten ties, leaves strung together on a thread, and even a blue spotted undegarment.

Celine made the mistake of opening one of the rags and reading the contents. She found the following,

Dear Celine,

Here is a poem for you,

Here lies buried not a he nor a she but an it.

Love

Woodbead

She read it twice and realised that was it. That one line was supposed to be the poem that was meant to win her back. She let the fact sink into her annoyed bosom and then asked Hopkins to build a fire on the doorstep of Blackthorne Mansion. She then threw all the poems that Philbert had recently sent her into the fire. She proceeded to cook a few potatoes in the same fire and eat them. Philbert watched the whole thing from his position on top of a fairly leafy tree.

Celine went indoors licking her fingers. The potatoes had been poetically delicious. She hoped Philbert would now get the message and leave her alone. Besides, the duke and Penelope had started asking questions about him and she hadn't known what to say.

Philbert did get the message, but it only seemed to fire up the creative wheels inside his large bony head. Celine watched in horror as he pulled out a violin and started playing it directly below her window. It was clear Philbert had never played the violin before in his life, but he had decided now was the time to try and take a stab at it.

Celine emptied a few buckets of water on the poet's head in order to deter him.

He was not deterred. Instead, he attacked the violin with renewed energy and frantic glee. His hands moved the bow rapidly over strings while water droplets sprayed from his hair like a dog shaking its coat after a long swim in a pond.

Celine tried begging, placating and even threatening him. She tried everything she could to make him see sense and leave her alone.

Philbert, in turn, spoke of his everlasting love and how this time it truly was everlasting. Poets, he informed her, had sensitive souls and romance and misery was their food and air.

Celine banged her head against the window in frustration until finally she had to ask the duke to do something. The persistent poet was driving her insane.

The duke picked him up and threw him into a carriage. The carriage now containing Philbert was sent to the other side of town to be deposited at a respectable inn.

Celine sighed in relief. Never again, she swore, would she fall in love with a poet. She also had to confess some of the facts to Penelope who was thankfully sympathetic and too distracted by roasted carrots to dig deeper into the matter.

With Philbert gone, an entire day went by without another incident. It was the next afternoon that Celine watched Philbert crawl back towards the Blackthorne Mansion. This time Philbert was more careful. He kept watch like a wild animal poised on hind legs, nose sniffing the air for a scent of danger. And every so often he would aim a flower or a poem wrapped around a pebble at Celine's bedroom window.

Which was why Celine had avoided the bedroom all day. But now it was bedtime. She tiptoed into the room and with the help of Gwerful and a single candle, changed into her nightclothes. She slipped into bed, pulled the sheets over her head and closed her eyes tight. She didn't think she would sleep a wink, but she did. Within a few minutes she was asleep and dreaming of poetry spouting poets chasing after her in a large green field.

It was past midnight when someone scratched at her window and woke her up.

Celine moaned into the pillow.

She decided that she had had enough. She would break the jade vase on Philbert's head. His persistence had stretched every nerve in her body. Every time she saw his long, thin face she wanted to thwack him.

Another scratch at the window had her throwing back the quilt and scrambling out of bed. She lit the candle and clutching the jade vase tiptoed her way to the window. Her eyes were red and wild, her lips almost snarling in frustration.

She pushed open the curtains, unlatched the window and with a barely contained roar brought the vase down.

It landed not as she had expected on Philbert's hard head.

Instead, it smashed into Nithercott's softer one.

CHAPTER TWENTY NINE

"I am sorry," Celine cried. "Did I hurt you? I thought it was Philbert. Oh, do come inside, Nithercott. I am awfully sorry about this."

Nithercott hung upside down on the ivy clutching the tendrils for dear life. It took a few moments for his vision to clear. Thereafter, he smiled apologetically and climbed in through the window.

"It is fine," he said wincing, "I deserve it for coming to your room at this hour, Miss. But if things were not so dire ..." He trailed off.

"Here, sit down," Celine said pushing him down on the chair. "I hope you are not bleeding ... no ... You are alright? Would you like a glass of water?"

"Truly, I have been knocked about worse. Don't worry about me," he mumbled embarrassed.

"I thought it was the poet."

"I sent him to the pub for a few drinks," Nithercott informed her.

"How did you manage that?"

"Was easy, I gave him a few coins."

She eyed him with respect.

Nithercott blushed.

"You said the situation was dire," Celine reminded him. "Is ... Is he alright?"

"Who, the poet?"

"No ... I mean ..." She bit her lip.

He waited for her to continue, and when she didn't, he said, "It is about Lord Elmer."

Her heart stopped.

"I don't mean he is dead," Nithercott soothed, noting her expression, "at least not yet."

Her feet gave away and she sank into a chair. "Could you ... could you perhaps start from the beginning?"

"It was like this. After leaving the Blackthorne Mansion, Lord Elmer secretly returned to his father's house. He hid in his room and came and went via the tree outside his window. Bless Lord Devon, he knew not a thing. He was looking all over England for his son," Nithercott chuckled, "and here was Lord Elmer staying right under his nose."

"Go on," Celine begged.

"Well, that was supposed to be the plan. He would stay hidden in the room until the pirates forgot all about him. That was until he found the poet and …" Here Nithercott paused.

"And we fought. Is that what you wanted to say?" she asked.

He nodded soberly, "After that Lord Elmer seemed to change. I have never seen him like that, Miss. He spoke about responsibilities and how he should accept them. He wanted to confront his father and take on his duties. He wanted to return the recipe to Sordid Sandy, and would you believe it, he wasn't even drunk."

"He didn't, did he?" Celine asked in horror.

Nithercott nodded, "I don't know what you said to him, Miss, but he refused to listen to reason. That evening after returning home, he opened his bedroom door, walked right up to his mother and hugged her. He hugged her, Miss, for no good reason. And then it gets worse. He promised his father he would return. He said he had something important to see to, and right after that he would come back home and take his place in society."

"Nithercott, has he returned to the pirate ship?"

"Yes, Miss. He took the recipe and returned to the ship. He told me to wait outside for him. He was only going to sneak back in, replace the recipe and then sneak back out. It has been two whole days since I left him, Miss, and he has not snuck back out."

Celine lifted a stricken face up to Nithercott.

Nithercott wiped his brow. "I thought you would be the best person to ask for advice in such a situation. I have seen you poke One Legged Tim in the eye with a kitting needle. Fast thinking that was. Clever too, in fact—"

"Nithercott, I have a plan."

"I knew it." Nithercott brightened.

"Listen to me very carefully. Only two people can help us now. One is Lord Adair and the other is the Duke of Blackthorne. I am going to try and convince the duke while you try and find out if Lord Adair has returned from his trip or not. If he has, then tell him everything truthfully. I am sure he will know what to do."

"Aye, aye picaroon," Nithercott saluted smartly before flinging himself out of the window.

***

Celine waited until Nithercott had safely climbed down the ivy and disappeared into the night. After that she quickly dressed in a dark brown travelling dress and soft brown riding boots and stuck a few pins in her hair just to keep it away from her face. A glance in the mirror confirmed her suspicions. She looked ghastly.

Shrugging her shoulders at her reflection she plucked an ostrich feather out of a blue satin bonnet and made her way towards the duke's room.

The duke and the duchess to the horror of London society chose to share a room together. The duchess' chamber was retained for Penelope's afternoon naps, whereas the nights she most assuredly spent with the duke. Hence, Celine needed a plan that would wake the duke and make him follow her outside without waking Penelope.

It had not taken long for Celine to come up with just such a plan, and accordingly she crawled into the duke's chamber, crept up to the duke's side and pulling out the ostrich feather tickled the duke's nostrils.

The duke swiped at the feather, but Celine persisted with the tickling until the duke's eyes snapped open. In a trice Celine clamped a hand over his mouth and with the other touched her lips.

His shock turned to understanding and he nodded.

She then jerked her head towards the entrance.

He nodded again.

She thanked god for giving the duke brains as she made her way outdoors still on all fours.

The duke followed also crawling on his hands and knees.

They stood up only after reaching the dowager's room which lay empty and on the other side of the corridor.

"Is everything alright?" the duke asked quietly.

"I am sorry, I had to wake you in such a fashion, but I did not want to distress Penelope, and it was an urgent situation—"

"Celine, calm down. What is it? Here, sit down, you are trembling."

SEEKING PHILBERT WOODBEAD

"I need your help," she blurted out. "Lord Elmer has been kidnapped by pirates. He is being kept hostage. Please say you can help."

"Tell me everything," he said shortly.

So Celine quickly told him everything that Nithercott had told her. She finished with, "I know the ship is called *The Desperate Lark*. Lord Elmer has mentioned it plenty of times, and Nithercott confirmed the name. The pirate's name is the Black Rover and Nithercott said that he is so frightening that every strand of hair on his head splits in two at the sight of him."

"I will leave as soon as the carriage is ready," the duke said calmly.

"You will?" Celine asked in surprise.

"Penelope's younger sister is as good as my own," he smiled, "and I cannot have your future husband shot before the wedding."

"Your life could be in danger," Celine warned.

"I am married to Penelope. My life is always in danger."

"I ..." Celine gripped her skirts, "I don't think this is a good idea anymore. I am sorry, I should have thought this through. I cannot put your life at risk ... I don't know what I was thinking waking you like this and—"

"Do you have an alternate plan?"

She shook her head.

"Are you in love with him?"

She nodded.

He sighed. "Then I have no other choice but to save the blasted man." Another thought seemed to strike him, for he brightened, "You don't think you could love someone else could you? I can produce a lot of fine specimens, and since I am the duke, they won't dare to refuse. Elmer is a touch evil don't you think? I know a lot of good fellows who are positively angelic compared to him. Let me see ... Perhaps Lord Harley? He has a remarkable physique or so I have heard Penelope say. And Sir Greenwood is the best shot in England. We went hunting together last winter. He shot down three pigeons and not a bullet wasted."

"Your grace, I think I have well and truly fallen in love with Lord Elmer. I don't think I will be wading out of it any time soon."

"I see, well then that settles it. I will have to go save that despicable second cousin of mine."

"You don't have to."

"No, I really do," the duke muttered.

"Will you let Penelope know?"

"I will leave a letter for her. I will leave it with Perkins and he can hand it to her if I don't return."

"But you will return."

"I truly hope so."

Celine nodded and soberly shook hands with him.

"I am glad you didn't spit before shaking my hand," the duke remarked.

"Eh?"

"Penelope had spat … Never mind."

"This is goodbye then."

"I am not going to die, Celine. Don't look so miserable."

"I hope not."

"This is getting morbid. I am leaving now … And, Celine, I know you Fairweather sisters. Don't you dare follow me."

"I won't," Celine lied boldly. She already had a plan on how best to follow him, and the moment the duke departed, she set that plan into motion.

CHAPTER THIRTY

Celine's footsteps pounded on the garden path. Her heart thumped in tune. Last evening's rain licked her ankles as she raced towards the stables. Sneaking past a snoring stablehand she made her way towards the fiery red mare called Storm.

The horse knew her, yet she approached the beast cautiously. A few precious minutes were wasted while she soothed the horse and saddled it. She tugged the reins and led the mare out into the open past the sleeping stablehand and towards the entrance of the Blackthorne Mansion.

She hid behind a large statue of Minerva, a tall marble figure which had an exquisitely carved owl perched on its shoulder. She stuck her head between Minerva's crooked elbow and watched the entrance, waiting for the duke's carriage to arrive.

The duke's carriage rolled out and came to a smooth halt near the entrance.

Her breath froze. She clutched the reins harder, inwardly begging the mare to stay quiet.

The duke, too, arrived moments later dressed in his travelling gear. He leaped into the carriage calling out something indistinguishable to Perkins standing by the door.

Perkins saluted in response, and the carriage started moving towards the road.

Celine clambered up on top of Storm and nudged the animal with her foot.

Storm ignored her.

According to Mrs Beatle a lady can have one fault provided she conceals it well from others. Celine's fault was that she was hopeless around horses. She knew not what in the blazes to do with them.

Celine spent a few minutes coaxing the mare to move.

The mare stubbornly stood her ground.

She tried bribery, trickery and soft spoken words, her heart sinking with every passing moment, for the duke's carriage was almost out of sight.

"Fine," Celine groaned, "do as you like. Stay."

And with that Storm started sprinting forward.

Celine quickly learned how to efficiently control the contrary horse. Her commands simply had to be opposite of what she wanted the horse to do.

With her nose pointed straight ahead, her eyes narrowed, and the wind streaking through her hair, Celine and not the mare tried to keep the duke's carriage in sight as best as possible. London unlike Finnshire had lamps lit on the side of the streets, and even though the moon was shy and hiding behind a hat shaped cloud, she could see fairly well.

Celine didn't know when they passed Gin Road, Mayfair Street or Marley lane. She knew nothing of London apart from Hyde Park and the Blackthorne Estate. If she lost sight of the duke for even a moment, she would be hopelessly lost.

The dark roads with double rows of twinkling gas lamps were a beautiful sight in an eerie sort of way. The swaying inky silhouettes of trees and the occasional shouts from drunkards kept her on edge throughout the journey.

More than once a night watchman spotted her and halted in his tracks. One of them was brave enough to abandon his declaration of 'Tis' past three and almost four, no thief shall come, for we watch the door' and chase after her. He leaped over potholes, rubbish and drunkards waving his stick in one hand and swinging the lamp in the other. He didn't stand a chance, for a man on foot is no match for a woman with a mission on a swift horse. She escaped unscathed.

She rode on even though the drays and carriages started rolling out onto the roads splashing her with dirty water. The milkmaids started appearing on street corners holding back yawns and squeaking out a few sleepy yodelling cries. A few mountebanks crept along the sides, while the musicians started setting up shop pulling out tambourines and whatnot.

The thought that gave her courage and propelled her through the streets was that at the end of the journey she would see Lord Elmer. Not Lord Elmer, she corrected herself, she really should start thinking of him as George.

"George," she said aloud, letting the wind carry his name. Her eyes briefly closed, and a delicious thrill went through her at the sound.

Her focus returned to the road, and in shock she realised that the duke's carriage had disappeared. Her heart in her throat she frantically searched the road ahead. She could see nothing but dark looming houses and an empty road. Where they even in London any longer? She felt as if they had been riding for hours, long enough to have left the city entirely.

Storm continued to gallop at high speed, turning neither right nor left but straight ahead, and Celine let her. She did not know what else to do but ride on in the hope that the duke's carriage was around the corner.

It was the scent of rotting fish and water that renewed her hopes. They were near a large body of water. She was sure of it.

A faint rosy glow in the sky indicated that the sun was about to rise. In the pink light she spotted small empty boats bobbing near the shore, and further down floating in deeper shimmering waters was *The Desperate Lark* with its pirate flag temporarily replaced with a friendlier one depicting a bunch of yellow mangoes on a white background.

Celine told the mare to keep moving, and the obedient animal halted on the spot. Celine leaped to the ground and quickly tied the mare to a nearby tree. She couldn't spot the duke's carriage, but it did not matter any longer. He would be on the pirate ship trying to save George, and she too had to get on the ship in case the duke needed to be saved in turn.

She moved towards the edge of the water wondering which boat to take in order to reach the ship. A loud rattling sound, a snort and a squeak made her whirl around.

A carriage had skidded to a halt behind her. It was not the duke's carriage. It was the duchess' carriage.

Penelope's happy head poked out from the window. Her equally ecstatic hand waved at Celine.

"Penny, what are you doing here?" Celine gasped.

Penelope carefully descended with the help of her maid Mary and the carriage driver.

"I will speak quickly for we have two men to save. I was awake when you entered the room and tickled the duke—"

"But I heard you snore."

"I am pregnant and that means mostly idle. I have been practising all sorts of things in my spare time and pretending to gently snore while I am wide awake is just one of the tricks that I have learnt. It is a talent worth acquiring."

"Continue," Celine muttered.

"I followed you both out of the room and into the dowager's room. I stuck my ear to the door, overheard most of the conversation and waited until the duke departed to ask Hopkins to get the carriage ready. I then woke Mary, got a second carriage ready and followed you here."

While Penelope paused to take a breath, Celine said, "Now get back into the carriage and go home."

"I will not."

"You are not coming, Penny."

"I shall wait here, and if you do not return soon, then I will go looking for runners or the king."

"The king?"

"I believe he is fond of the duke."

"I cannot leave you here alone and defenceless—" Her speech was cut short when Penelope pulled out a mean looking rifle.

"That is not enough," Celine objected.

Penelope quietly produced three dainty pistols from inside her corset. Two more were inside her riding boots, and yet another was retrieved from the hidden pocket in her skirt.

Celine took one of the pistols and pocketed it. "Still no—"

Celine didn't get to finish her sentence, for Penelope clapped her hands next and twelve maids poked their heads out of the carriage.

They showed Celine their weapons which consisted of rolling pins, cast iron kettles, more pistols, rifles, and a couple of exceedingly low gowns with large bosoms on display.

Celine stared at one of the maids in horror.

The tall, long faced bony woman with a brooding expression holding a spear fluttered her lashes back at her.

"Who is that?" Celine asked pointing to the woman.

"I am not sure …." Penelope frowned.

"I will tell you who that is, Penny. It is the blasted poet Philbert Goodbead in disguise. Why did you bring that fool along?"

"I didn't know what he looks like, Celine. I have been confined to the Yellow Room and only heard of the pest," Penelope replied testily.

"Well, the deuced man is moving towards me, Penny. Now, I don't have time to argue with you. Please return to the mansion and perhaps get the runners ready or the king's men. Hurry," Celine begged before racing towards the ship. She did not have time to untie one of the boats or the poet would be upon her, so she leaped into the cold, icy water and started swimming towards *The Desperate Lark*.

"Celine," Penelope called.

Celine spat out the water and turned to look at the duchess.

"Are you certain that you are doing the right thing?" Penelope yelled. "Is it proper?"

"An accomplished lady always follows her man in order to save him, and men always need saving," Celine shouted back. "And stop screaming or the bloody pirates will hear you. Go home."

Penelope grinned, and Celine turned back around and once more made her way towards the sloop style, hundred ton pirate ship that could easily hold seventy full grown men.

She used the rope ladder hanging on the side to climb up and slip onto the deck at the back of the ship.

She bit her lip and glanced at the pistol with a mother of pearl handle that the duchess had presented to her. Next, she looked towards the cannons dotting the deck and gulped.

Taking a deep breath she bravely moved forward.

Squelch, squelch, splurt went her water laden slippers.

She clamped down on fearful thoughts, pulled off the slippers and shoved them into her pocket. Any further exploration would have to be done on bare tippy toes.

She had never been on a ship before and knew not where to go or what to expect, and it was too late to turn back now, so she slithered forward and found what seemed to be a small cabin door on the right.

A sleepy, lethal looking creature opened the cabin door and looked upon Celine in surprise.

Celine quickly yanked her corset lower and smiled.

"Arr," the man grinned back, his eyes pinned to her bosom.

While he was thus entranced Celine grabbed the cabin door, slammed it on the creature's head, and as soon as he fell unconscious to the floor, she pushed him back inside the cabin praying that he would not wake too soon from his unwanted nap.

She once again slithered forward, keeping her eyes, ears and nose peeled at all times. She could hear a few men singing a pirate song. She caught an occasional line or two which sounded like,

'Barrels of rum, wenches and bum, together we shall sail to Ballynoonum.'

She stopped next to yet another cabin door and rubbed her arms. The wind flirting with her drenched clothes had chilled her to her very bones. She hummed the catchy pirate song as she spent a few precious moments planning her next step. Where, she wondered, did pirates keep prisoners?

She tried to attack the question from a different angle. If she wanted to imprison and torture someone in the Blackthorne Mansion, where would she hide him? The dungeon she concluded with certainty. Therefore, it was a great possibility that George too was hidden in the ship's equivalent to a dungeon.

She started walking again, and this time her steps were sure and purposeful. She needed to find the stairs that led below decks. Up ahead she spotted a man dressed in a red velvet coat, violet hat and dark green trousers leap through a hole in the ground. Only the captain could be so finely dressed.

She inched her way closer to the hole. Standing on the tip of her toes she leaned forward trying to see what lay below. She could see nothing.

She could see nothing because firstly she was too far away from the hole. So far away, in fact, that even if she lay prostrate on the ground, she still wouldn't be able to see it. And her upper body's eighty degree tilt was not helping matters except to give her calf a cramp. Secondly, she couldn't see down the hole because her eyes were squeezed shut. A sudden fright had ceased hold of her limbs.

She used her finger tips to prise open her lids.

She forced her form to unbend and straighten.

She pushed her legs to move forward until she reached the very edge of the hole and before her courage failed her.

She closed her eyes and jumped.

CHAPTER THIRTY ONE

She landed in what looked like a black pit, but once her eyes adjusted, she realised it was a corridor. A dying candle lying on a side table tinted everything in shades of orange and dark brown.

The muffled sounds of someone speaking reached her ears. She clutched the pistol with both hands and hugging it to her chest made her way towards the sound. It came from a partially open door on the right side of the corridor. She plastered her back to the wall next to the door and inched her ear closer to the crack. The voices became louder.

"Hand him over now," someone requested in a half-hearted voice that sounded like the duke.

"You don't seem to want him very much," drawled a bored stranger's voice.

"He is a pest, Rover," the duke replied.

"Then let me keep him."

"I would, but my wife and her sister are awfully fond of him."

"Why?"

"I ask myself that question every single day."

"I would like to keep him for a while and torture him. Surely you will enjoy that? You sound like you would. You can watch."

"No, thank you. I would rather wait here until you are finished with him. How long do you think the torture will take? You won't kill him afterwards, will you?"

"I haven't made up my mind yet. You see, the fellow stole my mother's recipe and my mother discovered the theft. She has not spoken to me since. The moment we docked here, she stormed off to visit her sister who lives in this town. When she returns, I will produce the thief in front of her and ask her what she would like to do with him. She may want to dine with his head decorating the desert table, who knows. I can make no promises."

"You are extremely well spoken—"

"Flattery shall not work," the Black Rover replied sharply.

"My men have surrounded this ship. If I don't return soon, they will come aboard and rescue not only Elmer but also take half your wealth."

"The ship has no treasures. We buried it. You are welcome to biscuits crawling with weevils."

"My men will kill you," the duke threatened.

"By the time we spot them approaching the ship, I would have shot you through the heart and tossed you overboard effectively turning you into flotsam. Thereafter, I will set sail for calmer waters."

"I don't like you."

"I already told you flattery will get you nowhere."

Celine closed her eyes in annoyance. The duke and the Black Rover were now discussing how they would kill each other. They seemed to be fighting over who could give the other a more gruesome death.

"My men will feed you to bloodthirsty flesh tearing fish," the pirate was telling the duke nonchalantly.

"My men will tie your wrists and ankles to iron chains and then using the latest torture instrument pull your limbs apart," the duke responded.

Celine shook her head in disgust and walked away. It seemed she would have to save George and come back for the duke later.

She tiptoed her way down the corridor feeling a touch braver knowing that the Black Rover was busy arguing with the duke and most of the men were singing pirate songs up at the top. Now all she had to do was find the stairs that led to the bottom of the ship.

She found the stairs easily enough. It was right at the end of the corridor.

She crept down the stairs wrinkling her nose as she went lower and lower into the belly of the ship. The fresh marine scent gave way to a damp musty smell, mingled with something that smelled like bad cheese and … She sniffed cautiously … a bit of rotten eggs, a hint of wet dogs, with a liberal sprinkling of freshly plucked roses.

She reached the bottom rung, the odour now strong enough to have wriggled its way into her mouth. With her nose and mouth scrunched up in revulsion, she stepped into the bilge.

This part of the ship was clearly kept for creatures no better than water rats. A single candle up ahead threw a measly glow illuminating a lump of dirty wood here, a broken bottle there and nothing much else.

She moved in further, the light grew brighter and she found doors on either side of the long passageway. George was certain to be in one of the rooms here.

She hung outside a couple of doors hoping for a sound or a hint as to what lay inside. Learning nothing she started opening the doors.

The first few rooms turned out to be no more than dark holes with a small chair and a cot. Still others were completely empty. She finally found one that contained a sleeping person. The violent red hair peeking out from beneath the sheets had her quickly back away. That was certainly not George.

The room right next to the carrot top contained yet another person. This one was awake. He looked like a potbellied grandfather, his smile angelic and his eyes inviting her to come closer.

She opened the door wider letting the candle light illuminate the room further.

He was a prisoner she realised. He was tied to a chair. An ally she immediately thought brightening. He looked like a kindly old man. He would be sure to help.

Smiling she moved closer to him, her hands inching towards the ropes that tied his feet together. She would free him and he would return the favour by helping her find George.

Someone growled.

She jumped in fright and turned around to look behind her.

Someone barked.

In horror she turned back towards the kindly old man.

"Did you just growl and bark?" she asked him nervously.

He beamed at her and asked her if she was a parrot.

A parrot she queried?

He gave two shorts barks followed by a short nod.

She smiled and nodded back and continued to smile and nod until she had inched her way out of the room.

In the passageway she waited a moment for her heart to stop racing. The loony prisoner had given her a dreadful fright.

Footsteps sounded behind her setting her heart racing once again.

She waited poised and quivering trying to ascertain if the footsteps were coming towards her or moving away.

The steps grew louder.

In another moment whoever it was would be upon her, and then she would be caught, imprisoned and locked in one of these rooms forever. Years later when her face had wrinkled and hair gone grey, she too would bark and perhaps crow at people and ask them if they were egg laying hens.

She shook her head dispelling the fog and dived sideways. With an inward squeak, she landed inside yet another room. Her shoulder complained as it crashed into the hard wooden floor, and her foot moved instinctively to close the door.

She lay stunned for a moment, her heart in her mouth.

The footsteps came to a halt outside the door.

She prayed that whoever it was had not heard her hit the floor.

The sound of shuffling feet reached her … Was he trying to open the door?

She gripped the pistol and aimed it towards the door.

"Celine?" a voice whispered behind her.

Biting down a scream she spun around … and found a cheerful George tied to a chair in the corner.

Her eyes widened and she lowered the pistol. "George," she mouthed putting a finger to her lips and pointing at the door.

He nodded in understanding.

They waited for a few more terrifying moments until the footsteps finally receded.

When all was quiet outside, she stuck the pistol between her breasts and pounced on George showering him with kisses. She was still too unnerved to speak.

"I am learning to love being the damsel in distress," George remarked.

The sound of his voice brought her back to the present. Her face suffused in a blush, she mumbled, "I should untie you."

"Not at all. Let me stay tied up for a touch longer. I don't think I have enjoyed being rescued quite so much before. No, no, truly don't untie me. A few more kisses and then you can do with me what you like."

"Oh, hush," Celine said, her hands busy tugging on the ropes to free him.

"Celine?"

"Hmm."

"Why are you drenched?"

"I was swimming."

"You swam? To come and save me?"

"No, for leisure. I was paddling in a pond with swans and ducks," she said in frustration. Unknotting the rope was turning out to be the hardest task of all.

"You are afraid of water."

"I am more afraid of losing you," she said with a catch in her throat.

"Celine?"

"What?" she asked in annoyance. If only he would stay quiet for a minute, she almost had him free.

"I have a knife in my boot."

"Why didn't you say so before?" she growled, lunging for his boots and pulling them off.

"Because I had missed you dreadfully. I wanted to spend a few minutes talking to you."

"Can we converse once we are on land and away from danger?"

"Once we are on land, will you stop being annoyed?"

"I will."

"And will you also tell me how much you love me?"

"You are free," she said instead.

He caught her around the waist and pulled her closer. "We should spend some moments kissing now to celebrate my freedom."

"No, we will go up onto the deck, and you will jump overboard and swim to the shore while I will go back and save the duke."

He sighed and released her, "You will swim to the shore while I will save the duke."

"Can we discuss this outside? I feel like someone will come around the corner at any moment and lock us both in."

He caught her hand and with a quick look outside raced up the stairs.

George knew his way around the ship, which was why they were soon standing in fresh air and morning light.

"I am staying, Celine," he told her firmly.

"How will you defend yourself?"

"I have a knife."

"And knitting needles," she said, producing a few from her pocket and handing it to him. "I still think I should stay. No one knows who I am, whereas they want to keep you as a prisoner."

"I am not letting you stay here alone and defenceless, Celine. The Black Rover is dangerous, and you won't even ... What in the—" George froze.

"What?" Celine asked turning around to look. She spotted a hand clutching the edge of the ship.

Someone was climbing aboard, and they were in direct line of his sight.

Celine grabbed George's hand and pulled desperately. They had to get out of here.

"I'll be bound," George gasped refusing to budge. "Isn't that Philly Slimweed?"

"Ack." Celine screeched spotting the long head and recognizing it.

"Philbert Woodbead," the poet corrected sourly.

"You took one of the boats," Celine said, noting that the maid's dress he still wore was dry.

"The duchess took my wig," he grumbled clambering over the rail and flopping onto the deck.

"What are you doing here?" Celine asked, her hands on her hips.

"I came to win you back," the poet replied.

"I don't want to listen to any more poetry," Celine said firmly.

"No more poems. This time I have prepared a dance."

"A dance?" George asked intrigued. "Please can we see it once?" he requested Celine.

She nodded grudgingly.

They watched the poet dance for a few moments.

"Perhaps you can describe what you are doing, it may help your case," George advised him.

The poet threw him a grateful look and said, "Do you recall, Celine, the time we met at The Devil's Pitchfork, I told you I wanted the poems back?"

"Yes," she replied irritably.

"Well, I told you that was because my poems were taken by a renowned highwayman called the Falcon. He told me that if I ever wanted to win a woman back, then I must do the falcon dance."

"So you are doing the falcon dance?" George asked in fascination.

"Yes, you see, you must bob and flap, bob and flap, and then bob, bob and flap, flap ..."

"I beg you throw him overboard," Celine pleaded in disgust.

"As you say," George bowed and then picked up Philbert and threw him back into the water.

After a moment, Celine asked, "Do you think he knows how to swim?"

"I hope so," George said looking down. He suddenly exclaimed, "Goodness."

"What is it?"

"Your poet is climbing back up the rope. He ignored the boat bobbing next to his head."

"He is a little persistent."

"A *little* persistent?"

"A lot then. How will we get rid of him?"

"Leave it to me and follow my advice. I am skilled in the matters of love." He threw a wink at her.

She rolled her eyes and nodded.

"Now tell him you love him,"

She didn't question him but poked her head over the edge and told the dripping poet, "I love you."

"Now tell him that you are so thankful that he still wants you, since you have nowhere else to go. The duke found out that you had visited him at The Devil's Pitchfork which is no place for a lady. And now that you are on a pirate ship he will surely disown you rather than have his family name besmirched."

Celine faithfully conveyed this to the poet.

"What is he doing now?" George asked.

"He has paused halfway. I think he is thinking things over."

"Wonderful, now tell him you are going to climb down the ladder and together you can run away to Gretna Green. Thereafter, you can live in a small cottage covered with roses and live on peas, since the duke has refused to give you a dowry."

Celine put a leg over the edge of the ship and once again repeated everything George had told her.

"Now what is he doing?"

"He is rapidly climbing down the rope," she informed George and then called down to the poet, "What did you say? Speak louder."

"What is he saying?" George asked hopping from foot to foot.

"He is saying goodbye. He suddenly recalled that a printer is waiting for him at the inn. He is now on a boat and sailing away." She pulled out a handkerchief and waved to the departing poet, "Goodbye."

"Was that fellow bobbing and flapping?" Penelope asked coming up behind her. "I knew it would catch on."

"Penny, what in the world are you doing on the ship?" Celine screeched.

"I think it was highly unfair of you to expect me to stay in the carriage when all of you are here having fun on the ship. Where is Charles?"

"We have to rescue him," Celine replied irritably. "Now the plan is that you will stay here. George will climb down the ladder and swim to the shore and get some help. Meanwhile, I will rescue the duke."

"What am I supposed to do with him though?" George asked.

Celine turned to George, "Him? Who him?"

"Him," George pointed behind himself.

Celine frowned and looked over George's shoulder and gasped.

One Legged Tim being a good head shorter than George had been standing and listening to them for some time. And all through that time he had kept a fully loaded gun digging into George's fourth lumbar vertebrae.

CHAPTER THIRTY TWO

Celine's eyes widened in fright.

"Don't be scared," George told her. "I can handle this."

"How?" she asked, her heart beating fast and loud.

George grinned. His hand shot up, gripped Tim's wrist and twisted it.

The gun slipped out of Tim's fingers and into George's waiting hand.

George pocketed the gun and spun on the spot. He spun so fast that Celine could barely see him, and while he was spinning, his leg shot out and kicked Tim's sole leg.

With a howl of annoyance, Tim crashed to the ground.

George dipped in an elegant bow, his dimple winking in satisfaction. It had taken him but a moment to win that particular battle.

Penelope clapped her hands in pleasure, "Oh, that was wonderful. Now do that again with the rest of them," she begged.

Celine turned to look at what Penelope meant by the rest of them.

She gulped.

The Black Rover with his menacing grey eyes, cruel lips and scarred cheek stood a few steps away flanked by at least thirty of his men.

The duke, too, stood in one corner staring at his wife in horror.

Somehow people always congregate where the action is. If two strangers start a brawl in the middle of the road, then magically a large crowd surrounds them. Here on the ship it was no different. Every one of the Black Rover's men and Penelope's blushing maids that were aboard *The Desperate Lark* raised their noses up in the air and smelled that something was afoot. They followed the scent and quickly arrived on the deck to witness the unfolding events.

"I wonder," the Black Rover mused scratching his cheek with the gun, "who to shoot first."

"You can keep me and let the rest go. I stole the recipe not them," George said stepping forward.

Celine's heart melted at her brave George. He was so sweet, she thought lovingly, wanting to give up his life to save them. She was pleased at how responsible he had become recently, though she had to admit she adored his mischievous side as well.

"I think Elmer is right," the duke spoke up. "Keep him."

"No, I have a better proposition," a new voice spoke up.

With the advent of this new voice, the wind seemed to perk up and pick up speed.

Everyone turned towards the spot from where the voice had originated. They spotted a man's hat slowly appearing over the edge of the ship.

The sun shone brighter and the early morning air became crisper as more and more of the black, exquisitely crafted hat came into view.

Everyone sharply sucked in air when the smooth dark forehead greeted them. The men straightened and the women brightened with the arrival of the nose. Ladies and gentlemen quivered in supressed excitement when finally the lips and the chin emerged.

Lord Adair's handsome looks and strong physique blasted them all in the face forcing a few to close their eyes against the beauty of it all. Three maids swooned and some of the pirates were moved to proclaim their patriotic side by shouting,

"May England's enemies be pickled in brine."

"Porcupine filled saddles to England's foes."

"Let the brains of the enemy bumfuzzle and their mouths fill with rotting fish from Billingsgate."

Lord Adair smiled and gracefully swung onto the deck followed by Nithercott and six old women.

"I have a proposition," Lord Adair repeated in a dark hypnotic voice.

The Black Rover ignored him, his eyes on the shortest of the old women. "Ma, ye have returned," he said worriedly.

The four feet tall, wrinkled person standing behind Lord Adair eyed her six feet five inches son in disgust, "Willy, what is this I hear, ye have decided to murder a duke? What shall become of yer future if ye go around killing important people? How many times have I told ye to choose yer victims carefully?"

"Can you please not call me Willy, Ma? At least not in front of them."

"I shall call ye what I like. And it was never this curly haired lad's fault. Lord Adair explained it all to me. Belcher made him drink. But ye, Willy, what excuse do ye have? What sort of a pirate allows an important artefact to be stolen under his watch?"

The Black Rover wilted, his mouth turning petulant. "I said I am sorry, Ma, what more do you want. I have your recipe back now."

Sordid Sandy placed her hands on her hips, a sign that she was settling in for a good long scold.

The Black Rover eyed his men from the corner of his eyes and hastily whispered, "Don't scold now. Not in front of them. My reputation is already wavering after the way you went on and on … I will have to shoot someone now, ma, to build it all back up. You have left me with no other choice."

His mother shrugged, "Do as ye like, but quickly now. I haven't had me breakfast yet."

The Black Rover hurriedly agreed. His gaze swept over the assembled interlopers finally settling on the duke.

Penelope waddled forward and took her place in front of her husband, "I would like to offer you someone remarkable in return for our freedom," she said bravely. "He will keep your crew entertained for hours, or you can shoot him. We won't mind either way. His name happens to be Philbert Woodbead and he is a brilliant poet. I saw him row away but a moment ago. If you look—Arrgh," she finished on a scream.

The Black Rover watched Penelope patting her belly nervously. "Do you have a babe in their?"

"No, I ate a horse on the way over," Penelope replied, her eyes red and her breath coming in shallow gasps.

"Har har," the Black Rover laughed in forced amusement.

No one joined him, their attention on Penelope who was now clutching her belly with both hands, her eyes squeezed shut and her face alarmingly scrunched up.

The captain stopped laughing and eyed the duchess fearfully. "When is the baby coming?"

"Now," Penelope replied.

"You mean soon?" the Black Rover asked hopefully.

"No, I mean now," Penelope insisted, glaring at the captain.

"What do you mean now?" the duke asked rushing to his wife.

"I am having the baby now," Penelope repeated through gritted teeth, "and don't you dare make me say so again."

"You can't," everyone screeched in horror. "Not on the pirate ship!"

Penelope replied with a full throated yell, "Oh, this ... blasted, blooming, rotten, flea bitten, beastly farting crackers. This hurts."

"No, no, Penny. You cannot do this now. I cannot have my child born on a pirate ship. You stay in there," the duke begged her belly.

"Get a chair," the Black Rover roared, his hands twisting together nervously, "with cushions."

"Get her some water," George shouted. "Hot water."

"Bollocks." screeched Penelope.

Sordid Sandy pulled out a gun from between the valley of her bosom and fired three times into the air. When all became quiet, she said, "It is time for someone older, wiser and more experienced to take charge. The baby is coming," she told the duke, "no matter how much you beg, plead or pray."

"But Dr Johnson, the midwife—" The duke was cut short by another curse from Penelope.

"Get Willy's chamber ready," Sandy ordered the six old women who were her lady's maids. "I want plenty of clean sheets, water, rum, a knife, and anything else you can think off." Next, she turned to the young maids who had arrived with Penelope, "Carry the duchess to the room at once."

"She is my wife, I will carry her," the duke warned striding up to the duchess.

The maids fell back and allowed him room to approach.

He went and put his arms around her legs. He heaved, pulled, exhaled and inhaled without moving an inch. He finally gasped out, "I will carry her with some help."

Thereafter, the writhing, screaming duchess was swiftly carried by the duke with the help of eleven maids into the Black Rover's private chamber. Celine raced after them.

"I want all the men to leave and anyone else who has a weak stomach or swoons at the sight of blood," demanded Sandy.

All the old women stayed, while six of the eleven young maids departed dragging the reluctant duke with them.

The door was closed, and Sandy after lighting plenty of candles turned to Penelope, "Strip out of yer clothes, wrap this sheet around yerself and open yer legs."

"No," Penelope replied in shock. "Not in front of everyone."

"Babe is squished inside. It will need space to come out."

"Does it have to come out between my legs?" Penelope asked.

"You could try and push is upwards and coax it out of yer nose, but I don't think yer nostril is big enough," Sandy chuckled.

Penelope did not laugh.

After that things progressed fairly slowly. Celine watched Penelope cuss creatively for what seemed like hours. A lot of prodding and poking occurred followed by some more screaming. When Penelope ran out of her more dignified oaths, Sandy taught her some shocking new ones. Most of the verbal abuse was aimed at the poor duke who stood outside, his ears glued to the door listening to every single word.

The sun inched upwards in the sky, sweat glistened on foreheads, and Penelope had no more energy left than to whimper every now and then. She tossed uncomfortably on the bed while the rest of the women breakfasted, sipped hot drinks and sang songs to please gods and hurry things along.

Once breakfast was over, Sordid Sandy looked refreshed and eager to attack the task ahead. She bounced around the room shouting orders. She made Penelope squat, kneel, sit on her hind legs and finally lie down flat on her back in the hopes of hastening the birth.

Penelope, tired out, slept for the next ten minutes while Sordid Sandy still bubbling over with energy turned her attention towards the maids and told them to lie on their backs and kick their heels in the air. Soon they had progressed to dancing around the bed.

"Is this necessary?" Celine asked as she hopped from foot to foot with her hands on her waist.

"I am trying to please the gods and speed things up," Sordid Sandy replied crisply.

"Is the duchess in danger?" Celine asked anxiously.

"No, but soon it is going to be time for my snooze. I would rather not forgo that."

Penelope woke to find flushed sweaty faces prancing in front of her eyes. The short sleep had done her good filling her with a burst of energy.

"Can I walk for a few minutes?" Penelope requested.

Sandy nodded, and with that single nod things spiralled out of control.

Celine watched what happened next in horror.

Two maids helped Penelope off the bed. Penelope stood up on shaky legs, her teeth biting down on dry lips. A single sheet was wrapped around her completely covering the upper part of her body but leaving her naked below the knees.

Sordid Sandy was not part of the London social circle. Hence, she had no idea that an upper class woman should be covered from head to foot and hidden behind curtains in a smoky, hot dark room at the time of giving birth. She did what she felt would keep the duchess most comfortable.

Celine, too, looking at Penelope's red face decided not to mention Mrs Beatle's chapter on confined ladies and birthing rituals for the elite.

Penelope prowled around the room, her steps cautious and her expression lethal. Everyone watched her hesitant steps become more confident.

"It doesn't hurt anymore," Penelope started to say with a smile …

The rest of the words froze in her throat, her face turned white and she looked down in horror.

The room stilled as they eyed the spot between the duchess' legs, the spot that was visible below the sheet and between the knees.

A heartbeat later everyone watched in shock as a lot of blood, gore, and with no prior notice … the baby gushed out.

Sordid Sandy was the only one who had the wits to move, and good god did she move. The wizened woman dived across the room and neatly caught the newborn babe in her arms before it could hit the floor.

The babe gave a full throated yell wrenching everyone out of their stunned state. A few maids snapped to attention and flew to see to the duchess, while some rushed to attend to the babe.

Celine paused long enough to ascertain that both mother and child were healthy before backing away towards the door. She pressed her lips together and flung the door open. She had to escape before she swooned.

George stuck his head inside, peeked over Celine's head and turned grey.

Celine pushed him out and weakly congratulated the duke. It seemed the pirates and the duke had become friends, for outside a feast was already in progress with plenty of rum doing the rounds.

"Was it a boy or a girl?" Lord Adair asked coming up to sit beside her and George.

"Hmmblurg," Celine mumbled, too busy guzzling a glass of rum.

After a minute of silence and wanting to desperately change the topic and erase the memory of the birth from her mind forever, she asked, "Will the pirates let us leave?"

Lord Adair smiled, "They will, for I have given the Black Rover an authorised letter from the sovereign declaring him to be a privateer. He is more than pleased with the promotion."

Celine understood not a word of what he said, but nevertheless she nodded. All she cared about now was being allowed to leap overboard into the cold water to wash away what she had witnessed from her mind.

"We will never have a baby," George's white lips suddenly announced.

"I wholeheartedly agree," she replied turning to him in relief.

"Never," he repeated.

"Ever," she echoed.

They smiled at each other.

Lord Adair tactfully left them alone.

George watched Lord Adair's beautifully crafted shoes walk away. "I know you are in love with me," he informed her.

All thoughts of the birthing flew out of her mind. "How can you be so sure?" she asked, her voice sounding high pitched and odd to her ears.

A dimple winked in his cheek, "You swam across to save me when you are terrified of water. You gave me your knitting needles to protect myself. You forgot to tie your hair back, you no longer care about propriety, you raced across England on horseback in order to save me and that too from pirates, you smell terrible—"

"Do you?" Celine cut in.

He understood what she was asking, "I came here to return the recipe, I promised my mother I will come home, I am planning to spend my life learning to be the Earl of Devon. What do you think,

Amy? Why would I agree to live a deuced responsible life?"

Celine took a deep breath, hope unfurling in her heart. This was it, she had to take the risk and tell him that he was right. She did love him. He may laugh at her, but she didn't care. If she didn't say it now, she could regret it for the rest of her life.

"Come and see the baby," a maid broke into her thoughts.

Celine lost her nerve and the moment was lost.

They stood up and avoiding each other's eye made their way back to the captain's chamber.

What they found was a far cry from what they had left.

The door to the chamber was flung open invitingly. A couple of pirates lay draped in the passageway holding bottles of rum softly singing celebratory songs.

Inside the room the windows had been flung open, and the bright sunlight flooded in illuminating the freshly made four poster bed with its clean white linen.

A few people stood in the room, but all Celine could see was the content duchess lying on the bed with a small infant curled on top of her chest. The duke sat kneeling next to the bed, his single large finger gripped by tiny newborn ones.

Tears of happiness and awe were streaming down almost every cheek in the room.

"Isn't she awfully ugly?" Penelope sobbed happily. "I still love her."

"All newborns are wrinkled and red. She will become prettier," Sandy remarked.

"She?" Celine asked approaching softly.

"I checked," Penelope confirmed. "It is definitely a girl."

"What will you name her?" George asked.

"Grace," Penelope replied promptly, "after my mother. Grace Mary Elizabeth Sandy Radclyff."

Sordid Sandy started bawling at this pronouncement, while Celine nodded approvingly. It was only right.

George came and put his arms around Celine and together they watched the duke and duchess cuddle the child.

"I changed my mind. Let's have one," George said, his fingers squeezing her shoulders.

"You have to marry first before you have one," the duke said. He didn't turn around, his eyes glued to his child.

"Will you marry me then?" George asked Celine.

"Because you want a baby?" Celine countered, resting her head on his shoulders.

"No, because you love me and I love you," he replied confidently.

"True," she agreed, turning her face up to receive his kiss.

With that single word, the matter was settled to everyone's satisfaction, and then they kissed and the pirates clapped, the angels sang, and the newborn baby let out a hearty healthy wail.

And in that room that day rang the happiest sounds in the world.

EPILOGUE

"I am glad you have become responsible," Celine said to her husband, "but not too responsible."

George lifted his four month old baby girl and wiped her face, "And I am glad you have become impulsive, a little mischievous and a lot more fun."

They smiled at each other.

"Do you know who I met the other day?" George continued. A young three year old boy with an adorable dimple raced up to him for a hug.

"Who?" Celine asked placing a cloth on the grass and sitting down carefully.

"Your poet, Philbert Woodbead."

"You said his name correctly," she said in surprise.

"I always knew it," he replied smugly. "I just enjoyed butchering it."

She shook her head in amusement, her loose curls glistening in the sunlight, "How is he?"

"He is marrying an American heiress who adores his poetry. She was hanging off his arm when I met him."

Celine grinned and patted her swollen belly. She watched three more children racing towards them and said, "Then it is a happy ending for everyone."

George now lying flat on his back with children of all ages crawling all over him replied in a muffled voice, "It always is, my love. It always is."

THE END

ABOUT THE AUTHOR

Anya Wylde lives in Ireland along with her husband and a fat French poodle (now on a diet). She can cook a mean curry, and her idea of exercise is occasionally stretching her toes. She holds a degree in English literature and adores reading and writing. Connect with Anya Wylde on Facebook, Twitter, Pinterest, or Google+ to be notified about her upcoming releases. Website: www.anyawylde.com

Book Cover designed by: www.lovelustandlipstickstains.com

Other Titles Available by Anya Wylde

The Wicked Wager
Penelope
Murder at Rudhall Manor
Ever After
Love Muffin and Chai Latte